What the Children See

Gregory Wolos

STORIES

Injuries and afflictions abound in The Thing About Men. Gregory Wolos keeps his compelling collection attuned to complications of recovery, while illuminating, with care and craft, the wounds most in need of wary monitoring: those that persist beneath 'the top layer of things.' In story after fine story, Wolos urges all of us to delve deeper.

Matthew Pitt, author of
These Are Our Demands

Wolos is at the pinnacle of his conspicuous talent, and that is really saying something because his previous short fiction collections occupy a prominent place in the pantheon of best short fiction. By any measure, he is one of the most original and adept writers at work today.

Michael C. Keith, author of
Pings and *Methods of Repair*

These wise, wry, and wildly entertaining stories will remind you why you fell in love with fiction in the first place. Wolos pays attention to our world, celebrates our fragile and complicated lives, and opens a space in front of us so we can see more clearly.

John Dufresne, author of
I Don't Like Where This Is Going

Wolos has done something necessary... storytelling, creation, frailty, and trying (and mostly failing) to see the world for what it really is. How have we gotten by all this time without it?

Matthew Thomas Meade, author of
These Are Our Demands

First printing, April 2025
Library of Congress Control Number: pending
ISBN 978-1-953136-96-1 Hardback
ISBN 978-1-965784-01-3 Paperback

Cover Photo, Design & Typography by **Kurt Lovelace**
Cover *Bauhaus Dessau* Alfarn by Céline Hurka, Elia Preuss,
Flavia Zimbardi, Hidetaka Yamasaki, and Luca Pellegrini.
Body in **Nimbus**, Chapter Titles in **Jenson** by Robert Slimbach
Flourishes set in Emigre Foundry **Dalliance**, by Frank Heine
Emigre Foundry **ZeitGuys**, by Bob Aufuldish, Eric Donelan
Typefaces licensed Adobe, Linotype, & URW GmbH

PSPRESS.PUB
PIERIAN SPRINGS PRESS, INC
30 N GOULD ST, STE 25398
SHERIDAN, WYOMING 82801-6317

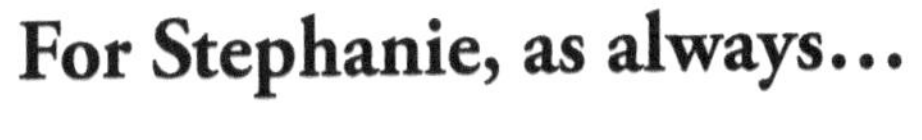

For Stephanie, as always…

CONTENTS

1 | Svengali 1

2 | Knothole 17

3 | Marigolds 27

4 | Appetite 47

5 | Leaving Loathsome Cave 65

6 | Old Yeller 83

7 | Claustrophilia, Outer Banks 91

8 | Nuzzi Great-Grandpa 111

9 | Iota 125

10 | Balance 137

11 | Glorious Vessel 155

12 | Blue Madeline's Version 179

13 | Pinocchio in New Hampshire, 1993 197

14 | Amabel's Children 205

15 | The Dry Boys—Paris, 1995 221

16 | An Evening with Willie Freeze 235

ABOUT THE AUTHOR | 251

ALSO BY GREGORY WOLOS | 253

Acknowledgements | 255

What the Children See

SVENGALI

It felt good to bug his eyes—to open them as wide as he could, exert pressure from the muscles around the socket, feel the tightness that threatened to launch them out of his skull, which couldn't happen, would never happen, was an impossibility, wasn't it? Barry loved mugging in the tall mirror on the inside of his parents' bedroom closet door—the mirror the boy had watched his mother pose in as she dressed until he was a kindergartner. Now Barry was nine—and here was his father's reflection, popping up behind his own. His dad dredged up some parental wisdom:

"You know, if you're making faces and someone slaps you on the back, your face could freeze." Though the threat was empty—his father rarely touched him, and never in anger or as punishment—Barry watched warily as the man lifted his hand to pat his receding hairline. When the hand lowered, Barry's face relaxed, and all that was left of his bugged eyes was a delicious throb. He watched his father wink, suck in his belly, and hitch up his pants.

"I've heard that if pug-dogs sneeze, sometimes their eyes pop out like champagne corks." His dad picked something from his ear. "Don't let anything I say spoil your fun, though. Bug 'em out—go ahead and see how long you can keep it up—maybe you'll make the Guinness Book of Records. But when you're done Mom says you need to clean your room."

After his father left, Barry discovered it was impossible to watch himself roll his eyes in the mirror—he *felt* them roll, but could only capture the "just before" and "just after." He stuck out his tongue at his father's warning about back-slapping, then watched his chest expand as he inhaled deeply. The closet exuded a stew of rich odors: leather shoes, stale perfume from his mother's dresses, a cheesy whiff from his father's suits that reminded Barry of dandruff. He bugged his eyes again, welcoming the irresistible pressure. But when he remembered the pugs, he frowned—without unbugging—and felt his lowering brow compress his eyes still further. And in the mirror? He gasped at the new expression: popped eyes under an angry brow. He couldn't look away and shuddered with exhilaration. This was more than just a pleasant feeling. This new face had *power*. It was genius, if he understood what the word meant.

A test: Barry turned from his reflection, vowing that when he looked again he'd react to the awesome expression as if it belonged to a stranger. He tried, and instantly fell under the spell of the face in the mirror.

⁂ ⁂ ⁂

Barry didn't keep his new face a secret. Later that morning while he spooned Cheerios from his bowl at the kitchen table, he trained his bug-eyed stare on his busy mother. When she noticed, she stopped suddenly between stove and sink, cast iron fry pan in hand.

"Barry!" she exclaimed, stricken, "what're you doing? You're going to ruin your eyes."

Her son, lost to the thrill of ocular tension, felt his brow rise and his eyes ease back into their sockets. "What?" he asked.

"You were making pop-eyes at me. Where did you learn that? You looked like Svengali." She poked the pan at him as she spoke as if fending off an intruder.

"'Svengali'?" The name was silly. It made Barry smile, which seemed to further agitate his mother.

"Svengali was the villain in an old movie I saw on TV when I was little," she said. "With Uncle Rudy one night when Grandma and Grandpa were out late. It scared me to death. Svengali was like a hypnotist—he controlled people with his eyes. He bugged them out in a spooky stare like you did. Who taught you that? Don't let me catch you doing it again, not in front of me or anybody else. It's not polite. It's bad manners."

"I'm sorry. Daddy saw me doing it in the mirror. He didn't like it either."

"I should think not." His mother pivoted to the sink where she ran water into the pan.

"He said my face would freeze if someone slapped me on the back while I was doing it."

His mother turned to him, hands on hips. "It just might. It would probably be unwise of you to take that chance, don't you think?"

"Is that what happened to Svengali? Did somebody slap him on the back—when he was making eyes?"

A shadow passed over his mother's face. Was she worried he was going to pop out his eyes again? Barry sucked in a breath. He could make his mother afraid!

"I don't remember," she said, shaking her head as she

slid back into the disturbing memory. "But I do recall that he led a beautiful young lady to a tragic end. A singer. That movie gave me nightmares. For years I thought men on the street were making those eyes at me behind my back. I never quite caught them—they'd smile when I turned to look at them, like they thought I was being flirtatious. I'll probably have nightmares about Svengali tonight. Thank you very much."

Svengali. The name caused electric ripples in the muscles and nerves of Barry's eye sockets that shot through his body all the way down to the toes.

"Barry!" his mother shouted. "What did we just talk about? Stop it right now! Do you want to be punished?"

"I'm sorry." He hooded his eyes with his hand and bowed over his cereal bowl. The sodden Cheerios reminded him of a picture he'd seen in a magazine of bloated cows drowned in a flood. "I was just testing—so I could stop myself."

❧ ❧ ❧

Ms. Hernandez, the new principal of Barry's elementary school, attentive to community concerns that she would abandon beloved traditions, announced that, in spite of a windchill near freezing, the annual Halloween parade would take place as always in the parking lot during afternoon recess. The children's fairy wings, superhero emblems, and sports jerseys were hidden under heavy coats. Witch hats were perched atop ski caps. The chase was on for windblown crowns. Costume parts that leaked out from under parkas flapped in the stiff breeze like the bunting draped around used car lots.

When the parade began, the children, prodded by their shivering teachers, shuffled along in line like prisoners in a labor camp. Faces clenched against the cold, they puffed frosty breaths as they marched toward a viewing committee that included the principal, the gym teacher, the nurse, and a half dozen PTO moms, one of whom comforted a sobbing damsel clutching a torn conical hat. While the moms thudded applause with gloved hands, the bareheaded principal, whose Dr. Seuss "Cat Hat" kept blowing off, dispensed the treats. Each child mumbled "Trick or Treat" for a bag containing an apple, a coupon for McDonald's French fries, and a fire-safety coloring book, then waited, freezing, for Principal Hernandez to guess their identity.

"Ah, Yolanda, you're Wonder Woman, right? I can tell by your boots. Your tiara won't fit over your ski mask, is that why you're holding it? And Randolph, is that you under that Patriot's helmet? Are you Tom Brady? He was traded, wasn't he?"

Ashley, a head taller than Barry—she'd been held back a year and was nearly eleven—clumped along in front of him. She wore earmuffs under an army helmet and a trench coat. She'd tucked her camouflage pants into a pair of oversized combat boots. Her toy M-16 rifle had been confiscated by their teacher and locked in a closet first thing that morning.

"A soldier, how authentic." Principal Hernandez's frozen mouth was stiff as a ventriloquist's. "'GI Jill'— is that who you are, Ashley?"

"GI *Joe*," the girl insisted. "The boots are my dad's. Trick or Treat."

"GI Joe, of course." Principal Hernandez nodded. "And be sure to thank your father for his service."

"What service?" Ashley snatched her goody bag and opened it to examine the contents.

"Why, military," the principal said. "In which branch did he serve?"

"None," Ashley said as she galumphed away. "He just likes army stuff."

Barry was last in line. He'd pulled the drawstring on

the hood of his parka tight to hide as much of his face as possible—he was trying to both protect his bugged eyes from the icy wind and to keep his expression secret until the last possible second.

"And finally—is that you in there, Barry?" the principal asked. Before he could answer, she turned away to shout instructions to the other students, teachers, and parents.

"Okay, we're finishing up here— excellent job, everyone. Teachers, you can take your pupils back inside—stay orderly, now, no running." She shook her head as the children stampeded toward the school entrance. Meanwhile, Barry was still struggling to unknot his hood's drawstring so he could reveal his full Svengali stare. The principal gave him a distracted onceover— the waiting PTO moms were stamping their feet and staring longingly at the children and teachers swarming into the warm building.

"Let's see, what have we here? I bet your coat is hiding all the important clues."

The only thing under Barry's parka was his regular school attire. But the drawstring knot wouldn't yield to his numb fingers, and he had to yank the hood back without untying it—which distorted the face he'd been trying to preserve. He'd kept his eyes bugged for so long he'd exhausted the muscles controlling them. The wind had wrung out tears that clung to his cheeks. He tried to restore pressure to his pop-eyed stare, but all he could muster was a wince.

Principal Hernandez noticed only the tears. Intending empathy, she hugged herself, and rubbed her upper arms. "Brrr! Not such a Halloweeny day, is it Barry?" She reached to the table behind her for a treat bag. "You should get a special award for being the most patient," she said.

Barry dipped his face into his shoulder to dry his

face before reaching for his goody bag. His skin felt raw against the fabric. His eyes burned.

The principal patted his shoulder and guided him toward the school entrance, then stopped. "Oh, she said. "I still haven't guessed who you're supposed to be."

"Svengali," Barry said.

Principal Hernandez cocked her head. "Sven? Like Sven from *Frozen*?" She laughed, or maybe just cleared her throat. "That's pretty appropriate for a chilly day like today, don't you think? I feel like Olaf the snowman myself. So—what happened to your reindeer antlers? Did they blow away?"

Barry shook his head violently, surprised to discover that he really was on the verge of crying. "Sven-*gali*, not Sven," he choked. Principal Hernandez draped an arm across his back and bent to look directly into the eyes Barry could no longer bug. And now his brow was stuck and wouldn't lower. The wind pushed a fresh tear across his temple toward a freezing ear.

"'Svengali.'" the principal repeated. "I'm afraid I don't know who that is."

"A scary guy—from an old movie. He hypnotized people—so they'd do what he wanted. So he could control them."

"Ahh—that explains your blinking—" Smiling, she squeezed Barry's shoulder. "You're not trying to hypnotize *me* now, are you?"

"Unh-unh. I was just trying to be the character."

"I see," said Principal Hernandez. "It must be hard getting the look exactly right." A fire safety booklet flapped like a wounded bird against the side of the school, and the principal picked it up before opening the door. She ushered Barry in ahead of her. "Well, the parade is over. You can relax. You can stop being Svengilly now."

When the interior warmth engulfed him, Barry's legs

jellied, and he almost sagged to his knees. But he found the strength to protest.

"Not Sven-*gilly*—Sven-*gali!*" His voice echoed in the tiled hallway. Some of the pink-faced PTO mothers lingering by the main office turned to see what the fuss was all about.

"Ah—I've got it now—" Principal Hernandez said, modeling a proper indoor volume. "'Sven-*golly*.' But— maybe you want to keep in mind for the future that 'controlling' people isn't such an appropriate idea. Now hurry back to class."

Barry moved like a sleepwalker down the corridor that led to his fourth-grade classroom. The fluorescent lights overhead twinkled at the edges of his squint like Fourth of July sparklers. He tossed his treat bag into the first trash bin he passed. Disappointed about the failure of his costume in ways he couldn't put into words, he heaved a shivery sigh. What, exactly, had he expected? What had he wanted?

❧ ❧ ❧

Festive sounds spilled from the open door of Barry's classroom. GI Joe Ashley, still in her camouflage fatigues, helmet, and boots, blocked the entrance.

"Halt! Who goes there?" she said, drawing herself to attention as Barry approached. Then she grinned and leaned against the doorframe. She took a bite from a half-eaten apple. In her other hand she held a wad of French fry coupons. "Take off your coat and stay awhile, dummy. You want your McDonald's coupon? I'll trade you my fire safety book for it. No? Who the heck are you supposed to be, anyway?"

"I'm finished with my costume," Barry said. "You probably never heard of the guy I was. 'Svengali'?"

"Nope. Don't know who that is." Ashley arched an eyebrow. "Everybody knows you were crying. Don't bother trying to hide it." She took another bite of her apple and studied the core before looking back at Barry. "So now you're just nobody, hunh?" She jammed her coupons into her pocket and nodded into the classroom. "Just like the rest of us. No shame."

Barry stepped by her into the organized chaos of a fourth-grade party. "The Monster Mash" blared from somebody's Iphone. Kids were drawing jack-o-lanterns and ghosts on the chalkboard at the back of the room. A half dozen crowded around Ms. Trilby, who sat behind her desk. She'd tied a colorful kerchief over the blond hair she'd braided into pigtails, and there were big red spots like a Raggedy Ann doll's on each of her cheeks. The fishbowl that usually sat atop the bookcase had been moved in front of her, and Burple, the class goldfish, hovered lazily above the blue gravel covering the bowl's bottom. Molly, a compact girl in a firefighter's hat, saw Barry nearing the teacher's desk and shifted over to make room for him.

"Ms. Trilby is making up pretend fortunes," Molly said. "Only good ones, right, Ms. Trilby?"

"That's right, Molly," the teacher confirmed, concentrating on the fishbowl, "only positive fortunes today."

"And it all depends on Burple," Molly whispered. "We're waiting for him to tell us Risa's fortune—if Burple swims up, she'll be a billionaire, but if he swims down, she'll only be a millionaire."

"I'm going to be Emperor of the Universe because he swam up for my turn," a kid in a Joker mask—Arthur?—said. "If Burple had swum down, I'd only become President of the United States. Look—there he goes!"

And the goldfish, lazily paddling its fins, rose to the surface, mouth gaping for a meal.

"Risa's going to be a billionaire!" Molly shouted, and

the kids congratulated the smiling girl in the skeleton suit.

"Whew," Ms. Trilby sighed, pretending to wipe sweat from her forehead with a checkered hanky. "Prognosticating is hard work. What about you, Barry? Do you want me to have Burple predict your future?" She winked, and the spots on her cheeks rose over her broad grin.

Barry felt the pressure of a body against his back a second before the point of Ashley's chin dug into his shoulder. Her helmet scraped his ear. She shoved him forward, and he stumbled, bracing himself on Ms. Trilby's desk. Only when the girl backed off could he stand up straight again.

"He's not Barry, Ms. Trilby. He's 'Salami,'" Ashley said. "Can't you smell him? He's all spicey."

The make-believe soldier's nasty tone deflated the mood. Barry wondered if the others had been about to tease him also. For being a crybaby. His face warmed—there was no escaping the tearful weakness he'd shown in the parking lot. But he chose defiance over defeat and crossed his arms.

"Not 'Salami,'" he declared. "*Svengali*. He's from an old black and white movie. My mother told me he was a famous scary guy. She said she still has nightmares to this day from when she was a kid and saw him on TV. Svengali made spooky eyes and hypnotized people to do his will."

"So what's your costume?" the Joker—definitely Arthur—demanded.

"Just regular clothes," Barry said. "But then I taught myself how to make my eyes like Svengali's just by looking in the mirror. The first time, I scared myself. Then I did the eyes in front of my mother, and she screamed a little. She told me about Svengali and made me promise to keep a *serene* face around her—that means calm."

Barry wasn't doing the eyes—not yet—but he was *picturing* himself making them so hard, he felt the power swell inside him, just like the first time he'd seen his reflection.

"Let's see, it then, Salami," Ashley challenged. "Do the face. I want to learn how so I can scare my father."

"It's Svengali, stupid, not Salami," Barry said.

"Barry—no name-calling," Ms. Trilby's clownish cheeks undercut her authority. A few of the kids chuckled nervously. But the name hung in the air—*Svengali*—

"Sorry, Ms. Trilby," Barry apologized. "Anyway, I don't know if I can do it right now—make the eyes, I mean. I did it for so long outside at the parade my eyeballs dried up and the muscles got tired. There are lots of muscles around the eyes."

"Don't do anything that makes you uncomfortable, Barry," Ms. Trilby said, but she sounded expectant. Did she like horror movies? Maybe somebody had hypnotized her once, and she'd enjoyed the experience. Whichever, the crowd had grown in front of the room as more students figured out that something special might be brewing.

"What's Svengali's super-power?" somebody asked.

"He controls people," Barry said. "He hypnotizes them to do what he wants. My mom says that in the movie it was women—at least one woman—that he used his power on. But I think it works on everybody." He paused, blinking slowly to lubricate his eyeballs. He flexed and relaxed his brow, and fresh energy surged into his sockets.

Ashley's breath heated Barry's ear. "Do your special face, Salami," she hissed. Without warning, she kneed him in the back of his thigh, and he wobbled, recovered, then spun to face her. From behind he heard titters and Ms. Trilby's admonishment to "simmer down."

Ashley's face hung above Barry like a moon, but

without pausing to register her expression, he struck her with the most concentrated Svengali-glare he could muster. The girl lurched backward as if hit by an uppercut, and her helmet flew off and clattered across the room. Sitting in a heap, confused and embarrassed, she looked down at her feet.

"Damn boots," she muttered, gathering herself. "My father lied—he swore I'd be able to walk in 'em." But as she met the blistering gaze Barry continued to level at her, she squeaked and plopped back down to the floor. When Barry finally relaxed his glare, the girl's eyelids fluttered as if she were emerging from a trance. She shook her head and got to her feet, eyeing her attacker with fear and wonder.

"Holy shit," she said. "It felt like you head-butted me."

"Ashley—" warned Ms. Trilby, "language—"

"Sorry—did you guys see that?" the girl stammered, wrenching her gaze from Barry's face and sweeping it over the students and teacher behind him. Then, cautiously, she looked again at Barry. "How'd you do that? Man, if I could look at my parents like that—you know what my dad said after I put on his boots this morning? 'For a daughter, you're one helluva son.' Then he took my picture." She sucked in her lower lip. "Mm—I taste blood— must have bit myself when I tripped. You can make those eyes anytime you want?"

Barry popped his eyes a smidge at her to demonstrate his control, unbulging them after she flinched. "Sure," he said. "I practice a lot."

Ashley lifted her chin toward the spectators. "Show them," she said. "You guys won't believe it."

Barry swung around. His scalp tingled, as if something—a crown?—had settled on it. The eager stares of his classmates washed over his face like the wet tongues of hungry animals, but Barry focused his attention on his teacher.

"What about *my* fortune, Ms. Trilby?"

"Do the eyes first, Svengali," Ashley urged. "Show everybody— I don't want to be the only one."

Ms. Trilby blinked, and Barry noticed that false eyelashes and blue eyeshadow were part of her Raggedy Ann face. Or was that how Ms. Trilby always made herself up? He'd never looked at her so intensely. She narrowed her eyes and licked her lips. Her cheeks flushed beneath the painted spots.

"You're causing quite a hub-bub, Barry," she said. "What have you got to show us?"

"Give me my fortune first," he said, more brazenly than he'd ever spoken to an adult. There'd be a consequence—but he wasn't afraid. The classroom lights seemed to dim—a dark mass like a shifting cloud composed of thousands of black birds rose between him and his teacher. Was she still there? Yes—he heard her voice, which seemed to come from a long way off.

"*Your* fortune, Barry? Or—who's that person you're pretending to be again?"

Barry tried to penetrate the thickening bird cloud— he'd marveled at such a sight before—birds rising together over a field at dusk. Was Ms. Trilby forcing him to make a choice? Who was to say his future was different from Svengali's?

"*Svengali*," he rasped. He peered into the black mass. It was one thing for Svengali to be *seen*, but how would Svengali *see*? Barry strained—the shifting cloud carried the weight of the deepest notes of the organ in church that always lifted the hairs on the nape of his neck. And then—and *then*—

"Barry?" Ms. Trilby's voice was nearly lost within the music of the whirling birds. "Whose fortune?"

"Look at his eyes! His eyes!" The children's cries rose and scattered like shingles blown from a roof in a storm. Barry's jaw tensed as he stared yet harder into the bird cloud—and then he was in its midst, still part of the mass and its power. But now, through Svengali's eyes, he could see every one of the thousands of birds individually—each pair of wings moving in synchrony with every other pair, every single pearled eye—and all of them at once—every beak and *all* the beaks, simultaneously. The organ groaned in his chest. Someone was sobbing—a girl's sob, not his.

"Burple's water—it's bubbling—" Then more voices, more cries. Among the thousands of blackbirds, a flash of gold.

"It's *boiling*—Burple's banging against the glass—"

Ms. Trilby's voice: "Barry—Svengali—stop—can you stop? Arthur, get the watering can. I'll scoop Burple into it—"

"Hurry, Ms. Trilby—the water's steaming. Barry, stop it, you're killing Burple!"

"Dammit—" Ms. Trilby wailed, "scalded my fingers. Where's the net? Has anyone seen the net?"

"Burple's *sinking*, Ms. Trilby—he's turning over!"

Ms. Trilby stood, swaying. The hand she shook flitted through the host of blackbirds like a lost dove. "Barry—"

"*Svengali—*" Had the voice come from inside or outside of him?

"Don't look at his eyes!" Ms. Trilby cried.

Hands pawed at Barry's shoulders, but he shrugged them off. Somebody tried to pull him backward, and he held his ground.

"Stop pulling me!" he ordered, meaning the children, not the massed birds. But the cloud was sliding away, morphing into unrecognizable shapes, and though Barry longed to immerse himself within it once again, to *see* it from inside and out just as Svengali would have, its low tones had faded to silence.

What had happened to his fortune? Where was Burple? Barry's forehead ached as if he'd gobbled a pint of ice cream, but he glimpsed the class pet floating belly up in the fishbowl.

Then utter darkness fell without warning: Barry smelled cloth and stale sweat, and for a moment he thought he was back in his parents' closet, staring into the magic mirror where he'd first seen Svengali's eyes. But a buckle whipped against his ear, and he remembered the trench coat Ashley had worn during the parade. Somebody, probably Ashley herself, had wrapped that coat or another around his head. Then Barry's arms were pinned against his sides—the whole class, maybe even Ms. Trilby, must have joined in. The darkness he glared into now was different, impenetrable, and all he could hear was his heart, each beat a sharp crack, like the breakup of a frozen sea. Barry panicked—if he lost his Svengali-stare now, could he ever recover it?

What were the voices around him chanting? "Barry" or "Svengali"? He stared into this new darkness until his skull seemed to open, and it poured into him. Was this what his mother dreaded in her nightmares? His father said a sneezing pug might pop out its eyes. Would they dangle down to the floor, bouncing like marbles at the ends of a pair of stretched out nerves? But his father had said something else, too: he'd given a warning—or had it been advice? Those words burned through Barry like a lit fuse—if he could echo them— make himself heard through the layers swaddling his head, he might be saved yet.

"Hey," he bellowed. In his mind's eye the hands restraining him belonged to Ashley, his parents, Ms. Trilby, Principal Hernandez—everybody he knew. "Slap my back—slap it hard! *Now*, slap me on the back before it's too late."

And then, out of breath, uncertain if his message had gotten through, he waited with aching eyes.

KNOTHOLE

The boy whose gloved hand I hold as we cross the busy street on the way to his elementary school is my ex-wife's son. To him I'm Uncle Jim, his emergency babysitter. He's no blood of mine. I don't think Austin knows how sick his father is, that the man's knocking at death's door, that he's on a ventilator, that he's probably never going to return from the hospital where Janet keeps vigil. Austin, odds are, will never see Robert alive again. I'm taking the boy to school because his father had signed up as the "volunteer helper" months ago, when the thing that's killing him seemed only a minor discomfort in his groin, the kind of pain anyone would laugh off in the gym.

Trees lining the street suffer from splintered branches and raw amputations, the results of the recent "Superstorm" and the power company's line repairs.

There's an atmosphere of loss I'm familiar with—but this neighborhood regained its power after a day. It's believed that new leaves will hide the tree damage in the spring.

Austin's half- brother Jesse, the son Janet and I raised together before she announced her decade-long love for her co-worker and divorced me, is in his third year of law school in Boston. He's engaged to a lovely Swiss girl who's studying veterinary medicine in the same city. Jesse was twenty when the little boy keeping pace beside me was born. Both boys inherited my ex-wife's heart shaped face. Jesse has my height and his mother's black curls. Austin's hair is blond like his father's, nearly white at the neck-nape his ski cap doesn't cover. I'm a dozen years older than Janet. Somehow, she and I now belong to different generations.

❧ ❧ ❧

"Robert and I are in love," Janet had announced on the ride home after we'd dropped our son off for his freshman year of college, "and, now that Jesse's out of the house..." She loved me still, she reassured while my tightening hands on the steering wheel seemed to compact everything in my chest into a ball of ice—but she was no longer *in* love with me. During their ten years together at work, she explained, the easy familiarity she and Robert shared had blossomed into feelings there was no longer any rational reason to suppress.

Jesse now splits his vacations between households: his mother, half-brother, and Robert get him for holiday meals; I get his study time, during which he works in his old bedroom, while I show myself to be a good father by turning down the volume on the TV. I wonder if Jesse's memories feel as hollow as mine often do. His mother's simmering passion for Robert didn't necessarily overshadow her maternal love. But Jesse must have sensed a shifting dynamic that I missed. He seems to think I need healing, and, as if I were the son and he the father, he's tried to explain the world to me.

"'Reality' is bigger than we think," he told me last semester break. "Imagine if you'd never seen a baseball game, and you were watching one through a knothole in a fence—but you could only see third base. What would you be looking at? The fielder's feet? Dirt kicked up by a runner? Maybe, if you were lucky, a ball. You wouldn't have a clue about other bases or players or what the crowd was cheering about. You wouldn't get the game at all. That's life, Dad. We only get a glimpse of things, and we have to infer the rest. We invented religion and philosophy and science to fill the gaps."

"Hm," I nodded. "Very smart." But I was thinking, and I'm thinking now, that Jesse's got things backward. I'm not *looking* at third base, I'm *standing* on it. I'm anchored there on the field, and everything that "baseball" has to offer I see perfectly well. But there *is* a knothole—it's far away in the outfield fence, beyond the players; it looks like a pinprick from where I'm stuck. That knothole's the only "gap" I'm interested in— if I could free myself from third base and peek through it, maybe I'd see that there's more to the world than "baseball."

❧ ❧ ❧

I'm a large man, and I fill the doorway of Austin's classroom, where his teacher Ms. Gunderman meets me. She props the door open with a low-heeled foot while she thanks me for coming. Her dark hair is pulled back in a pony tail, and she's tweezed her eyebrows into sympathetic angles. Austin trots by us to hang up his coat and hat and join his classmates. Ms. Gunderman glances up at my gray hair and down at my big belly as if they might answer the question she doesn't ask about my relationship to the boy. Janet has informed her that "Uncle Jim" would be standing in for Austin's father, whom Ms. Gunderman knows is gravely ill. But who, I'm sure she wonders, *is* Uncle Jim? Am I intimate with the family's circumstances, or am I only hired help?

❦ ❦ ❦

Before I knew of Janet's feelings for him, I'd been friendly enough toward Robert. At company picnics we'd done horseshoes and shared burgers, beer, and potato salad. I'd even invited him to play golf, twice, and beaten him once. He'd never been married, he told me over nineteenth-hole drinks. He wasn't yet forty then, and wouldn't be much past it now. Regarding family, I told him he didn't know what he was missing. "There's nothing like it," I said, and Robert's cheeks dimpled thoughtfully as he stared into the beer mug cupped in his hands. It's not difficult to believe Janet fell in love with those dimples. But what might he have been thinking? What plans had he and Janet already made? Was our golf date intended to throw me off the scent? Or was it a failed attempt to come clean?

I haven't visited Robert in the hospital. He's lost fifty pounds, my ex-wife says. Nothing but skin and bones. I don't know the impact wasting away has on dimples. A mummy has sunken cheeks, but never dimples.

❦ ❦ ❦

"You Austin's grandpop?" asks a brown-eyed girl with braids like a nest of shoestrings. I'm passing out crayons and construction paper, glue sticks and snubbed scissors. The children are making cards. At first I think they might be Get Well cards for their classmate's father, then I think Thanksgiving cards, but Ms. Gunderman explains they're Congratulations cards for the newly re-elected President: "Maybe he'll pay us a visit," she says with a wink. "Or at least send us a thank you note. On White House stationery. We're also letting him know of our donation to the victims of Sandy!"

"I'm Austin's Uncle Jim," I say to the girl with braids. When she said "grandpop" I pictured my own father. Jesse and my brothers' kids were his only grandchildren. Austin is no relation to him at all.

"I'm Pria, and I love Bobama," she says as I pass, her attention devoted to the giant red heart she's crayoned onto her blue paper.

Austin is busy on his card. I can't see what he's drawing from my vantage point in front of the classroom's long bookcase, but he finishes each stroke with a flourish. I'm to read the children a story. I slide an old Dr. Seuss, *McElligott's Pool*, from one of the shelves. It was a favorite from my own childhood, and I read it probably a hundred times to Jesse. After Austin was born, Janet claimed all the children's books stored for years in Rubbermaid tubs in our basement. *McElligott's Pool* is a hymn to the imagination: the story's young fisher-boy, his line cast into the tiniest of puddles, hypothesizes an array of wondrous fish, all eager to take his bait. "They *might* be there" is the story's moral.

***

There's no guarantee that Austin knows exactly how we're related. Or *un*-related. He should be aware that I'm the father of his very much older brother Jesse, but I know how such facts can run parallel to one's life without actually intersecting it: when I was a teen, I'd been shocked to discover that my mother's father—my Grandpa George— was actually her *step*-father. Mom's father had been killed in a factory fire when she was two. "We thought you knew. It wasn't a secret. Your grandpa adopted me. He's the only father I've known," Mom said. "Of course you knew," my older brothers insisted. Grandpa George never knew of my ignorance, but I felt awkward in his company for the rest of his life; it was a relief when he passed away.

❧ ❧ ❧

Austin wasn't yet four when Janet called me as a last resort to ask "a tremendous favor." She knew the kind of solitary life I'd been leading, but she and Robert were desperate. It seems that they'd been about to leave on a two-week vacation to Paris when their trusted nanny had come down with adult chicken pox. "She has to be quarantined," Janet said. "We stand to lose a lot of money. There's no one else we trust. We never had a honeymoon." I didn't bring up the honeymoon she and I shared; I've blotted out most of that memory, except for an argument in a restaurant parking lot. Of course I would take care of their little boy, I said. Have I mentioned that, since beginning her second-chance life, Janet looks younger every time I see her? Even now, with the burden of a dying husband.

❧ ❧ ❧

"What do you *do*?" demands a small boy wearing a striped polo shirt. He's coiled into himself like a cobra among the twenty students who've gathered in front of me on the story-telling carpet. *McElligott's Pool* rests on my belly like a shield. The boy in the striped shirt seems to forget his question the second after asking it, but Austin, seated nearby, tilts his blond head, as if ambushed by the fact of my existence, and his mouth gapes with interest.

"What do I do?" I repeat. "Austin knows—" The other children look at him, and he squints, grinning slightly. "I *uncle*," I say. I'm a professional *uncle-er*!"

"You w*ha-aat*? You're a *wha-aat*?" a dozen voices demand. It's a belligerent chorus, and Austin withers. His gaze drops to the carpet. His cheeks flame. We're both paralyzed by his sudden consciousness of what he doesn't know: *who's the old man in front of my class? What's his claim on me? When is my father coming home?*

⁂ ⁂ ⁂

While his parents enjoyed Europe, Austin and I passed our time together quietly. We held to the letter of the routine Janet had prescribed: meals, TV, baths, bedtime. I half-closed my mind's eye for the duration of my stay and pretended that Austin was a blue-eyed, fair-haired version of Jesse. At night I read to him from the books that connected me to my own childhood and my son's: in my extended dream-memory, Austin was a ghost child—a placeholder. When his parents returned, the smiles we passed around like souvenirs confirmed a successful mission and stamped me as an official emergency babysitter. Robert shook my hand; Janet hugged me in a way that felt both familiar and distant. Austin grasped one of my fingers and murmured the "Thank you" his parents encouraged. I politely declined the Thanksgiving dinner invitation they extended.

⁂ ⁂ ⁂

Ms. Gunderman arrives to save the day and explain to everyone who I am. "He means he's Austin's *uncle*," she smiles to the children. She's placed a hand on my shoulder to both comfort and guide me. "The boys and girls would like to know what kind of work you do," she stage-whispers. "How you're employed. That's what the parents usually share."

"Of course," I say. I squint over the children's accusing eyes at the dusty, sunlit windows. "I'm a consultant. I work with numbers on a computer. I can do it at home. I help people with questions they have about money and investments and taxes."

Faces go blank. Mouths open and nostrils flare with yawns. But when Austin bites his lip I see his father's dimple. I clear my throat, open *McElligott's Pool* outward to show the pictures, and I narrate from memory. I'm soothed by my own voice as I reveal fish after miraculous fish.

Ms. Gunderman is still at my side. Her hand leaves my shoulder like a bird taking flight. I'm sharing a story about fish, but my thoughts drift to a different Dr. Seuss book, one about a zoo full of fantastical animals. Then I drift further and see myself at an actual zoo with my family. Jesse is Austin's age. I'm slimmer. Janet has yet to meet Robert. There are no animals visible, but there's no mistaking we're at a zoo. Other families stroll along paved walkways past fences and obscure buildings. Boys and girls hold balloons or ice cream cones. Parents hold bags of food pellets or the hands of their children.

Jesse pulls free of my grip and rushes to a steel fence with yellow caution tape threaded through its links. His fingers lock in the fence wire, and he lifts himself onto his sneakered toes, craning his neck. A uniformed guard approaches and lays his hand on my son's shoulder, and the gesture pierces my revery for just a moment, reminding me of Ms. Gunderman. Then back to the memory: Janet and I join Jesse at the chain-link fence. "The African wild dogs," the guard says in an accent I don't recognize. "A baby fell in last week. The dogs got him. Exhibit closed. It was on TV. All over the papers."

I scoop up Jesse, and he wraps his arms around my neck. His skin is cool, his scent blue cotton candy. Janet and I lock horrified gazes—how did we miss this? We look at the other families milling about—did they all know?

"They shot the dogs," the guard says, as if he'd held the gun himself.

And that's why I think that I'm not such a fool, when I sit here and fish in McElligott's Pool," the young narrator of Seuss's story admonishes a skeptical farmer. I'm hoarse from reciting and fuzzy-headed from remembering. The children are expressionless.

"Are there any questions for Austin's uncle?" Ms. Gunderman asks. She stands beside me. Soon it will be time for me to leave. I'll have lunch in the diner down the block from the school and wait for a call from Janet to see if she'll need me to walk Austin home.

"I thought there'd be a shark, and it would eat everybody," the polo-shirted boy says, and growls. I start to flip through the book, revisiting the amazing fish.

"Don't you know a story with monsters?" another child asks, and I lift my head.

"Austin fell into a pit of African wild dogs at the zoo once," I hear myself say. Austin's eyes bug. His classmates gasp. "Did your mom and dad ever tell you about that?" I ask him. "You were just a baby. They were probably waiting to tell you until you got older." I pretend Ms. Gunderman isn't in the room, but I'm waiting for her touch. "You fell in, and the dogs, there must have been six or seven, went for you, growling and barking. And you know what? Your dad jumped in and fought them off. He punched and kicked until zookeepers with stun guns shot them all. It was all over the news!"

Austin's eyes bore into mine as if we're staring at each other through opposite ends of magical binoculars that somehow make both of us bigger.

"Your dad's shirt and pants were torn to shreds, but you didn't have a mark on you. He still has scars on his arms and legs. Some of them have faded." Ms. Gunderman's hand finally arrives. I resist shrugging it off; I've gone too far not to finish. "But never *ever* ask about those scars! I shouldn't have said anything—if your parents had wanted you to know, they'd have told you. So—you have to keep what I've said a secret, okay? Between us. Between *us*." I make a circle with my arms as if to embrace Austin and all of his classmates. They shift in their places on the reading rug. "And act surprised when Mom and Dad finally decide to tell you, if they ever do," I warn. "You don't want to give me away."

MARIGOLDS

Sol knelt at the edge of his garden contemplating the grub that lay on his palm, so plump he could pop it in his mouth; it would burst against his palate like a grape. He tossed it aside. What would his mother, gone for decades, have thought of *that*? Ma hated "vermin"— anything smaller than a cat. Rodents and bugs terrified her, but the invisible attack of "germs" did her in. In her last years she withdrew to her bed, distrusting her own flesh. The visiting nurse removed Mama's gauze mask before reporting that she had passed "peacefully."

Sol would never eat a grub, but imagined the flick of his tongue, the warm, soft marble rolling in his mouth. Look how the senses were linked to his memory—a grub craving brought back his mother. But if a bug was so stimulating, what about his marigolds? The flowers' golden heads bordered his garden, and Sol patted the half dozen in reach, then sniffed his fingers. The sweet scent, his gardening magazine said, kept out pests. In the pictures, the bloom burst like anti-aircraft fire: and for a moment he floated off to the other plot he'd surrounded with marigolds. Sol's mother rested here, safe, he hoped, from contamination. Beside her tombstone was another, his daughter Emily's. Hadn't he been headed here since the first imagined lick?

Sol bent to the nearest marigold and inhaled deeply.

Ten springs past their oaks had been invaded by tent caterpillars. They spilled from their lacy nests, to Emily's delight. Before her death, she'd had a final bloom. She flushed with each heartbeat, it seemed to Sol. Her dark eyes were huge, her lips too red, her smile too wide. She begged Sol to gather the caterpillars as they crawled hungrily up her arms. "No leaves here," she said as they reached her fingers, and Sol looked away.

"Hey Daddy," she called. Emily shimmered through his wet lashes. Sitting cross-legged beneath an oak, she wore a caterpillar under nose. She shut her eyes as it drooped over her lips. Her lids were purple. Her black hair hung to the grass when she tilted her face to the sun. "Heil Hitler!" she said, saluting stiffly. Sol's grin hurt his cheeks. The caterpillar reared and dropped into her lap.

"Damned cutworms," Sol muttered from his knees. His wife stood on the other side of the garden. She hugged herself against the morning cool. Had it really been ten years—ten gardens? "Half the lettuce'll be gone before it's ready to pick. Don't we qualify for a government subsidy if we don't grow anything? Maybe we can just raise grubs and sell them as house pets." But he was still thinking of the cemetery plot ringed by marigolds and the pair of tombstones they guarded.

Lena wouldn't have left the house unless she had something to tell him. She wasn't exactly agoraphobic. She preferred the house, was all. She looked out of place wincing in the sun. She lifted a hand to shade her eyes, but Sol pictured her as he always saw her: bent over the stove or kitchen sink or the dinner table, listening to details of his day at the bank, or watching television, its changing light reflected in her glasses.

Dutifully, she'd accompanied Sol to the cemetery for a few months after Emily's burial, but never left the car. If they'd discussed the end of her visits, Sol couldn't remember. Mourning was personal. The plot was where he expressed his devotion. Lena must have found her own way to grieve.

Lena's eyes were hidden by the shadow of her hand. "The boy is coming this afternoon," she said, and smiled.

❦ ❦ ❦

An hour later, after showering, Sol paused with a sock in his hand. The boy—Jeffrey. Lena's enthusiasm had made it impossible to forget, but he was unprepared nevertheless. It had started with a Lifetime movie. He'd fallen asleep with his book on his chest. Lena woke him. She picked up his book and marked his page, speaking quickly with a rhythm he hadn't heard in a long time. A foster child? Such a foreign idea. Why had he agreed? Had Lena's excitement exhausted him? It seemed too unreal.

And now Jeffrey was a fact. Sol scooped his toes into his second sock. His toenails needed a trim. Badly. If he were barefoot at the beach he could hide them in the sand, but he'd be embarrassed for Lena to see them in this condition. Lately his feet seemed far away. His toenail rasped the fabric. Was this age? Was it starting from his feet, as if he'd abandoned himself to the earth, and would it rise cell by cell up his legs, through his stomach and chest, his arms, all becoming as remote as his toes, until his humiliated head refused to acknowledge the rest of his body? Funny thought.

Jeffrey. Sol remembered Ms. Sokol from the Department of Social Services. Behind thick glasses, long lashes fanned her blue eyes. He scratched his shin—flakes of dead skin sifted onto his sock. So dry rot had begun—he thought of his mother and her terror, and then of his daughter, dripping with caterpillars as she grasped at bits of life.

"The danger lies," Ms. Sokol had said, "in growing too close to a foster child. That would be misleading and unfair to him. The responsibility of the foster parent is to provide an appropriate and natural home environment. Often the child is awaiting adoption. In many cases, as with Jeffrey, the child's home situation has become untenable, and the courts have ordered that he or she be removed from that environment. What's important to remember is that yours will be a transitional, not a permanent, home for the child. So what you're really being asked to do is provide a nurturing situation without establishing an overwhelming emotional bond." She had taken off her glasses, which Sol was shocked to see had reduced the size of the eyes that now flooded her face. You could drown in them! "Frankly, Mr. and Mrs. Warren, this ideal is almost impossible to achieve. One would think that a nurturing home environment would be based on love, wouldn't one?"

They nodded. Ms. Sokol replaced the glasses, stemming the tide. "The successful foster parent finds an appropriate balance. We at D.S.S. hope that every experience will be a happy one. Thus, the lengthy and somewhat painstaking procedures involved in ascertaining that the foster situation will meet certain standards—"

She shed the glasses again, and her eyes spread like the wings of a butterfly; it threatened to fly from Ms. Sokol's face into Sol's, and he lifted his arm to swat it away.

"Yes," she asked, "question?" He really hadn't one, but while Sol watched her resettle the glasses and tuck the wings away with her little finger, he asked if she thought his wife and he were qualified. "Highly qualified," she said. "I have the greatest hopes for you," she said.

Qualified? Lena squeezed his fingers. To do what? Withhold love—that's what Ms. Sokol had said, hadn't she? Or were they to love and not show it? He patted his wife's hand. They had agreed that he would stay in the background. He had his job and his gardens. This show would be hers.

So a strange child would be living in their house: a business arrangement, like the loans Sol approved at the bank. An applicant's numbers couldn't lie. He trusted Ms. Sokol's paperwork. No "overwhelming bond" would interfere with the healthy distance he meant to keep. Lena's agenda would be less relevant than the memory of a winter's storm he might have while weeding in his garden.

❈ ❈ ❈

But when Lena opened the front door, Sol's palms were damp, and he rubbed them together. He would present a dry hand to shake. Ms. Sokol, masked in sunglasses, stood alone. Couldn't Sol hear wings beating against the black lenses? Did blue powder sift onto her cheeks?

"Jeffrey's in your backyard. I sent him back to take a look." She lowered her voice. "A nice yard is a new experience for him. I'm sure it will do him good!"

"Oh—we have a vegetable garden," Lena said. "Maybe he can help you out, Sol?"

The women stared at him. He felt trapped. "Sure," he said. They waited while he shuffled off. "Why don't I go round back and give him a little welcome…"

Scarecrow, Sol thought at first sight of the boy standing beside his garden. Sol had slid along the shadow of his house and looked at the boy's back. He wore new jeans and an oversized black T-shirt. His thin arms and neck were pale, and his hair stuck up like dark straw. Sol let his heart go out to the kid—he needed some fresh air. Was he big enough for a thirteen-year-old?

Then the boy raised his sneakered foot over the marigolds and brushed it across a row of lettuce. Flushed out of the shadows, Sol saw the kid flick something into the garden. He turned to Sol as if he knew him and had known he was behind him, pursed his lips and blew a streak of smoke toward his new foster dad. Sol met his gaze, then both of them looked at the garden.

"These are mostly vegetables," Sol said without introducing himself. "We'll have them for dinner." Should he mention the cigarette? The phrase on the tip of his tongue was "private property."

"I hate vegetables," the boy said in a harsh falsetto. A cartoon voice, but Sol stumbled as he took another step forward. Their eyes pushed away from each other, like magnets of the same pole. There'd have to be some ground rules, Sol thought.

"Why would anybody want to mess around with all these fucking bugs?" The boy flapped his arms, like he was catching his balance. "You got stinking bugs all over the goddamned place."

"It's been so long since we've had children here,"

Lena whispered. Jeffrey was in the den watching TV. Sol waited at the kitchen table while his wife made a sandwich, poured a glass of milk, placed two, then a third cookie on a silver tray he hadn't seen in years. "It's his first day—I don't think a little extra treat will spoil him. Sol shrugged. He hadn't told his shimmering wife about the smoking or swearing. Maybe the kid was nervous. Maybe that was all. Maybe he would act differently with Lena. Who knew? But better to let her discover on her own what they'd welcomed into their house. Overwhelming emotional bond? If that was foster parenting's gravest danger, he stood on pretty safe ground.

Lena left with the lunch, as excited as a schoolgirl greeting her first date.

"I'll be in the garden," Sol called.

Lena stopped short. "You won't come get to know Jeffrey?"

This is not TV, thought Sol. I'm no actor. This is no show. It's my house. "The boy's got food and television. If he wants to help me in the garden when he's done, send him out." Ask him for a cigarette, Sol thought.

"He's got food and television and me." Lena said and floated off.

TV music blared from the den, louder than Sol had ever heard it. An unfamiliar show—a cartoon? The sound changed to guns and shouting, then to ballroom music, then to grinding, screams, then an old pop tune shortened for a car commercial...

❧ ❧ ❧

The marigolds had failed. A large pest had invaded the garden. Plants had been uprooted. Sol found the damage at the plot's center while searching for Jeffrey's cigarette butt. Now he squatted over some young beans, patting the cool soil back over their roots. They would survive if the pest didn't return. To deter the vandal he would sprinkle pepper along the rows and stick mothballs into the earth like poisonous seeds.

And Sol's other plot? If the marigolds were impotent, then a tulip or lily might fall as easily as a bean stalk. Why not seek the brightest flowers if your goal is to ravage? He blamed himself for his misplaced faith. The thing he imagined was nearly the size of a cat, lumbering on rodent legs through the marigolds, hair plastered as if had swum through an oil slick. It crawled with mole eyes over his mother's heart and stopped at Emily's stone, lifting its snout to sniff her flowers.

Sol found himself on all fours. His hand crushed a pepper plant. The air smelled like baked earth, and he was short of breath. He'd gone hatless at midday, a serious mistake. He licked his lips and looked toward the house, feeling he was being watched. But Lena wasn't at the kitchen window. He searched the other windows, one by one, first floor, then second, den and bathrooms, bedrooms, until he forgot what he was searching for. He sat back, his focus lost. Then he caught Lena's head in the last second floor room, Emily's room, which was odd, because his wife never went there. Neither of them did. It had been emptied of their daughter's personal things by silent mutual agreement within weeks after her death. Now it was a guest room. No leering teddy bears, no pink ribbons, no motherless dolls. There was nothing threatening in the room, but no one went in. So why now, Sol wondered. Would she want to start visiting the gravesite again, too?

Then Sol realized that the head belonged to Jeffrey. He'd forgotten his foster child. Why hadn't Lena put him in the other guestroom? He cringed at the thought of the stranger wrapped in sheets on his daughter's bed. But Sol waved. If the boy had nothing to do but spy on him, Sol would meet the challenge. Coward, he thought, when his wave went unreturned. Of course it might have been the back of the boy's head he saw. Maybe Sol was the furthest thing from Jeffrey's thoughts.

"The room is larger," Lena said. "The closet is empty, so Jeff has plenty of space for his things." She seemed to slip away, then squinted at Sol.

"Your eyes look strained, dear. It's too hot today, isn't it? Didn't you wear your hat?"

Sol had nothing to say. Lena had her own expectations. Cigarettes, foul language—what she'd learn about the boy she'd learn. Really, had there been anything so serious? Nothing criminal in the boy's record. Some property damage, one dismissed shoplifting episode. If he really thought the boy a threat, he'd tell his wife, wouldn't he? What he needed now was a glass of something cold.

"You rest and I'll go up to Jeffrey," Lena said.

❧ ❧ ❧

The cemetery plot was untouched. Flowers blossomed beneath Emily's headstone. But for how long? Sol's loss of faith in the marigolds had made his trip to the gravesite difficult. He worried for a week about what he might find—scattered petals, withered stems, desiccated roots clawing at the sky: he saw this devastation in spite of the fact that nothing was disturbed. Didn't the marigolds alert the invader that something valuable lay beyond them? They were an inducement, not a protection. Sol had half a mind to uproot the marigolds himself.

What portions of routine, love, and dread had drawn him to the cemetery? As he was leaving, Lena had stopped him at the door, and it felt like rescue. Maybe she did want to join him. Maybe there was an emergency that would keep him home.

"I asked Jeff if he wanted to go for ride with you," she said. "Just to give him a change of scenery. I thought maybe you could stop for a hamburger on the way back. You two should be spending more time together."

Sol froze: the boy alone with him in the car; standing beside him at the grave; across a table chewing. "—but he chose to say home," Lena had said.

Sol hadn't exchanged a word with the boy since the first afternoon.

"You talk to him, don't you Lena?" Sol asked. He sank into his recliner. Nothing on television held his interest. "I think he's afraid of me."

"Oh, I don't think so." Lena lay her knitting aside. When had she last knitted? "Why should he be afraid of us, after the kind of life he's had to live?"

"But you talk to him," Sol said. "What's he say?"

Lena blushed as she smiled. She picked up the knitting. "Nothing at all, really—sometimes it's not even like talking—it's more like we're whispering together, but not really words—" Then she giggled. "He swears, you know," she said. "It's his background, what else could we expect? But—I imagine that I cuss right along with him!" She kept her eyes on the points of her busy needles.

"You swear together?" Sol felt he'd been stripped of a weapon that was now being used against him. "So we're encouraging profanity? What will social services think? I just wish he'd look me in the eye. He won't do it. It's unmanly. And if I'm not looking at him, I feel his eyes on me. It makes me feel like showering. I need a shower." Sol wrung his hands and rubbed them together as if dissolving sanitizer.

A month of the summer passed.

"Why doesn't he have any friends?" Sol asked. "He's been here for weeks, and I haven't seen another kid in the yard!"

"He doesn't know anybody. It's the summer—children are away at camp or on vacation with their families. We're all he has until school starts.

Sol pushed his plate away. He'd always loved eating his own vegetables, but lately his appetite had deserted him. "He doesn't go outside. He's pale as a leper." Across the table were a full plate and an empty seat. "And what does he eat? He's got a filthy mouth that he doesn't fill. What'll they think if they get him back starved?" Can't we give him back, Sol was thinking.

"Shh—he'll hear you," Lena said. Sol watched her eat. Her appetite was another new thing. For years she'd only picked at her meals. But here she was, spreading butter on a roll and pushing it through the gravy. Okay, so she had a cause and had rejoined the living. Good. But shouldn't he remind her about becoming too attached? She was setting herself up for disappointment.

"He won't hear a thing. He's up in his room again. Does he spend all day in there? He does, doesn't he?"

Lena chewed and swallowed. "He's secure there. But now he roams, too."

"'Roaming'?"

Lena's potted window plants blocked Sol's view of his garden and mocked him with their health. He had given up on his plot. "For the year," he said, blaming the heat, his work schedule, even his age. After dinner and on weekends he reclined—in front of the TV or in bed. He'd ignored the cemetery, too, the first time because of a steady rain. After that, without an excuse. He pretended he'd sacrificed his garden to save the cemetery plot—

an offering, but he knew the invader would be encouraged rather than appeased by his defenselessness. He'd abandoned both his mother and his child.

"'Roams'?" Sol repeated. He could see the boy gliding through rooms, pausing to fumble through drawers and closets. "Where does he 'roam'?"

"You know, around the house," Lena said. "It makes him feel like he belongs, I think." When, Sol wondered, had Lena grown so plump? He hadn't noticed her breasts in years, but there they were, buoying up her crossed arms. "Soon," she said, "He'll realize that he needs us."

"I don't want him to need us!" But Lena had left the table, humming, like mothers on old sitcoms. Had he actually spoken?

❧ ❧ ❧

Sol wore gloves when he finally visited his garden. Lena had insisted on fresh vegetables for Jeffrey even though he wouldn't eat them. The plot was severely neglected, but not otherwise disturbed: weeds, rot, and stunted growth couldn't be blamed on a vandal. But the lack of damage didn't mean the thing, whatever it was, didn't visit nightly to assert its claim, lording over the territory as if it were Sol in his recliner. Its shit would cover everything. Sol picked through brown and shriveled vegetables, bitterly aware that only the marigolds flourished. Returning with nothing but contaminated hands and a shrug for Lena, Sol sat in front of the television. He would try to remember to wash up before dinner.

As for the cemetery, Sol regretted that Mama would also be repulsed by the interloper. But it was too painful to think that he'd allowed the creature dominion over his daughter. Pushing the thought into the shadows exhausted him, and he sat and did nothing.

The bank president suggested Sol's leave of absence. He had vacation time coming, no? He might have his health checked, that would be a good idea. He could relax, enjoy his gardening, recharge his batteries, spend time with Lena and the new boy. Had Sol been losing weight? Really, that checkup was in order.

So Sol took the time off. Work was no more than serving people with demands, forms, figures, the glow of computer monitors. Dragging his arm across document after document, his signature an effort. Why bother? Who would miss him? Lena rose before him for the first time in their marriage. Bed forever? Why not. He would ignore his wife's suggestion of "a nice family trip somewhere with Jeffrey."

❧ ❧ ❧

Sol's car keys were missing. He lay in bed staring at the square of blue sky the window framed. The color was so pure he wanted to fill it with thoughts of Emily, but he hadn't the strength to pull her from the shadows. The blue was the blue of eyes. It was the blue of the wings Ms. Sokol's glasses trapped. She had brought Jeffrey. The flying thing the social worker kept hidden now clung to the edge of the roof, and its giant wings covered his window. It really wasn't the sky after all.

But it couldn't be too late. He knew where to find his daughter. He'd clean out the weeds, clip the grass, replace dead flowers, and remove all evidence of an intruder. Sol climbed out of bed. The carpet pricked the soles of his feet. Opening dresser drawers and his closet left him panting. But when he nearly fainted and saw stars, he glimpsed Emily among them, and he shuffled forward with determination.

Then he couldn't find his keys. He checked the usual places: the hook by the back door; the mail basket on the table in the foyer. He dug around the cushion of his recliner and turned out the pockets of the pants he'd worn for the last two weeks, when he bothered dressing. He circled the house, checked the same places over and over, began to swear, "Dammit," a tic or incantation. But soon the word was just a sound, and both meaning and feeling disappeared like a pair of turtles slipping from a log into dark water.

He passed by Jeffrey. The boy stood in front of a closet in the unused guest room, his hands clasped behind him as if they'd been cuffed. When his eyes met Sol's, a smile opened like a wound. "Not in there," he said.

Sol moved on. His failure calmed him. He was trying, but he was the victim of fate, and surely he could be excused. Absolved. Forgiven. When Lena offered her keys, bringing to Sol's attention "how big a help Jeffrey is trying to be," Sol declined.

"I need mine." He dropped into his recliner. "I wouldn't be able to think of anything else." He closed his eyes. He was blameless. But the boy's face rose before him like a scarred moon. "That boy's into everything now, isn't he?" he heard himself sigh.

"Yes," Lena said. "He's right at home here."

❧ ❧ ❧

Lena was folding laundry, piling it on the bed beside her husband. "Would you like some breakfast?" she asked. "Do they still call it breakfast when it's afternoon?"

Sol thought it over. He wasn't hungry—the opposite, really. The thought of food made him sick. If he said nothing, maybe Lena would leave. But then maybe she'd bring him something on her own, something that would turn his stomach...

"Oh my goodness—Sol?"

She wasn't leaving. Sol's bones felt like cold lead.

"Sol, look at this—" Lena stood at his dresser. The top drawer was open. A black sock hung from her hand. "Look at this—" She was staring into the open end of the sock. She shook it, and it jingled. "It's your keys! Here—" She tossed the loaded sock at Sol. It landed by his side like a little sack of gold. His keys slid half out. He stared at them. His veins carried ice to his heart. Lena bent over him and shook out the sock.

"Look at all that," she said. "When did you do that?" She laughed. "And why? What else have you got there?"

"Have *I* got?" Sol covered the pile with his hand, protecting it, then peeked under his fingers and saw the keys, red ceramic earrings, a silver chain, and a wedding band.

"Those are my earrings," Lena said. And the wedding band was Mama's. She'd worn it on string after arthritis had swollen her knuckles. The string was missing. The silver chain he'd chosen himself for Emily's tenth birthday. She'd worn it on special occasions. Why was it here? Sol stirred through keys and jewelry with his stained fingers. His black nails curled like talons.

"It was the boy," he said, and when he heard himself, he knew it was true. "Him and his roaming." He slapped at the pile. "This is a crow's collection—shiny things. He's a thief!"

"Don't be silly," Lena said. "They only accused him of shoplifting a candy bar. But after that's when his mother's boyfriend beat him, 'trying to teach him some discipline.' Thank God he's with us." Her crossed arms rose and fell with her breasts when she sighed. She smiled. "And what in the world would he want with one of your socks?" She left Sol with the glittering things he was afraid to touch.

※ ※ ※

Night fell and Lena joined Sol in their bed. "Wouldn't it have been nice if the two children could have known each other?" she asked.

"What? *What*?" Half listening, Sol didn't understand at first.

"I think Jeffrey's smoking in his bedroom," she said.

Both statements were outrageous. "Dammit!" Sol muttered, and wriggled onto his elbow. "He's doing *what* in Emily's room?

"It's Jeff's room, dear." Lena's statement was like a great stone Sol couldn't lift. "I should have mentioned the health risk. It was a teachable moment. It's a little thing when you think about his background. I should at least bring him an ashtray."

The stone Sol couldn't lift pressed him into the mattress. "It's unhealthy," he said.

"Maybe you should talk to him about it some time. You could tell him we're concerned. He admires you so much."

Admired. Of course. Sol had made himself easy to admire. It was the respect due the defeated. In the space he'd vacated, why not erect a statue to the "nobly vanquished"? Raise it next to his daughter's grave, where the marigolds could mock him.

"I'll talk to him now." It was the voice of a Sol from the past, and the act of ventriloquism that made it seem his own gave Sol courage. "Why not? He's not asleep— the light's never off in there." Was he dreaming? He'd tossed off his sheets and risen, cast off the impossible weight and stood at the door. Lena seemed to have shrunk under her blankets.

"Maybe he keeps it on because he's afraid—I'm sure he's asleep," she said.

"What does he do all day that would tire him out? *Roam*? How much energy does it take to pilfer our personal things? We've got to tolerate smoking?" Sol rose like a balloon on a taut string. He didn't feel his legs. "It's all turned inside out," he said. "I can fix that." And he moved into the hallway.

There was a slash of light under Emily's door. A long time ago, when it *had* been her door, Sol had hesitated, afraid to knock. What if she didn't answer? But she'd be reading, of course, no matter how exhausted, refusing to lose a moment left her to sleep.

Now Sol knocked. No response. He knocked again, then opened the door and passed inside. The bright light disoriented him, and he felt himself dip. But there was the boy on the bed, brushing at the sheets with the back of a hand. He wore yellow pajamas. He looked at Sol but didn't speak.

"Jeffrey—" Sol's pajamas were decorated with little crowns. Maybe he should have worn his robe. The room smelled like stale smoke. He reminded himself whose bed this child was in. "Excuse me—I saw your light on, so I thought I might as well—" He cleared his throat, and the boy might have murmured something he didn't catch. It might have been "asshole."

Sol still floated. He wanted to sink, but couldn't. Jeffrey's tongue darted in and out like he was sampling Sol's unease.

"Okay—okay, then. What I've got to say is, well, if you're smoking in this room, I'm going to have to forbid it. You know," he said, "it's not just that we don't like smoking in the house—even though we don't—or that we think you're too young—which you are. It's not even the fact that it's been proven, medically substantiated, that cigarette smoking will kill you—" The boy was staring at Sol's hand, and Sol looked at it himself. His nails curled like claws. He shifted his hands behind his back and scratched himself clasping his fingers. He might either rise or sag.

"In the past, smoking, swearing, maybe that was part of your world. But not in here." The boy rubbed his upper lip with his middle finger.

"This used to be my daughter's room," Sol said. "Did Lena tell you? She died, you know. When she was about your age she passed away right there, right in that bed you're lying on." Sol longed to sit on the bed. Could he put his arm around this boy, comfort him, draw comfort from him? "Emily," Sol said. He reached toward Jeffrey. If they could shake hands, make a pact to start over. If Sol could just touch him...

"Jesus!" The boy slapped his hand, and Sol pulled it back. "Keep your dirty hands off me!" It was the voice of something cornered. "Don't touch me, ever. You think I don't know what you want?" He recoiled with round eyes and a frightened half-smile. "What'd she, kill herself? What'd you do to her? Stay away, I swear to God! Lena—" he called. "Lena!"

Sol sank to the floor—or just above it, because he felt nothing beneath him. "You're stealing from me, you little bastard," he whispered.

"She warned me—" Sol heard. "She told me to watch out—Lena!"

Sol felt her in the room. She helped him to his feet, whispered something to Jeffrey, and guided her husband back to their bed. She tucked the comforter under his chin. He was panting— how awful he smelled. Lena kissed his forehead. There were so many vile things.

"Shh, dear," Lena soothed. Her voice was as sweet as flowers. "You've got to let her go, Sol," she whispered. "Let her go."

And he knew he would never leave his bed. A shower of petals covered him. A last golden blossom hung over his head like mistletoe. Was that why Lena had kissed him? Then the blossom dropped, and he shut his eyes but saw it anyway, a dislodged star streaking deeper and deeper into the dark, until, a prick of light, it disappeared.

APPETITE

When Drake turned eleven, he bought himself a pair of gerbils with his birthday money. He'd wanted a dog, but his mother was pregnant with what would be his first sibling, and puppies and babies don't mix. The day itself had been a dud—his father had just lost his job after a merger that left him "redundant," and to make ends meet had turned his candle making hobby into a full-time at-home job. Drake's birthday breakfast was served while giant pots of strawberry-scented paraffin boiled on the stove. His dad had set eleven lit candles on the kitchen table, each a foot tall and as thick as a man's wrist. Drake had to blow them out one at a time and was out of breath by the time he finished.

Drake named his new pets Adam and Eve, though he couldn't tell them apart. Even the pet store clerk had only been "pretty sure" that the pair Drake had purchased were male and female. Truth be told, he didn't like the gerbils from the start. They offered little to love—most of the time they hid in burrows dug in their cedar chip bedding. When they snuck out to their food dish or water bottle, they paid him no mind and scurried back into their tunnels the moment they'd satisfied their appetites. Nighttime was unpleasant. Knowing that he wasn't alone in his bedroom, Drake couldn't seem to quiet his mind down. Instead of counting sheep, he inventoried the sounds of the house. First, from their bedroom down the hall came the hum of his parents' voices; probably, they were preoccupied with his mom's health and his dad's job situation. When they quieted down, Drake listened to heat sensors tick, refrigerators hum, floors settle and beams creak. But if he held his breath, beneath all the other sounds, Drake imagined he could hear Adam and Eve rustling in their burrow.

Eating breakfast was like having a meal in a candle-making factory. The boiling wax polluted the air like car exhaust. The greasy eggs his father prepared for Drake each school day morning tasted of strawberry scent. The odor saturated every meal and everything else in the house, including Drake's clothes. "What's up with the strawberry smell?" his classmates asked. He felt lucky that the nickname "Strawberry Man" didn't stick. When his mother worried that the overwhelming odor might be unhealthy for the baby, Drake's dad showed her the label on the scent bottle.

"It says 'non-toxic,' see?" he said. "I'm not sure about the paraffin. I think it's okay."

The second set of gerbils—at least a dozen, though Drake never attempted an official count—arrived in a twenty-gallon terrarium and came with a water bottle, a carton of food pellets, an exercise wheel, and a book about gerbil care. The animals and the supplies were a "bonus gift" from Drake's mom's Fuller Brush salesman and came with a bottle of conditioner for her "that avoids the chemicals that are dangerous for pregnant women." When Drake came home from school and shrugged off his strawberry-tainted coat, hat, and scarf, his smiling mother told him to "go upstairs and check out the surprise the Fuller Brush man left on your dresser."

The new terrarium had been shoved up against Adam and Eve's smaller home and blocked most of Drake's mirror—he could only see himself from the neck up. His stomach clenched when he saw how many little beige bodies there were: half a dozen or so had wedged themselves into one of the corners; several burrowed in the opposite corner; another handful stood like prairie dogs in the center of the terrarium as if they were waiting a turn on the occupied exercise wheel. Lying atop the tank's cover screen was a thin paperback, *Know Your Gerbil.* It pictured a handsome, upright rodent nibbling on a pumpkin seed. Drake tossed the book on his bed among his schoolbooks and turned his attention to Adam and Eve's smaller abode, where the pair were hidden deep in their bedding. He was about to knock on the glass when both popped up like a pair of Whac-A-Moles and froze. Maybe, Drake thought, the oldsters would enjoy the company of the newbies. And vice-versa.

Drake removed the covers from both habitats and dumped Adam and Eve into the new tank. They landed softly and scrambled instantly to an unoccupied corner, where they began digging furiously. The Fuller Brush gerbils didn't seem to notice. The pace of the one on the exercise wheel never slackened.

Drake watched the pair disappear into the cedar chips, then climbed onto his bed. He rubbed his jaw with his shoulder—strawberries. Had he absorbed so much of the artificial scent that it was leaking out of him? His nostrils flared at a wet-dog stench underlying the fruitiness, recognizable, but a hundred times worse than the odor from Adam and Eve's habitat. Too many bodies in the Fuller Brush terrarium, and their defecation saturated the cedar chips. The two pungent scents—overripe strawberry and acrid cedar—didn't blend well. Drake tried breathing through his mouth instead of his nose, but it didn't help much.

Drake picked up the gerbil care book, *Know Your Gerbil.* He opened to a random page, and under the heading "Gerbil Teeth" he read: "Gerbils teeth never stop growing." He frowned at the idea, imagining his own teeth lengthening like Pinocchio's nose did when the puppet told a lie. Before long he'd have walrus tusks hanging over his chin. How would he eat? Or kiss? His face got hot, and he squirmed under his covers as he envisioned the limber strides of girls wearing jeans or short skirts in the hallways of his school. Giving the gerbils cardboard to chew will keep their teeth filed, *Know Your Gerbil* said. Why hadn't Adam and Eve's teeth been growing, he wondered. He hadn't seen any cardboard with the Fuller Brush gerbils either.

The exercise wheel squeaked—something else he'd have to get used to along with the stew of stenches he tasted when he yawned. Sleepily, he turned the pages of the gerbil book, looking at pictures he hoped would make the creatures more appealing. He stopped when he came to a chapter titled "WARNING."

"Because gerbils are cannibals," Drake read, "it is necessary to take certain precautions." *Cannibals?* He shuddered at the word. If gerbils aren't properly fed, they will eat each other, he discovered. Colonies will attack and devour strangers. Mothers will eat their newborns "without a qualm," the book said. The exercise wheel ceased to squeak. Why? What else were the gerbils up to? Were Adam and Eve safe? Drake was afraid to look. He threw *Know Your Gerbil* to the floor and reached for his math book. But he couldn't concentrate on the assigned problems. He kept *listening*, for exactly what he didn't know. Would he hear *munching*?

Drake started avoiding his room. He took to doing his homework at the kitchen table and stayed up later and later in front of the TV, outlasting both of his parents. When he finally dragged himself upstairs, he changed into his pajamas in the dark, scrambled under his covers, and tugged his pillow over his head; he tried to think about anything but gerbils. As he lay, the twin odors of strawberry and gerbil wound around him like a strait jacket, and he struggled to keep from writhing, as if the noise might stimulate the rodents' appetites. The darkness, plump and full, hung over him like a storm cloud, and though his parents' bedroom was silent, his thoughts shifted to his mother's swollen belly and the baby growing inside. Would it look like him? By the time it was his age, Drake would be a man, whatever that meant.

Mornings Drake dressed with his back to the big terrarium and used the mirror in his bathroom to comb his hair. Instead of investigating the fate of Adam and Eve, he got rid of their empty habitat. Eventually, routine conquered guilt, and he came to ignore the gerbils completely. Drake convinced himself that an "invisible hand" he assumed was his father's was secretly caring for the little animals. Side glances suggested their numbers were dwindling, but most were probably hiding in the cedar bedding. The water bottle looked full, and seed shells scattered around the food dish came and went, which implied that someone must be feeding them. Drake kept mum on the subject of cannibalism with his dad, afraid that too much information might affect the invisible hand's generosity. In fact, he never mentioned the gerbils at all. Silence and ignorance made things nearly tolerable, and as Drake hardened himself against pity, he grew more and more comfortable with the part of his life he'd abandoned to the shadows. His mom and his dad attributed his silence to the anxieties each of them fretted over, and never mentioned the gerbils.

"Are you worried about the new baby?" his mother asked. "Don't be jealous—you'll always be my first."

"I know you're not crazy about the candle business," his father said. "But it's just temporary—we'll be back on our feet before you know it."

Days went by without a sign of life in the terrarium, but still no comment came from the invisible caretaker. The deserted tank became a symbol of something, but what? Why was it still in his room? Then, one afternoon, a surprise resurrection: two gerbils sat next to the exercise wheel as if it was part of their daily schedule. *Adam and Eve*, Drake thought, convinced that they were his originals. And a new feeling, pride, surged past his suppressed guilt and revulsion. Adam and Eve were survivors! At that moment, the idea for his school science project was born.

Of course, the project was a hoax in every way imaginable, but it fit perfectly into the shadow world of half-truths that had claimed Drake since the gerbil invasion had begun. For his "experiment," Drake pretended that this surviving pair had been fed a healthy diet of seeds and nutritional pellets, while a secondary group of gerbils had been fed only sugar and candy. Adam and Eve thrived. Those given sweets didn't make it.

Drake scribbled a poster for his display at the science fair: "EATING ONLY SUGAR IS DANGEROUS." He illustrated his point with a skull and crossbones like the ones on cartoon bottles of poison and attached pictures of the Disney chipmunks Chip and Dale, labeling them "ADAM" and "EVE." Since the entire experiment was a lie, what did it matter that chipmunks were the wrong species?

Drake's father dropped his son and his experiment off at school for the event Drake had told his folks was "just for kids." His dad would spend the two hours of the science fair at Jimmy D's, the neighborhood tavern that had become his hangout when he wasn't pouring hot wax into molds or delivering candles to gift shops. Drake had heard his father tell his mom that the tavern was "great for networking."

The science fair was in the school cafeteria. Drake's project shared a table with a towering papier mache volcano that belonged to a kid from a lower grade. An easel in front of the volcano displayed a cardboard clock that announced the time of the next eruption. The volcano kid's mother, a tall woman with dark-rooted blond hair, guarded her boy and his project. When she caught the tank's animal odor—or was it the strawberry scent emanating from Drake?—her nose wrinkled. She read his poster and gave him a chilly look.

"Isn't it cruel to starve innocent animals?" she asked. Her son's smirking face poked out from behind his volcano, and he stuck out his tongue at Drake.

"These are the ones that had the good food," Drake told her, trying out his fib aloud for the first time. "They got a variety of healthy seeds and nutritional food pellets. Did you know that gerbil teeth never stop growing, so you have to give them stuff to chew on to wear them down?"

The mother's eyelids dropped and rose like window shades. "Of *course* the others died if you didn't feed them. Did you watch them starve? Did they die right in front of you?"

"They stay burrowed in the cedar chips pretty much all the time," Drake said. His face heated up. "Mostly, they come out at night, so I don't see much. I hear them, though."

Just then, Drake spotted his teacher, Mr. Leeds, who'd be grading his experiment. Mr. Leeds had stopped at the first table in Drake's row, where he studied a half-dozen small flowerpots under a poster that read "THIS 'MOSS' BE THE PLACE!" Sally Jeffers, who sat in front of Drake in class, nodded at something the teacher was telling her. Mr. Leeds made some marks on his clipboard, shook his head, and moved toward Drake's table. Drake smiled stiffly at his teacher while trying to ignore the volcano-mom's harangue:

"You *must* have had an inkling that they were dying. You let them suffer cruel, painful deaths!"

"It's for *science*," Drake hissed like a ventriloquist through his teeth. Mr. Leeds reached Drake's table and began to read his poster.

"Volcano eruption in one minute!" the volcano kid shouted. He ducked behind his project and mounted a stool. He held a vial of clear liquid over the volcano's mouth. The handful of spectators attracted by the announcement looked at Drake, assuming the project was his, until the boy's mother warned Drake to "quit blocking the show."

"They eat their babies, you know," Drake confessed to her under his breath. "I hear them at night when I'm trying to sleep. They keep nibbling away. Not just the ones that got the bad diet. These healthy ones, too. It doesn't matter that they've been well fed. They just like to eat babies, I guess." Drake had spilled so much information so aggressively that he was dizzy and could feel his heart pounding in his chest.

"Eruption time!" the volcano kid shouted. When Drake shut his eyes, the darkness was red and swirly.

A loud belch gurgled from the papier mache, and a puff of steam rose toward the ceiling. Thick gray slime slurped over the lip of the volcano, dribbled down its side, and congealed.

Volcano-boy's mother clapped. "Oh, that was beautiful, Struther! See the lava, everyone? Doesn't it look real?"

But Mr. Leeds frowned. "Another volcano," he sighed and made a note on his clipboard. "Where's the supporting information? You could have at least mentioned 'our living Earth.' C-plus, Struther, and that's generous." He waved his clipboard at Drake's terrarium. "Now, 'survival of the fittest' is a theme we can all sink our teeth into."

"But—but—" Struther's mom stammered, then fell silent. Her eyes narrowed at Drake. For a second he thought she might slap him, as if her son's lousy grade was his fault.

"So—where are your survivors?" Mr. Leeds asked Drake. "Are those the little devils, half-buried in the corner? Can you wake them up so I can assess their health. What precisely was the diet of the, uh, 'non-survivors'?"

"Cookie crumbs," Drake replied, ready with a host of lies. "Also crushed M & Ms. I filled their water bottle with Pepsi."

Mr. Leeds paused. "Did I hear you say these rodents are cannibals? Any conclusions about that?"

There were *Eews* and *Yucks* from the spectators who'd come for the volcano, but Drake had an answer. "Maybe the sugar in their parents' diet made the babies that got eaten really delicious."

Mr. Leeds smiled and patted Drake on the shoulder. "Very good! Sweet babies! That answer takes you from B-plus to A-minus. Best in the class so far."

"I think murdering God's creatures shouldn't be

encouraged," Volcano-mom grumbled. "I can't tell you how many hours Struther's father and I—"

"I've actually been to the rim of real volcanos," Mr. Leeds interrupted. "Believe me when I tell you that your son's project is subpar and unoriginal. But let's see how these little critters are doing. He reached around to the back of the terrarium and knuckle-rapped the glass. "Rise and shine," he sing-songed, the way Drake's dad did when he called his son for his strawberry-flavored eggs every morning. But the gerbils didn't move. "You're certain they're okay?" the teacher asked.

Before Drake could answer, a short, wiry man wearing a baggy track suit stepped through the crowd and pressed his nose against the terrarium, leaving an oily spot on the glass when he backed away. It took Drake a second to recognize his mom's Fuller Brush man, the guy who'd convinced her to take the extra gerbils in the first place. How many afternoons had Blake come home from school to find this man in their living room surrounded by his open cases of brushes and supplies?

"Hey, I think I know these guys," the Fuller Brush man announced. "Where are they all hiding?"

"They're all dead," volcano-mom said. "*That's* his experiment. He starved them until they ate each other. They probably even ate their babies."

"Survival of the fittest," repeated Mr. Leeds, who lingered near the display. "No room for sentimentality."

"Had to get them out of my house," the Fuller Brush man said. "Wife and kids couldn't stand them, and they wound up in our basement, where we'd kind of forget about them for a couple of days at a time. The smell of that cedar crap stunk up the whole house, didn't it, honey?"

Drake caught his breath—the "honey" the Fuller Brush man addressed was none other than Sally Jeffers, who'd left her moss-filled flowerpots and wandered to

Drake's table, probably to see the volcano. Who would have thought Fuller Brush men had children? When Sally saw the terrarium, her face turned white, and her whole body seemed to shimmer like an image on a broken television.

"That's why you did moss for your project, not rodents, right, kiddo?" the Fuller Brush man said to his daughter. "'This moss be the place!'— that was my idea. And who do you think lugged the little buggers up to your bedroom, young man? Not your mom, not in her condition."

"Dad was out selling candles," Drake said, instantly regretting his apologetic tone.

"Yeah, the strawberry scented ones. Your house reeks of it. Your Mom says she's sick of it, too." The Fuller Brush man closed his eyes, lifted his nose, and sniffed. "You can even smell it here. I wouldn't be surprised if the stuff is poisonous. Hey, don't I see your dad at Jimmy D's? I go there for lunch a lot. What, does he use the bar as his 'office'?" He chuckled and clapped his hands as he tried and failed to catch the volcano-mom's eye.

Drake couldn't shake the image of the Fuller Brush man poking around in his bedroom. He pictured the guy setting the terrarium on his dresser next to Adam and Eve's tank, then grinning at his reflection in the mirror. Maybe he looked through Drake's drawers, touching stuff.

Sally turned her back on Drake's display. Her black hair slipped over her shoulders like spilling oil. She probably owned a million brushes, Drake thought. Her eyelashes sparkled with caught tears.

"I had them in my room at first, but they made noises at night," she said quietly. "I pretended they were crying."

"Next eruption in five minutes!" Struther cried.

"Wait until this group leaves," his mother said to her

son. "These aren't volcano people. They're just cruel." She looked at Sally. "Don't fool yourself, miss. What you heard wasn't crying. It was starving parents eating their own babies."

"I wouldn't eliminate the possibility of tears," Mister Leeds said. "Tiny antelopes in Africa use their tears to mark their territory. And it's a fact that there are moths that feed on the tears of sleeping birds."

No one spoke. Drake imagined those soft moth wings batting against his cheeks, and a thrill ran through him. Sally blew her nose with a tissue her father handed her. What, Drake wondered, if Sally had been in Drake's room with her father? Maybe she'd sat on his bed. Maybe she lay down with her head on his pillow and stretched out her long, white legs across his comforter.

Mr. Leeds tucked his clipboard under his arm. "I would have liked to have seen a little activity from the survivors," he said as he walked away. "But you can't predict Mother Nature."

"He'll miss the eruption," Struther said. "And this is going to be a big one!"

The Fuller Brush man clapped his hands again. "Tell your mom I've got a new electric carpet sweeper to show her," he said to Drake. "It's almost weightless. I'll stop by next week. Not that she should be pushing anything around in her delicate condition. You and your dad should be helping out more. Where is she, anyway? At Jimmy D's with your dad? She's staying away from alcohol, I bet. Good advice for all mammas and papas who care about their kids." He shifted a look between the terrarium and Struther's mother. "You think those baby-eaters care about theirs, ma'am? Now where's that volcano?"

"He's waiting for new people," the angry mom said.

Drake tried to picture his father at Jimmy D's, sitting

at a booth with other men. What did "networking" look like? Then, as if conjured out of his thoughts, Drake heard his father's voice.

"Looks like I got here just in time for the show!" Drake's dad sidled up and nudged his son. The air was thick with strawberries. "You said two hours, so here I am." He looked around the cafeteria. "I think you got the wrong message about parents attending." He peered inside the terrarium. "Where's the gang?"

"Adam and Eve are sleeping." The Fuller Brush man winked. "Who knows what they're up to."

Drake's dad looked at the short man. "I'm sorry—you must be one of Drake's teachers?"

"We've never been officially introduced, but I've seen you around." The salesman stuck out his hand but Drake's father must not have seen it. "I'm Lou Jeffers, your wife's Fuller Brush man. You can thank me for that beard trimming kit you got last Father's Day. And for the passel of gerbils I gifted you, though I've been looking at your boy's experiment, and I'm not so sure how well they've fared. Hey, congrats on the new one, by the way. Due practically any minute, right?"

"The rotten fruit smell is getting worse," Struther said, screwing up his face.

"Smells like a strawberry daquiri," the Fuller Brush man said. "Not exactly a man's drink."

"It's just scent," Drake's father said. "I make candles. Smelling like one is an occupational hazard. We don't even notice it anymore, do we Drake?"

"Rub-a-dub-dub!" The Fuller Brush man grinned. "How are the butcher and baker? You see them at Jimmy D's?"

Drake bit his lip, but his father's reply came with a cautious smile. "You mean what do *they* smell like? I don't know. Raw meat? Cake? What's a Fuller Brush man smell like?"

The salesman stood up straight, but he was still a half a head shorter than Drake's dad. "We smell like whatever the customer wants us to smell like," he said.

Struther suddenly sneezed like a machine gun, five times in a row. He wiped his nose with his sleeve. "Mom," he whined, "I think I'm allergic to strawberry. Can I do the volcano now?"

Drake's father's smile faded. "So you're the one who brought these into our house."

"Your wife said your boy had some already and would love a few more." The salesman stuffed his hands in his pockets. His eyes were as wary as Drake's father's.

"'Love' is a little strong, I think," Drake's father said. "And the ones you gave him turned out to be a bunch of duds, if these two are the only survivors. I don't keep track of them, but that's what it looks like to me."

"Adam and Eve." The salesman tapped the pictures of Chip and Dale.

Drake stood mutely. His dad hadn't "kept track"? No "invisible hand"? But he'd suspected that all along, hadn't he?

"Cannibals," Struther's mom murmured. "Just plain cruelty."

The Fuller Brush man waved at the air as if he were swatting flies. "Man, I don't know what's worse, the gerbil stink or the strawberry."

"Volcano time!" Struther, from up on his stool, emptied his vial into the volcano. Again there was a gurgle and belch from inside the papier mache shell. But this time nothing else—no smoke, no lava.

"No! Don't let it!" Sally's sudden cry broke the silence. She buried her face in her father's chest.

The source of her alarm was immediately apparent: one of Drake's 'survivors' had unburied itself and stood atop the cedar bedding. Smoothing his daughter's hair protectively, the Fuller Brush man squinted inside the terrarium. "What's that it's got in its mouth? What the Hell *is* that?"

Struther's mother screeched "Cannibals!" into her hands. The gerbil stood placidly. The thing dangling from its mouth was shiny and smooth, the size and color of a kidney bean.

"It's moving!" a spectating kid shouted, and everyone stared. Had the tiny pink head gyrated slightly?

Struther stared gloomily down the mouth of his volcano. "It didn't work," he whimpered, but his mom wasn't listening.

"That's its baby," she wailed. "Don't you see, it's eating its baby. Somebody *do* something!"

Parents pulled their distressed children away from the display. Sally heaved with sobs. What if she really had been in Drake's room—in his bed—when her father had delivered the gerbils? What if Drake had found her there, the way the three bears had discovered Goldilocks at the end of their story? Then it might have been *his* arms wrapped around her now, instead of her father's.

"No!" Drake exclaimed. "It's not what you think. That's just a candy gummy, I swear. It's left over from my experiment. That's from the sugar diet that the other gerbils couldn't survive on. It's just a gummy bear." Drake's admission was no less true than the bulk of his gerbil details.

The commotion had drawn Mr. Leeds back to Drake's table. The teacher checked the terrarium, where the gerbil still stood at attention. "Survival of the fittest," Mr. Leeds said one last time, and strolled away. Finally, only Drake, his dad, and the Fuller Brush family remained. Even Struther and his mom had vanished.

"A gummy!" Drake insisted. Hadn't all of it—the lies, the cruelty, even the guilt Drake had struggled to hide from—been about survival? All he wanted now was to ride home with his dad on a wave of strawberry scent.

They could light dozens—hundreds!—of candles, all over the house, and then invite Drake's mom from her bed rest to share in the splendor.

The gerbil still stood like a statue. If there had been a tear in its tiny eye, it was too small to see. The thing in its mouth had lost its luster. Without warning, the critter ducked, spun around, and dove back into its burrow with its burden.

"So this is what you bring into people's houses?" Drake's father asked the Fuller Brush man. "This is what you do?"

The salesman was still patting his daughter's head. "Mostly it's brushes. But the animals were free. And didn't your boy here say these here were his originals? Nobody took care of mine. Ask her. Ask your wife." He pried his daughter from his chest and took a step toward her display. "Come on honey. Let's clean up your mosses and get out of here. This is over."

"Whoa-whoa-whoa—" Drake's father grabbed the salesman's elbow. "We're not taking these things home. Nobody ever asked me what I'd let in my house. They stink—way worse than strawberry." He dropped the Fuller Brush man's arm and looked at his son. "You want these things? You're sick of them, aren't you? Experiment's over."

Drake's heart beat feather light. "They can have them," he said as he followed his father toward the exit. They left the Fuller Brush man and his daughter without a goodbye.

"Wait—" the salesman called, but Drake's father held up his hand. Then he stopped and pivoted.

"Listen," he said, "What about this Fuller Brush thing? I'm interested in how it works. I'm looking for something. You want to tell me about it, come to Jimmy D's tomorrow afternoon. You can meet the butcher and the baker."

The salesman didn't answer. Sally pushed her hair from her face, which was blotchy from crying. Something new filled her eyes—a kind of pleading. Drake touched his father's hip, still staring into Sally's eyes. It was mercy she pled for. And Drake understood that she shouldn't ever have to listen to anything crying in the dark, even if it was just pretend.

"Dad," Drake said, "I changed my mind. I want to keep them—Adam and Eve. I need them."

LEAVING LOATHSOME CAVE

We, the youth of our county, grew up with the story, at least the naked bones of it—how over a hundred years ago the Winston Dam crumbled without warning on the first sunny day after a week of torrential rains. Until then, Winston Creek had babbled lazily through the field and forest, where it had cut, over millennia, a mile long tunnel through Hallowed Mountain. The well-worn footpath that accompanied the creek into and out of Loathsome Cave had provided a shortcut through the mountain for anyone with a torch. But, on the day the dam collapsed, Winston Creek had in the blink of an eye swollen into a river, flooding the cave and leaving its entrance and egress several feet underwater. The water gushing out rose up the hillsides, forming what's been known ever since as New Lake.

Before the flood, the worst casualties connected with Loathsome Cave were the scrapes and twisted ankles sustained by the daring participants in the "Dash through the Dark," an annual race through the cave without benefit of torches or lanterns. On June 24, 1916, the day the dam burst, the race had ended without mishap, and all the contestants had joined their families and friends for the usual picnic celebrating the race and the summer solstice on the banks of the creek not far from the cave's exit. This particular race day, the congregants of St. John the Baptist's Evangelical Church swelled the number of picnickers. They awaited a torch-lit procession of eleven children, ages ten through twelve, who were being led through the cave by their teenage youth adviser. After the procession, the children would be baptized in the waters of the creek by their waiting pastor.

But instead of marching children, something akin to a tidal wave exploded from the cave. The surging water inundated the picnic grounds and chased the horrified celebrants onto higher ground, where they watched the flood carry off their pies, potato salad, and roasting pigs. There wasn't a sign of the children.

After the water settled, rescue attempts proved futile: a powerful current invisible from the new lake's placid surface pushed divers away from the cave's egress, and not even the most accomplished swimmers risked the turbulence at its entrance.

For a few weeks, parents, congregants, and concerned members of the community camped among the trees around the new lake's perimeter, praying for some sign of their children. But the water never receded, and Loathsome Cave yielded none of its dead. On the first anniversary of the tragedy, a memorial plaque, set in a granite outcropping as close to the cave's entrance as possible, was dedicated:

"For The Dozen, Taken To Heaven On St. John The Baptist's Day, Where They Sit On The Right Hand Of The Lord."

The plaque is now more than a hundred years old. Trails of rust from its iron frame stain the rock. St. John the Evangelist Church, divided over the eternal fate of the unbaptized children, did not survive the tragedy.

※ ※ ※

We, three girls and two boys, sit around a campfire on the littered shoreline of New Lake, rehashing the junior year of school we've just finished, making plans for the summer we've just begun, guessing at the excitements and disappointments our senior year is sure to bring. None of us is thinking that we've built our fire on the very spot desperate family members had waited a hundred years ago for signs of their children. Our blaze animates the nearest trees, creating a screen of dancing light and shadows that hide the forest's depths. The lake reflects nothing on this starless, moonless night. We might as well be perched on the edge of the earth. We've all pledged to our parents, our church, and our school administration that we will refrain from alcohol, but the boys have brought beers that only one of the girls samples. She spits it out, claiming it tastes like gasoline.

After a while, a heaviness descends that squelches our festive mood, and we grow melancholy before the fire, each of us retreating to thoughts of our own uncertain futures and unfulfilled desires. One of the boys, slightly drunk, suddenly leans back from the fire and lets loose a howl that echoes off the escarpment of

Hallowed Mountain. We catch the gleam in his eyes when he lowers his head and wipes his mouth with the back of his wrist.

"This place *has* to be haunted," he insists. "All those unbaptized kids caught between heaven and hell. So, where are they?"

"Pastor Mel says those kids *are* saved," one of the girls says. "He says that god grants special dispensation to victims of natural disasters. He says their souls are all in heaven where they belong."

"It *is* haunted," another of us says, "or it used to be. I heard that the kids' parents used to come back every year on the anniversary of the flood for prayer meetings, and once they heard what sounded like a bunch of children singing 'Happy Birthday.'"

A mighty splash startles us— it sounds like someone cannonballing into a pool, and our eyes jerk to the lake, but we see nothing. We rise, feigning courage. One of us picks up a rock, and the rest choose among the thick branches we've collected for the fire.

"What do you do for bears?" one of the boys whispers.

"Stay by the fire. Bears don't like fire."

We wait, as still as statues. A burning log crackles, spitting embers like tiny fireworks. We hear sloshing— something is moving through the water. None of us breathes. The sloshing stops. We brandish our weapons.

And then, as if caught in a sudden spotlight, he emerges from the darkness. Ignoring us, he stretches his arms toward the fire—to warm his hands? He is as tall as our tallest boy and naked. His wet, tangled hair hangs past his shoulders. None of us know him, though he appears to be around our age. His narrow chest heaves, as if he's just finished a long race.

Why doesn't he notice us? Frowning, we test the heft of our weapons. But he's concentrating on his hands. He turns them over, flexing his fingers as if he's just discovered them. In the firelight his glowing skin is the pinkish-gray of canned tuna, including the penis hanging between his legs like a sleeping bat. Some of us think of nude statues we've seen.

"Hey," one of us calls with a cracking voice. Our visitor, pivots and faces the speaker, his hands grasping like pincers. Then he finally notices the rest of us. His outstretched arms sweep back and forth as if he's conducting a band. We watch him shake his head violently like he's got water in his ear, sink to his knees, and collapse.

He lies on the packed earth, eyes closed, knees drawn up to his chest. We drop our branches and stones and approach him. One of the girls shakes out the red and white checked tablecloth we've been using as a blanket and covers him. She kneels by his side, announces that he's breathing, and lays her hand on his forehead like a mother testing a child's temperature. When he moves slightly, she yanks her hand back, waits, then touches him again, this time sliding her hand under the tablecloth to feel his shoulder.

"He's cold," she says. "His skin is cool and hard. Weird hard, and wet-ish. Like a dolphin, you know? Come feel." Within seconds the five of us squat or kneel around our visitor. We scootch our fingers under the cloth, run our palms along his shins, squeeze his feet. His toenails and fingernails are long and curl under like talons.

"He was just swimming," one of the boys says unconvincingly. "He's okay, right?"

What does "okay" even mean, we wonder.

Our visitor shudders and we shuffle back, forming a ring around him. He props himself up on one elbow. He squints at us at an angle, as if he's trying to look at us and the fire at the same time—the light seems both irresistible and painful to him. His lips move, and we lean toward him, expecting him to speak, but he doesn't. He notices the cloth covering him, picks at the red and white squares, then flicks it off as if it irritates his skin. He sits up and crosses his legs. We look at each other with firelit eyes to avoid staring at his genitals.

"Are you okay?" one of us asks. "Do you need help? Are you lost?"

"Is this—?" he hisses and pauses to take a breath. "We know about light," he says. "Is this how you make it? It —paints—everything." He holds his hands toward the fire again as if to demonstrate what he's talking about, then rubs his arms and legs like he's soaping up in a shower. His lip curls—is that a smile? When he looks at us one at a time, our faces warm. "And I look like you— we all look like you." He turns his head in the direction of Hallowed Mountain, then back toward us, wincing. "I'm the first to know that. Inside, there's no seeing. Does light always hurt this much?"

We don't know what to tell him, because he's mistaken— we are not just like him. *Inside where*, we wonder.

❦ ❦ ❦

"We know about fire," he says. "Light is hot, right? We've heard of hot, too."

"All light isn't hot," we tell him. "Like the stars and moon. They're just—light. Most nights you can see them in the sky. When it's clear they're reflected in the lake."

He cranes his neck and stares up into the darkness. "The sky—" he murmurs.

One of us turns on her smartphone's flashlight and points it at the ground beside him. "Not hot," she says.

He paws at the pool of light, then lets it sift through his fingers.

"I've heard of the moon and the stars. And the sun," he says. "And something called an 'electric torch.' We never had one. Light was the first thing we lost, we're told. We touch. We hear." He blinks into the void. "This is night. And then there'll be day. And colors? Something called a 'rainbow'?"

"Look at our clothes," we say. "See the different colors? They don't show so well in the firelight."

As if he's learning to see, his eyes bulge, then squeeze shut. His mouth hangs open. Can he distinguish the reds and blues and yellows of our T-shirts? What does he make of the words printed across them: the name of our school, of bands we like, of places we've vacationed?

"We know about clothes," he says, then suddenly covers his face with splayed fingers and rolls his head like we've seen blind people do. "Too much," he grunts. "It hurts my head."

We are silent a long time, watching him. "How old are you?" one of us finally asks.

"How old?" He lowers his hands, but keeps his eyes closed. He hesitates when he speaks—an accent or impediment? Or is he just mulling. "We had 'time' for a while," he says. "A gold watch came in with the first ones. It 'ticked,' they say. They counted the ticks, then added them up and scratched the rocks to show that a 'day' passed. We're told they kept track for twenty years. Then the watch stopped ticking. We don't have it anymore. But we can still touch those scratches to see what time felt like. How old am I? I'm generation four, same as my partner. Our daughter is generation five."

What he's telling us about light, about color, about time, leaves our heads spinning: a partner? a daughter?

"Do you go to school around here" one of us asks.

"School? That's what we *are*—the Saint John the Baptist Evangelical School. Who else would we be?"

One of us gasps. The earth seems to shift under us. The fire flickers—it needs more wood. The one of us with the phone flashlight points it at the escarpment, but its beam doesn't reach. We suspected from the first, didn't we? But we've been afraid to accept it: *He's telling us he came from the cave.*

⁂ ⁂ ⁂

We stare at our visitor, who sits before the dwindling fire, the checked tablecloth heaped beside him. When he opens his mouth, we hold our breath. What next? But all he does is yawn. His eyelids flutter and shut, and, as he'd done earlier, he sinks onto his side. He snores lightly, his ribcage rising and falling.

"What the hell?" blurts one of the boys.

"He's asleep," says one of the girls. "Look at how smooth his legs are."

"That Sunday school class—is he saying there are still people in the cave?"

"For a hundred years?"

"Nobody lives that long."

"They never found bodies.

"'Generations'?"

"How can you not know what light is?"

"Or time."

"Maybe this is just a huge practical joke," one boy says. "Maybe he's an escaped lunatic."

"No—look at him—" one of the girls says. "Look at his skin—he's different."

"He just kind of tipped over and went to sleep."

"If it's always dark—if they don't have day and night, maybe they just doze whenever they feel like. Maybe they just disconnect."

As one, we turn toward the escarpment, staring hard, as if the power of our concentrated attention will drill through the stone. We hold our breath, listening for pulses that have been beating beneath the stone, unheard for a century.

It's late. Some of us have curfews. We make phone calls and send texts, composing foolproof alibis about spending the night at each other's homes. None of our parents are suspicious. We stare at our slumbering visitor. A fishy odor wafts from him that we hadn't noticed before.

How did he escape, we wonder. *Why is he here?*

⁂

When the fire goes out, the stars and a half-moon emerge in the night sky. What would our visitor make of them? Without knowledge of light, what does he— what *can* he—dream? The dark of the mountain and the woods across the lake seem a solid presence. We wait for morning in the company of a legend that has unexpectedly come to life.

⁂

Dawn's pale fluorescence absorbs the moon and the stars. Our visitor still sleeps. The mountain blocks our view of the rising sun. But we are impatient—there is so much we are eager to share with our guest, and there are so many questions to ask: Does he really come from the cave? Are we the first living creatures he has ever seen? Does he have a name?

Across the lake, a flock of geese rises, distance separating their flight from their honking. They fly east toward the sun we won't see for hours and disappear behind Hallowed Mountain. We hadn't planned on an overnight, and the five of us are shy with each other in the daylight. One at a time, each of the three girls stands stiffly and heads into the woods to pee, then reclaims her spot next to the cold fire. Then the boys leave and return together. We're all pasty-mouthed and hungry, but we've no food or drink left for ourselves or to offer our visitor. Still, as the world wakes up around us, we're as excited as children on Christmas morning—we're about to present him with the world. How long will he sleep?

Wait until he sees—everything! we think.

✿ ✿ ✿

"I'm sure I didn't sleep last night," one of the girls whispers while we crouch around our visitor, waiting for him to wake, "but it's really weird—I remember dreaming."

"Me too," says another of us. "So did I," says a third. Neither boy admits having dreamt.

"In my dream," the first girl says, "I was inside Loathsome Cave. I knew it was supposed to be pitch dark, but I could see somehow. Deep in the cave there was sort of a raised shelf—the Saint John the Baptist Sunday School kids must have discovered it and scrambled up on it before their torch went out. I heard water rushing by below, but I couldn't see it. I saw how they ate—they made nets out of the clothes they'd worn in. They sat huddled together, biting into fish they held like corn on the cob. The whole scene looked like one of those paintings, the ones on—"

"The ones painted on black velvet?" the next girl says. "That's how it was in my dream, too. Everyone in the cave was squatting or sitting cross-legged up on a rock platform, like you said. All of them had long hair, and they were all busy twisting each other's braids. Their fingers worked really quick, but their eyes were closed, and I remember there wasn't any light."

We look at our sleeping visitor's long hair—it's disheveled, but there's crimping that hints at braids. His skin gleams, nearly iridescent.

"And—" the second dreamer continues, "all of the

braiders were taking turns speaking. I couldn't make out everything they said because of all the water splashing by and the echoes, but I heard bits and pieces. I heard them say 'Moses' and 'Jesus' and 'Abraham Lincoln.' Somehow I knew that they were *reading* the braids they were fingering, just like the blind read Braille. I think they were having some kind of school."

One of the boys interrupts. "Won't the sun hurt his eyes—and his skin, too? Won't he burn?"

We consider this and conclude that, when he wakes, we will lead him into the shade. We have sunblock, and at least one of us imagines coating him with it.

The third dreamer among us, the girl who'd shown our visitor the flashlight, speaks up. "I dreamed of the cave, too. Like you guys said, I knew it was completely dark, but in my dream everything and everybody sort of glowed like ghosts in movies. All of the people in the cave were packed together and squirming like octopuses —their arms and legs were wrapped around each other. It was just touching, touching, touching." Pausing, she glances over her shoulder at the shadowed escarpment of Hallowed Mountain. She pulls up the collar of her T-shirt, trying to hide the blush spilling from her neck to her chest.

"Sounds like an orgy," one of the boys says.

"I guess," the dreamer says. "Did you ever see maggots in rotten meat?" We groan, but she's shaking her head. "No," she says, "it didn't feel like a bad thing. Like they were just *luminous*. There were babies, too, squeezed in here and there—you know how things are in dreams. But nobody looked any older than him—" She nods at our visitor, and we all stare at him.

"Maybe they don't live long," one of the boys says. "Imagine living in the dark just eating fish. They're naked and trying to keep warm. And they've got no way of keeping track of time. Time's just old scratches on the wall, like something you'd see in a museum."

"Well, I didn't have any dreams," our other boy says. "And dreams aren't facts. When he wakes up, we can ask him what's true and what's not. If this is all a hoax, he'll probably laugh his ass off at us for being so gullible. He probably goes to North High, or Jefferson."

"Look at him," says the girl who dreamed of touching. "You ever see anybody who looked like him *anywhere*?"

We haven't.

"We need to do something with him, don't we?" our doubting boy asks.

"Find out what he needs. He must have come here for a reason."

"And then show him everything we see, like the lake and the trees and flowers and birds. We'll have to tell him about all the new inventions, like television—"

"What about all the wars? And nuclear weapons?"

"Wait until we tell him we got to the moon!"

"Then—when he's ready—we'll ask him if our dreams are true."

"Okay, but who are we going to tell?" asks our doubting boy. "Our parents? The police? If he's what you think he is, we better notify *somebody*. If there *are* people in the cave, don't we have to get them out? We've got the technology now to do it—like scuba equipment and mini-submarines. They got those Korean kids out of the cave they were trapped in."

We exchange looks. "Do we have to say anything right away?" asks one of the dreamers. "I mean, they've been in the cave for a hundred years. We don't even know if they *want* to get out. Remember what happened to ET when the authorities found out about him? They almost killed him."

"ET was an alien in a movie," our doubter dismisses. "Whether or not this guy is an actual cave dweller, he's definitely real."

"But why rush?" asks the girl who dreamed of fish-catching. "Wouldn't it be fun to watch him discover things? Couldn't we just share him, just for a week, maybe? He could stay a couple of days in the barn at my place. You—" she says, jutting her chin toward the doubter, "your parents are away, and you've got a finished basement with a fold-out couch—and the rest of us, you know, we'd just find our own secret places. We'd get him some clothes, first, of course..."

Both boys are quiet. They kick at the ashes of the campfire. Suddenly, we're slapped by brightness—the sun has edged over Hallowed Mountain. We squint up at it, lost in our own thoughts. Then one of the girls screams.

"Jesus—look at him—he's all blue!"

We panic: "Is he okay? Is he breathing? He's not breathing!" We wring our hands. "Who knows CPR?"

❧ ❧ ❧

The girl who dreamed of fish-catching has been a lifeguard at a summer camp, and she kneels beside our visitor. "Damn-damn-damn-damn-damn," she mutters, struggling to remember the Red Cross lifesaving steps. She places her ear next to his mouth and listens. She shakes her head. "I don't hear anything," she murmurs. She checks his pulse, first at his wrist, then at his neck, and shakes her head again. Hunching over our visitor, she tilts his head back, pinches his nose shut, seals her mouth over his and blows hard twice. We watch his chest rise and fall, and for a second feel a twinge of hope. But our lifeguard lifts her head, wipes spittle from her lips and pushes her hair back. She places her palms flat on our visitor's chest and presses with all her weight — ten, twenty, thirty times. She stops. Our visitor is as lifeless as a store dummy.

"Can you help?" she asks our doubter. "Thirty times, just like I did? We need to get his heart started. You do the compressions, I'll do the breathing."

So many compressions and breaths, we lose track of time. The girl who dreamed of touching watches her friend's mouth clamped over their visitor's and wishes she'd learned CPR. None of us has ever witnessed life pass into death. Finally, our lifeguard sits back on her heels. She's given up. But the doubter keeps thrusting, grunting with each push. Our lifeguard reaches out and squeezes his shoulder, but he doesn't stop until the other boy steps forward and gently pulls him away. Tears and snot smear the doubter's face.

⁂

Our boys half-lift, half-drag the naked body to the lake, wading in with it up to their hips. The water appears still on this windless day, reflecting the midmorning blue of a cloudless sky, but the boys can feel the drag of the current that has traveled through the cave and runs powerfully beneath the surface.

His body will follow those who died in there, runs the argument that has won out. *The bodies must get stuck underwater somewhere, or else get washed way downriver. Maybe they get to the Mississippi. Maybe they wind up in the Gulf of Mexico. But it's got nothing to do with us. We did the best we could. If we hadn't found him, he would have died anyway. And if we tell? He'd just be a John Doe, and if we reveal what we believe might be true, everybody will think we're nuts.*

"At least," the doubting boy says, "he got to see light. Too bad he never got to see the sun."

But, some of us are thinking, *what if it was the light that killed him? We insisted he look at our colors, and that's when he collapsed. And what if he wasn't a reckless adventur-*

er, and the descendants of the St. John the Baptist's Evangelical Church Sunday School Class desperately need help? What if they aren't just a dream?

Our boys splash back to shore. The body glides down the lake like an abandoned beach float, somebody else's problem if it's ever found. We resist looking back at Hallowed Mountain and the escarpment's stone face. How hard will it be to keep our secret—that a colony of cave dwellers has existed right under our noses for decades?

❧ ❧ ❧

Summer passes. The five return to school for their final semesters. By graduation, they will no longer be a "we." First, it is the routine of senior year that absorbs them: classes, homework, sports they play or watch, parties, choices regarding alcohol, drugs, dating, and sex. Slowly, the bond that linked them one summer night on the shore of New Lake loosens, fades, and disappears. When any of the five pass in the halls, settle in seats in the same classes, bump into one another in the cafeteria, wind up at the same parties, in the same plays, or on the same sports teams, they ignore confessional urges. No body is ever reported found. Couldn't it all have been just a dream? Without moving, four of the five pretend they have moved on, until pretense becomes habit, and habit hardens into fact. But the weight of the truth they suppress anchors them in time and place; they are no less trapped than the occupants of Loathsome Cave.

❧ ❧ ❧

It is the fifth witness, Britney, who refuses to forget, the girl who dreamed she saw the cave dwellers squirming together, *like maggots, but not in a bad way*. The red and white checked tablecloth that had covered their visitor's nakedness curtains her bedroom window and filters both daylight and darkness. He'd shrugged off the unfamiliar fabric, consumed as he was by the painful thrill of the firelight.

Some nights while Britney lies in bed, she pretends the checkered cloth is a net spread across the swollen creek's torrent, and she dreams of leaping fish. Other nights she discovers herself twisting among the bodies writhing in the cave and remembers how she'd longed to coat the visitor's shoulders, arms, torso, and legs with lotion. Recalling his revelations of a daughter and a partner, Britney moans and bites her lip. When she drains a can of tuna in the kitchen sink, the oil glitters over her hand; later, she will blush with guilt and pleasure as she catches the slight odor on her fingertips.

Only Britney of the original five returns to Loathsome Cave. It's the day before she's to leave for college. Rain threatens, and New Lake reflects an ashen sky.

She stands on the shore. Mud stains the new sneakers she'd hoped to keep pristine for her first day on campus. *This is where I saw him discover light*, she thinks, though there are no signs of the campfire. The trash of later picknickers is scattered in the weeds at the forest's edge. She scans Hallowed Mountain's escarpment and pictures a giant fist descending from the clouds and rapping on the rock. *Anybody home*? She listens: where is the chorus of children's voices? the thrum of imprisoned hearts? One of the boys had howled that night, before *he* came. She clears her throat and opens her mouth wide, but can't produce a sound.

Her gaze tumbles down the face of the escarpment to the juncture of rock and lake. The way back into Loathsome Cave is beneath the surface. Had he meant to return? Do those he left feel his absence, or is the sense of loss forgotten, like light and time? Her heart pounds. She's leaving too. Their visitor's compromised vision had reminded her and the other four of their world's beauty, but what had blinded them to his frailty? How had they not seen that he was dying?

Britney releases a shivery sigh. She kicks at a rusty can and remembers the plaque placed so long ago on the far side of Hallowed Mountain, as near as it was possible to get to the submerged entrance to Loathsome Cave. But the memorial lied about the lost children being in heaven: at the very moment the plaque was being fixed to stone, the Sunday school class had been learning to live without light.

Her sneakers—she'll never be able to clean them. The easiest thing to do would be to throw them out. But she knows she won't. She'll wear them stain-streaked, waiting to be asked why she wears such filthy shoes. If she's able to keep the story straight in her head and heart, she'll tell all about the tragedy of Loathsome Cave.

OLD YELLER

We've just finished watching *Old Yeller*, my boy and I. A classic film, exhumed from my childhood. I'm dabbing my eyes, my throat and nose still too full to ask Carl what he thought. He lies quietly as the credits and music run, belly down on the sofa, his heels close enough for me to grab. I can't see his face, except for the curve of his cheek. The bowl of chips sits on the floor beneath his dangling arm. If it were his head near my hand, maybe I would tousle his thick black curls.

Carl usually becomes subdued the last few hours of Sunday afternoons before his mother picks him up. That's why we fill that lull with a film. This slot, I've told myself, is my opportunity to teach the boy about movies. They're my business, after all. And though he's spent time with me on sets and has an idea of how movies are made, there aren't too many of my own films

I'd let him see. Except for *Son of Kong*, my PG crossover blockbuster remake of the classic sequel, the slasher movies associated with my name earn their R rating. Gratuitous violence and brief frontal nudity are marketing prerequisites. I've never brought Carl to the set when we film breasts. Except once, because of a scheduling snafu, but I had Hans the make up genius take Carl aside and plant a bloody ax in the boy's forehead. As a distraction. His mom gave me Hell for letting him wear it home.

The blood on the set never bothers Carl, nor should it. He can see the canned carnage squirted out of bottles and cans.

"It's like Halloween!" he said, his eyes bright, the first time I brought him with me. He watched Ralphie Di-Giorgia, my assistant director, lay out a murder victim and strew an armload of severed limbs around the set. With all the scaffolding and lights and cameras, who could confuse a movie set with the real world? When you see a ghoul chatting with a gaffer and sipping a Diet Pepsi a second before your dad yells, "Action!" it's impossible to take it seriously when the same ghoul whacks a rubberized torso with a hatchet and kicks a mannequin's arm down a pretend gutter while whistling Wagner's "Flying Dutchman." Not if the actor returns to his soft drink and conversation a second after Daddy calls, "Cut!"

But Carl isn't allowed to see the product—two months of filming boiled down to 90 minutes of gore choreographed with brilliant psychological insight to induce audience nightmares. That's what they pay for, but it's not for my boy. What kind of father would I be? He can watch when he's older if he chooses.

Christine, my darling ex, accuses me of sending Carl home every weekend depressed. I try to explain that the sadness at the end of movies like *Old Yeller* is the culmination of a kind of joy—a triumph of spirit it's nearly impossible to experience in everyday life, but she doesn't get it. She's neither literary nor spiritual. It seems that late every Sunday night I get the same phone call:

"He's crying into his pillow again, Raymond. How can you do this? Are you trying to sabotage your relationship with him? Don't you want to see him? You're trying to poison *my* relationship with him. And Klaus's, too. Is that it?"

Klaus is Carl's chess master stepfather. I don't bother trying to defend myself anymore. Once in a while by way of retaliation I'll complain about my successor teaching my boy to "think in chess," but I'm not really worried about it. My comments manage to set Christine off, though.

"And what are *you* teaching him to think about, Raymond? Violence? Sexual perversion? What's he get from watching you play out these horrible juvenile fantasies?" I'm not sure she can distinguish between Disney classics and the movies that keep the support checks in the mail.

I want to say that what Carl gets from me is a father, but I really don't want to undermine his relationship with Klaus (whose talent I genuinely respect), even though the international chess circuit keeps my boy's stepfather out of the country for weeks at a time. And with Christine managing *MindGames* —"the 'zine for intelligent game players who enjoy playing intelligent games"—Carl is being raised by Greta, his caregiver. Christine works at home, but when she's busy, which is nearly always, nobody's allowed near her. At least I take the boy to work with me.

But here it is, the end of *Old Yeller*, and as soon as I shiver out my last sniffle, I'll tell Carl to load up his backpack so he can be ready for his mom. Theme music plays on, as do memory shots of the big yellow dog romping with the boys, that crazy hound, mischievous and courageous, and I bite my lip again. It's dizzyingly sappy, and I'm ashamed of myself and the movie for softening the impact of the young hero's call to man-hood: shooting his beloved, rabid dog is as solitary and clean and generous a gesture as George's shooting of Lennie. Maybe next week we'll graduate from animal movies to *Of Mice and Men*. I could tell Christine after-wards that I thought the story was about pets.

I wish I could see Carl's eyes. If his leg didn't rise and fall rhythmically into the sofa like a lazy ax, I might think he was asleep. How much of what he feels about the film can he put into words?

"Son of Kong," I say after the credits have spooled out and the music stops, "time to get a move on."

"Yes, Papa Kong," he answers. He hoists himself onto the sofa, his dark eyes still on the black screen. He's thinking. What if he's assessing *Old Yeller* through the patterns of chess?

"Dad—" he says, blinking lazy lids, "—I want to be an actor."

There's a mature set to Carl's lips that reminds me of the mantle photograph of a smiling corporal I never knew. Your Dad, Mom insisted, a War Hero. He was also my first Doubt. But my foundation of disbelief cracks a little each weekend as I watch the Hero's smile develop, as through time lapse photography, on my boy's face.

It's hard to deny my son; I'm mired waist deep in the film industry. But an actor? Is it possible he's miscon-strued his own feelings after watching *Old Yeller*? Being an only child is lonely, I know. Your imagination is your only companion.

"Listen," I say, "maybe you could talk your mom and

Klaus into getting you a dog. Or maybe I could get one here for you to play with on weekends. I suppose Sylvia could walk and feed it." My middle-aged housekeeper spends half her day hunched on the back stoop, huffing her generic cigarettes. She might actually enjoy having an excuse to get outside. I can see the little rascal tugging at his leash—

"No, Dad. You're away too much. And Klaus is allergic. Really allergic. He's always worried about getting a sinus infection right before a big match, like, he'd be sitting over the board, and his nose would drip. Right on the pawn, he says." My son smiles faintly as he mimics: "'The king and queen or the brave knights—no they are too noble too be dripped upon.'" I forgot how recently Carl had lost his lisp. I have to admit, he's got Klaus's accent down, though it pains me to hear how thoroughly the man has been absorbed into my boy's life. "'The bishop—ach, he would have me excommunicated! Only the lowly pawn remains—it is his lot in life to receive the fluids of my nose!'"

Carl captures Klaus's perplexed concentration with an arched eyebrow. I'd forgotten my son's memory is nearly photographic. Or "phonographic." He can repeat what he hears, even if he doesn't know what the words mean." His face relaxes, and he is ten year old Carl again.

"What's 'excommunicate'?" he asks.

"It means to get thrown out of the church."

"You mean like for talking too much in class?"

"Sort of—" my thoughts are elsewhere. Does Carl treat his mom and Klaus and Greta the governess to imitations of me? "—but, no, not really. Not just thrown out of any one specific building. It means you're not supposed to be part of that religion any more. It doesn't recognize you."

"Who doesn't recognize you?"

"I don't know. The powers that be."

"What powers? God?"

"I suppose so," I say. "The Big Fellow himself gives you the boot. Just like I'm about to do. Get your stuff together, Son of Kong, and your rear in gear. Your momma will be here in a minute."

When Carl stands up he upsets the potato chip bowl.

"Don't worry," I say. "The imaginary dog will clean that up."

"What about acting?" he asks.

"We'll talk to your mother. I'm sure she'll have plenty of excellent ideas about it. You know how she loves it when you join me on the set."

Carl gazes at me a second with an ambiguous smile. First one eyebrow lifts, then the other. They ride up higher on his forehead than I've ever seen them. It's another adult look. It's not surprise or dismay, exasperation or tolerance. I don't know if it's an imitation of somebody—it *is* oddly familiar—or a personal expression he's grown into. Then he's off to fetch his bag.

The clock on the DVD player reads 6:15, which means Christine will be here in ten minutes. When it comes to removing my son from my company she will be remarkably punctual. I hope it's because she misses him. I turn on the TV and the screen brightens to a doll-faced newscaster. Her porcelain cuteness dooms her to weekend anchor. Has she satisfied her ambitions?

"Another—" she shrills, and I mute her with a quick thumb.

Carl wants to act. I know a dozen casting agents, and half of them owe me favors. If I put Allison, my assistant, on the case tomorrow, she'd have a gig for the boy by sundown, even though she can't stand him. Children frighten her, she says, flaring yellow smoker's nostrils. Since Carl is the only child she ever sees, I take it personally for him. And Carl distrusts her. He never ate the licorice sticks and lemon drops she foisted on him when he was younger. "She maketh them out of dead children," he'd lisp to me privately. He kept the candy in a glass bowl on his dresser at my place. The sight of the stiff red and black twists and the hard yellow pellets made my skin crawl.

I could give Carl a job myself. It wouldn't be so hard to script a small role for him in the untitled quickie we're shooting now. He could be a victim's narrowly escaping child or little brother, sent running down a dark alley in a futile search for help. Later we could have him round his deep brown eyes in terror at the discovery of a body, or parts of one, and then disappear down the same alley. We economize by recycling alleys and limbs, the fundamental raw materials of my genre.

I'm thinking of ways to use my boy, considering the virtues and problems, when I sense him behind me. His breath tickles the bald spot I pretend isn't there, but glimpse in mirrors and store windows. (When I watched myself on the "Making of *Son of Kong*," I followed that patch of flesh as if it were the bouncing ball under the lyrics of a sing-a-long.)

When Carl doesn't speak, I gather that he's focused on the TV. The doll-faced anchor is gone. Instead, there is a pair of photographs, school pictures of a boy and a girl not much older than Carl. The children look alike. Maybe twins: they share the same gap between large front teeth, the same lank hair and protruding ears. The same pale eyes, the girl's slightly crossed behind her glasses.

A woman stands on uneven porch steps, grasping a collapsing iron rail. Paint flakes from the door behind her. To one side is a battered trash can. On the other a bush shrivels against the porch like a starving mongrel.

Microphones labeled with the letters of local TV stations urge my focus to the woman's face. Curious neighbors crowd the frame, a grandmother with a purple scarf and scabbed nose, a boy with a Florida Marlins hat straddling a bicycle, but the shot is locked on the first woman. Of course she is related to the two children, the twins from the photographs. She squints with incomprehension or grief behind glasses like her daughter's. Her nose is red and her loose cheeks quiver as her gapped teeth clamp again and again on her lower lip. Her ear slides through her dull hair like an actor peeking through a curtain.

Something very bad has happened. As in my slasher films, the possibilities are limited, but all point toward a tragic end. An accident, a kidnapping, a murder. I shut off the TV. Carl doesn't need to see this. It's not a movie under production; it's life. There's no theme music. I try to deflect any difficult questions.

"A story that was on before you came in," I say. "Very sad. A couple of kids lost their dog. Nobody can find it." I feel my throat constrict around my fiction, and my eyes sting. "It's thought to be dead," I add, as solemn as any anchorman.

I feel Carl at my side and allow myself a sidelong glance, wary that he'll read my lie. His features sag with grief. Has he taken my dog story to heart? Maybe he's devastated by his discovery that his father is a liar. More likely, he has sensed the tragedy I tried to conceal. His chin is trembling, and I reach to console him. But then I see his face: his lips have drawn back and exaggerate the size of his teeth; his nose is red and swollen; a pale ear sticks out of his flattened curls. A trick of lighting has rinsed color from his irises. He wears the face of the mother on the news.

The doorbell rings. Christine has come to claim her son, but neither the boy nor I move. Tears well in Carl's eyes. My God, I think. He's *acting!*

Claustrophilia, Outer Banks

I

Two uniformed men stand on the deck of the U-boat, close enough to hail, Dad and I know, because we can hear them talking. The blond one smokes a cigarette. The heavyset one gestures with his hands. The sky's icy blue, and the sea between the motorboat we've been fishing from and their sub is black and calm. When I look the other way, west toward the Outer Banks shore we'd see if we weren't so far out, the glare stabs my eyes like a polished knife. It's possible but not likely that this glare hides us from the U-boat men. Now each of them shields his eyes with a hand—they seem to be staring right through us. Maybe we're just too small for them to worry about.

"They're probably looking for shore," Dad says. "They want to brag that they saw America. They'll probably lie and say they did."

Dad had cut the engine when the submarine surfaced, and we rocked in its swells for a minute or two. Then our Germans had emerged.

"Reel in your line," Dad whispers. "We don't want to catch something now and get them curious." The sailors' voices carry, but we don't understand their language. "Don't hook yourself," Dad says when he sees me flip my bait minnow onto my rubber boot. I can't stop staring at the Germans.

Dad has been planning this father-son fishing trip since he decided to enlist "before the draft gets me." Tomorrow Mom will drive him off the Outer Banks, and he'll be bussed to boot camp. He'll miss my tenth birthday party.

"Lie low," Dad says, and we slouch, but there's nothing to hide behind. "Can you imagine being crammed inside that thing day and night? The whole crew must be dying for fresh air—maybe they're coming up two at a time."

The U-boat takes up the middle third of the horizon. The thin, blond sailor points his cigarette at something overhead. I look up, too—there are gulls, way, way up. I don't like the sky, and I don't like the ocean. They're both too big, and they're meant for birds and fish, not human beings. I think I'd like it inside the U-boat, where I could huddle in the dark in a bunk pressed tight to the ceiling, engulfed in the engine's thrum.

"You've got yourself an indoor-boy," Mom said to Dad when I told him I'd rather read than play catch. I'm not really sporty, though I'm not afraid of the ball, and I don't get picked last in gym when we choose up teams. But these are serious times, war times, so when your dad tells you you're going fishing, you go. The U-boats have been sinking oil tankers in the Atlantic for a year now, but nobody's reported seeing one yet off the Outer Banks. Before this one surfaced I'd been waiting to hear important things that fathers are supposed to tell sons, like, "You'll be the man of the house while I'm gone, Billy."

The German with the cigarette throws it overboard, holding his arm like a salute as he follows its flight. The sailors face each other.

"Maybe they're deciding what to do with us." Dad tosses me an orange life jacket, which I duck into and buckle. It smells like mildew. He holds his life jacket without putting it on. Every other breath I take is shivery. If the Germans take us prisoner, they'll probably bring us below deck.

Once, when I was a little kid, I fell asleep in my parents' bedroom closet. I'd crawled in looking for Christmas presents and shut the door on myself when I heard Mom on the stairs. In the dark, I made a nest out of a pile of soft towels. The cool fabric of her dresses brushed my cheeks. The smells of leather and shoe polish and mothballs made me sleepy. I listened for my mother and counted to one hundred... and woke to harsh light and her too-close silhouette. "My, oh my," she sighed. "Should I tell your father about this when he comes home?" I stood up on wobbly legs, clinging to a dress, and she stooped and hugged me.

The bright spring sun warms my face, and I've closed my eyes, picturing the way the U-boat had emerged: the sea boiling from black to green to white, its tower taking shape like a magical castle, water spilling off the long deck as the submarine rose and settled.

"Whoa—man overboard!"

My eyes snap open at Dad's whispered cry, and I squint at the U-boat's deck. I count Germans: one—just the blond, who bends over the rail like he's seasick.

Dad's straining to keep his voice low. "The big one's overboard—I think the skinny one pushed him."

There are splashes at the U-boat's waterline. The German in the ocean is shouting. My arms and legs feel suddenly heavy, as if something's hanging on them.

"His friend better get him out of there," Dad says. It feels like we're watching a movie. "He won't last long—the water's still winter-cold." The blond German pivots from the rail and disappears down a hatch. "He's going for a life preserver or rope—you'd think they'd have something like that on deck." Seconds pass, then minutes. There's no movement aboard the U-boat, and the commotion in the water has stopped. With a grinding rumble, the German boat slides to our left, north, pushing a lip of foam, then veers out to sea.

Dad's surprised: "They're leaving him? I don't get it." The wake reaches us, and our boat nods up and down.

Barely breathing, I stare at the U-boat shrinking into the distance. I remember a newsreel I saw a month ago, "Perils of Flight." It showed plane crashes and zeppelin disasters. The worst accident, worse to me than the burning of the *Hindendburg*, involved a blimp that a group of about twenty soldiers were trying to hold on the ground with a rope. But the huge blimp had a mind of its own—it dragged the landing crew across the field, nosing into the air as it shook off soldier after soldier. The blimp soared up and away—with one soldier still hanging on to the rope! I gasped along with everyone in the theatre as we understood that the dangling soldier had made a snap decision and guessed wrong. The blimp rose, a hundred feet, a thousand, towing us up with the desperately clinging man. We were all praying for a miracle, but the newsreel camera was the only thing that caught the soldier when he finally fell, a speck.

"Dad?"

I feel like I'm a link between the blimp-man and the drowning German. Maybe I'm a mirror—maybe the German sinks into me, a reflection of the blimp-man who's being pulled up into the sun. *Let go*, I think, but it doesn't make sense.

My father frowns at the horizon, his arms folded over his chest. "God-damn bloodless Nazis," he mutters. "We're going back in." He shifts to the boat's console, presses a button, and the inboard engine sputters and catches. I'm kneeling now, keeping my balance with a hand on the side of the boat. The deck vibrates under me.

"We're at war." Dad raises his voice so I can hear him over the idling engine. "*You're* at war, too, because you're an American. You have to be hard. Having enemies is hard. We saw something terrible, but we're not going to tell about it. It'll be enough to say that we thought we saw a U-boat. But we're never going to mention the other thing. Not to your mother. Not to each other. You understand?"

I shrug, and Dad turns to the wheel. He shifts a lever, the motor whines, and we start forward. I fix my gaze on his back—I feel the distance widen between our boat and the spot we'd last seen the splashing German. Dad will be leaving tomorrow, and I practice the silence I've promised him.

II

Fat Victor, go home. I'm lying on my back, half inside the castle on hole fifteen of the miniature golf course my stepfather Victor Stockman abandoned a year ago when the Jockey's Ridge sand dunes finally overwhelmed Stockman's Gulp and Golf. Tonight I slipped out of our apartment in Nag's Head Village and bicycled through the deserted streets and across route 158 to the site.

Victor's not really fat, but he's a big man, and he limps because he had polio when he was a kid. I don't really want him to go home, either—that would be to Canada, where he's from. He's nice to me and my mother, and there are things to admire about him, like his ambition. And people like him, even the locals who snickered when he bought the cheap land abutting the dunes and built the snack shack and mini golf course. They knew the little storm fence he'd constructed around the property would be useless. He'd been right, though, about vacationing tourists flocking to the Outer Banks after the war ended. If we'd been able to keep the course dug out, he'd have made a nice profit. Now he and Mom run Stockman's Nag's Head Diner that's right in the middle of town, under our apartment, where I help out weekends and after school.

Victor salvaged everything he could from the snack shack—freezer and stove, tables and chairs, then flattened the building and sold the wood and bricks and shingles. The dunes ate up the mini-golf course. But every once in a while the winds shift, and word gets out that the tower of my castle—I think of it as mine—is poking up through the sand. When and if I can, I sneak there with a shovel and clear it out, usually in the dead of night. Now my legs stretch along the putting surface, my hips on the bridge over the sand-filled moat, and the rest of me inside the castle's wide mouth. The cup must be under my neck. I've burrowed my fists through the sand-filled east and west wings, out of which mis-hit balls used to roll back to the putting surface. I feel like I'm a hand in a glove.

The castle's central tower rises straight up over my head, and I gaze through it at a dish-sized circle of night sky. Sometimes I imagine that my castle and I are buried under a tremendous dune, and the tower tunnels up a hundred feet. A few stars creep through my view.

When a bright one shows up, like the one I see right now, I make a wish by it, though I don't always have a good one ready. I settle on *Fat Victor go home.*

I guess the wish comes out of loyalty to my father, who never made it back from the war. I remember my arm being tired from waving as I stood on our porch with the neighbor who'd be watching me while Mom drove Dad from Nag's Head to the mainland where he'd catch his bus. It was the only time I'd ever seen him in our car's passenger seat, and he didn't seem to like it, because his smile was more of a frown. At the last second, as they pulled away from the curb, Dad pointed his index finger like a pistol at my chest, screwed one shut, and pulled the trigger. The only thing I could guess was that he was reminding me to keep quiet about the enemy we'd left out in the ocean the day before.

The star I just wished on has almost edged out of the circle of midnight blue above me. I struggle to conjure up a memory of Dad from before the fishing trip and the pointing, but it's as if my history with him started with the rise of that U-boat. I know he died in a German forest half a dozen years ago, which made him a war hero. I remember hearing Mom cry in her bedroom late at night and that we changed churches, "because the God in that one didn't do us any favors." And I know that she eventually met Victor in the choir of our new church, and that they got married without much fuss two years ago.

There's a sudden brightness— I grunt and try to move, but my arms are stuck in the castle wings. I kick my legs uselessly. Then I see that it's not an intruder's flashlight beam sliding down my castle tower. It's a silver moon that's crept over the opening, a first. I wince against its harshness. A wish on the moon: how about a girl? What if one showed up now, someone from school, and found me here like this? I picture girls flushed and shiny-faced, spinning with the junior and senior boys at school dances. Katherine, who sits in front of me in Civics: sometimes I spend the entire class staring at the mark pinched on her upper arm by the short sleeve of her white blouse. What if she were outside the castle now, tiptoeing around the sand, about to straddle my lap with a flaring skirt? With a thrill in my thighs, I imagine her sudden weight. "Who's in there?" she asks. "Is it you?" I stare wide-eyed into the moon until it hurts, until the feeling turns from good to bad, and I think I'm falling. Stare at the sky too long, and you'll always see a man who made a bad decision dropping from a blimp. And there's my father, pointing at my chest with warning in his eye, a German in the water our only bond.

III

Mom is upstairs in bed, dying, but the smells of coffee and frying in Stockman's Diner cover up the scent of it. And the clatter of plates and glasses, the buzz of chatting customers, the grease sizzling on the griddle can't muffle the silence that weighs on Victor and me from above. "Woman's disease," Mom called it, when she still had the strength to speak. "Cancer of the ovaries," I've heard frowning regulars whisper after I turn from their tables. As I bring their orders, I see "orphan" in their eyes when they meet mine. But I've got Victor, and we've got the diner. Mom's illness made it convenient for me to postpone college, which would have meant leaving the Outer Banks. Victor couldn't run this place alone, especially with the beginning of summer: vacationers have joined the regulars, and our tables stay full.

For the supposed entertainment of our customers, Victor snares me in dialogue while he sweats over his griddle. Droplets slide down his jowls like tears, but he never loses his smile.

"Who's on first, Mr. Smith?"

I shake my head, rolling my eyes at the grinning customers whose orders I'm taking. "I don't know."

"*I don't know*," Victor mimics. "That's the most I've heard out of you in a week. You've got to work on your social skills if you want to get ahead, Billy. And it's 'I don't know, *Mr. Stockman*.' Try again." He waves his spatula. "Show a little enthusiasm: Who's on first, Mr.Smith?"

"*I don't know*," I practically shout as I grab dishes and glasses on my way to post the last order.

"'I don't know'...?" Victor spins from his griddle, his hand on the hip of his bad leg. If it's aching, he's not letting on. In spite of his sweaty face and grease-spotted apron, he's well-groomed. Patrons regularly compliment the cleanliness of Stockman's Diner.

"I don't know, *Mr. Stockman*," I correct. I dump my armload of dirty plates into the tub next to the pantry door. Terrance, who prepares cold salad plates and washes dishes, will slink from the kitchen for them when he gets a chance. I glance at the pantry door. There's a calendar posted on it with Outer Banks' scenes. June is ocean waves. May was the dunes at Jockey's Ridge. Before Mom got too sick to do the bulk of the waitressing, I'd often sneak into the phone booth-sized pantry during slow hours. I'd do my schoolwork under a bare light bulb at a little desk wedged beneath shelves loaded with paper napkins, ketchup bottles, and soup cans. When I was needed, Victor or Mom rapped on the door.

"Here comes the mummy," Victor would say when I emerged, or "Look out for Dracula—he's escaped from his coffin!" Victor hasn't made coffin jokes since Mom's been sick, and I haven't had time for the pantry. Even with school over, it would be a nice place to sit and think.

Not so long ago, when Mom was still working, I'd stepped out of the pantry after a long night of studying. Victor bent over the counter, leaning on his elbows. Mom sat on one of the stools, swiveling herself back and forth with a toe on the floor like a schoolgirl. Both of them had tired eyes, but grinned at me.

"You know what that boy is?" Victor asked my mother. "He's a claustrophiliac."

"A closet-*what*?" Mom asked.

"A *claustrophiliac*—he loves closed in spaces," Victor said, and both of them stared at me, still smiling, like I was some kind of science experiment.

Mom's taking a lot of drugs now and is almost always asleep. A hired nurse comes in twice a day to change her nightgown and her bedding. Victor or I run upstairs to make sure she's as comfortable as possible every chance we get.

"*Third base!*" Victor shouts suddenly over the spitting, smoking griddle long after everyone in the diner, including me, has forgotten the routine he started a quarter of an hour ago. I'm busy seating a family of vacationers.

"Hey, claustrophiliac—" my stepfather calls, turning with a little hula to disguise his stagger. I shrug, slipping my curious customers a look to let them know everything's okay.

"The cavalry is on the way, Billy—we've got a new waitress coming at noon. She'll be on half-days for the summer. She's the daughter of a lady who just joined the choir. They're new here."

IV

Mom passed away on the Friday of Labor Day weekend, and Victor closed up the diner for the funeral. He taped a black bow on the window where Mom had hung a wreath last Christmas and a red heart on Valentine's Day. Some of our regular customers have set bouquets against the door. The funeral service is brief. Mom is being laid to rest in her family's plot in the cemetery of the church she'd left after Dad died, and it's a little awkward. People tell Victor and me "It's a blessing," and we nod, because they're right. We were sad for a long time, but we finished mourning long before she died. Dad is buried in Arlington National Cemetery. I've never been.

I stand next to Victor while they lower Mom's casket into the ground. He's wearing a snug gray suit I've never seen before, and he seems deep in thought, but when someone approaches with condolences he finds a quick grin and a "Thank you." As the coffin descends, I remember the U-boat. It's been eight years, and I've kept my father's promise—Mom never knew about the drowned German. I drop a shovelful of dirt on the polished coffin and picture Mom inside, cushioned in satin, then hand the shovel to Victor. I support his back while I listen to the thud of earth on wood. We listen to the minister's words. My thoughts return to the U-boat, its sleeping quarters, the bunks no more than shelves. A hand on my shoulder, Victor's, startles me.

"Your castle's up. I meant to tell you. I saw it yesterday, when I drove past the dunes," he says, waving his hand as if he's holding his spatula, "while I was making arrangements. It's probably still there. You should go see it. Take Helen. Tell her what we had there that we lost."

I'm tongue-tied and blushing when I see that Helen and her mother are on the way over. Our summer waitress has a year of high school left, and only now, outside the diner, do I feel the weight of the crush I've got on her. I'm so flustered by her approach that I'm slow to process Victor's news about the castle. It's been buried off and on for a long time. How does he know that it's mine? Helen's wearing a flowered dress, the brightest at the funeral, but a black shawl covers her shoulders. The red hair she keeps in a bun at work spreads over the shawl. Victor interrupts the condolences she and her mother murmur.

"Thank you. Helen, Billy's got something to show you, out on the highway. Your mom can help me set up the food for the mourners back at the diner—" He looks at Helen's mother, who nods. "Take the car, Billy. Stick one of these shovels in the trunk."

⁂ ⁂ ⁂

"Victor says I can work after school whenever I can, and on weekends," Helen says.

I stop digging and lean on my shovel, trying to hide that I'm catching my breath. I've loosened my tie and rolled up my sleeves, but the slick soles of my dress shoes have been slipping in the sand. To the east, behind Helen, the sky is lavender. To the west it's so swollen with blue the razor outline of the white dunes threaten to slice it open. Out here things are different than in the diner, where Victor's banter gives me something to cling to when Helen's around.

"Nice," I say.

"So there was really a restaurant here, and a whole golf course?

"Miniature golf. And a snack shack. Stockman's Gulp and Golf."

"And all that's left is this little castle." Helen's skin is the dune-white of most redheads, almost blue over her cheekbones. Her green eyes stand out because there are no trees or grass nearby.

"'Little castle?' It's a matter of how you look at it," I say. "If you saw it from far away and didn't have anything to measure it against, you might think it was huge."

A smile blooms on Helen's face. "It would be like that in the ocean."

"I guess," I say. "But you don't build a castle on water. I don't like the ocean."

"Why not?"

"Lots of reasons. It's too spread out—you can't see where it begins or ends. Plus you can't see below the surface. You don't know what's down there."

"Couldn't those be reasons for liking it? It's a mystery."

The flowers on Helen's dress look wet, as if they'd stain my arm if I held her around the waist. I grab the shovel and dig away at the castle's base. "It's—all—a—matter—of—perspective," I huff. I don't bother clearing all the way down to the putting surface. I kneel before the entrance of my castle, poke the shovel inside, and scoop out as much sand as I can.

"You're getting dirty," Helen says. She's got her hands on the waist I wish I had my arm around.

"Can't be helped. You need to see how I used to crawl inside." Our gazes brush, too briefly for me to tell if she thinks I'm ridiculous. I turn my back to the castle, lie down, and wriggle my head and shoulders through the opening. It's a tighter fit than I remember. I force my arms down the clogged castle wings before I allow my-self to look up through my tower, where I see the sky. *Blue plate special*, I think.

"Hey in there." Helen's voice is muffled.

"Hey," I grunt. My words shoot up the tower. If we were children and this was a playground, I'd worry about Helen wandering off to find more interesting playmates.

"I'm sorry about your mother, Billy. I didn't get a chance to say so before."

"Yeah."

"Billy—tell me about your father."

"Victor? He's a good guy." Helen knows that—she spent her summer serving the orders he prepared and laughing her throaty laugh at his corny jokes.

"Not Victor. Your real father."

The circle of sky atop my tower seems to freeze solid, blocking my air, and I'm breathless. Nobody ever asks about Dad. It's as if they sense something in me that warns them not to. "What's to say? He died in the war. In the Battle of the Bulge. In the winter. He's buried at Arlington National Cemetery. He was tall. He sold cars." *He took me fishing*, I don't say.

"I lost my father in the war, too," Helen says. "He's not dead, not that I know. He's just kind of no good."

"Yeah," I murmur. I know something about this. You gather gossip when you wait tables. Helen's dad had been in the Navy and stayed in Japan after the war ended. He'd picked a new Japanese bride and started a new family.

"I guess he's still overseas," Helen says. "Mom packed us up and we left Indiana. We moved to Cincinnati, Ohio; Knoxville, Tennessee; Greensboro, North Carolina—and places in between I can't remember. Always further east. She wanted to get as far away from Japan as she could. I never made friends I could keep. When we hit the Outer Banks and the Atlantic Ocean, Mom figured he'd never be able to find us if he ever came looking. This year will be the first time since we left Indianapolis that I'll be going back to the same school. I remember my Dad has green eyes like mine. I think my mother sees him sometimes when she looks at me."

I don't know what to say. I lick away the sand on my lips and grind it between my back teeth.

"Victor's funny: '*Who's on first—*'" Helen says. It's a relief and a disappointment that she's shifted the subject from herself. "He's a foreigner, right? His accent is funny."

"Canada isn't so foreign."

"He says 'a-boot,'" Helen says, and giggles. "'No doot a-boot it.'"

At first I think she's said "U-boat" and my legs shift involuntarily. How must I look to her? Like some stupid ostrich with its head buried in the sand?

"Billy—don't you have any secrets you want to share?"

We let somebody drown. Why not come right out with it? I'm trying not to squirm. What if Helen's mocking me now, outside my castle, standing over my thighs, hoisting her dress, pretending to lower herself onto my lap like one of those girls I used to dream about? *I once saw a man soar away on a blimp*, I could say. *He made a mistake—he should have let go. Everyone else did.* But I choose a different secret.

"I'm a claustrophiliac." My words echo as if I'm wearing a helmet.

"'*Castle*—?'"

"*Claustro*. Philiac. I love tight spaces."

Quiet. Then a whistle that gives me goose bumps. "You love tight spaces, so you wear a castle." A laugh. "You're the king of the snails!" For all I know, Helen's dancing over my headless body.

"I used to stargaze through this tower," I say. "That's another secret. I'd sneak out of the house late at night and lie in here and stare at the sky."

"Wait—I can't hear you." Something thumps, and I flinch. Helen's slapped the castle. And there's scraping —she's climbing it. "What's this made of, anyway?"

"I don't know." I picture her as a giant, scrambling up the turrets, her flowered dress billowing, her red hair like a flag. "Some kind of rubber."

"What?" She's pummeling the walls.

"Rubber!"

Helen's face replaces the sky. Her features seem to ripple, as if I'm underwater.

"Peekaboo!" she says. "It's dark. Can you see me?"

"Yes."

"Close your eyes," she says, and I do. Something pea-sized hits my cheek. Then my nose.

"Hey—" I call, "—no spitting!"

"Not spit," Helen says. "We're kissing. Our first kisses. They're long distance."

"Oh—" I'm defenseless. I pucker and wait. The next drop pats my forehead. I smell spearmint gum.

"You like that?" Helen calls down the tower. I can hear her breathing. "I'm getting dry—you like that, King of the Snails?"

"Yes."

"Your 'castle' thing—crawling into them—that's permanent?"

I open my eyes. Her face is in shadows. My cheeks are wet, as if I've been crying. "I don't know," I say.

V

There's a sealed urn on the fireplace mantle in the den of our house on the Nag's Head shore. On nights like this one, just before my four-year-old son's bedtime, while I'm reading to him or telling his favorite legends of the Outer Banks, the brass urn seems to absorb the light of the fire burning in the hearth beneath it. The urn's reflection floats in the black picture window we watch the ocean through in the daytime. The water is just a few hundred yards from the house. It's the reflected urn Thomas gazes at as he cuddles against me. "What's in there?" he asks for the hundredth time.

Who's on first, I think. Some nights I say "A genie," and we laugh while Helen shakes her head from her seat near the fire. Usually, I say "Grandpa Victor's ashes," and I tell Thomas something he's never heard before about his grandfather. He knows I have two fathers. Someday he'll ask why. Tonight, Helen is in town—she's in class, earning her realtor's license. I look at the urn hovering within the dark glass. "Grandpa Victor," I say. "And some secrets."

"Ghosts?" Thomas asks.

Everything's a ghost, I think. Outer Banks' lore is full of stories about pirates, Indian princesses, abandoned colonists, fishermen, animal spirits. In his will, Victor had stipulated that he be cremated, which meant transporting his body to the mainland— the first time since I'd known him that my stepfather had been off the Outer Banks. But it was a nonplussed representative of the crematorium who guided me into his office when I arrived to pick up Victor's remains.

"I don't understand it," the little man in the neat suit said, shaking his head. His hand was on the urn that's now on my fireplace. "You can be assured we followed our normal procedures for—preparing Mr. Stockman's remains."

"And?"

"It seems that when our cremator opened the furnace, there was nothing there. There should have been ashes, as always. As in one hundred percent of the cremations I've supervised in the twenty years we've provided our service."

"You lost Victor's ashes?"

The crematory's representative craned his neck as if his collar was too tight. "Not lost. That would be impossible. They just weren't there."

I tapped the unadorned brass urn sitting on the representative's desk. "What's in here?"

The little man shrugged. The sealed urn he presented me, "without charge, due to the cremation's irregular conclusion," was, and still is empty. And I'm the only one who knows it.

"First I'll tell you again about how Nag's Head got its name," I say to my son. "Then I'll tell you the secret." The bright urn reflected in the window must have reminded me of the legend of the land pirates who posted ponies along the shore with lanterns tied to their heads. The pirate's goal was to convince ship captains at sea that the bobbing lights were safely moored boats. The ships would get too close, wreck themselves on dangerous reefs, and the land pirates would row out and plunder them.

I finish the story: "The nags and the pirates and the plundering—that all happened right out there on our beach." The fire is dying, and the urn fades in the dark glass.

"What about the secret?" Thomas tucks himself under my arm and looks up at me. His elbow is sharp against my ribs, but I don't ask him to move. You never know what someone's going to remember forever.

"I'm getting to it," I say. "Some people believe that the land pirates used the wood from the wrecked ships to build their houses."

Thomas's eyes flit from ceiling beams to door frames to the fireplace mantle. "Our house?" he asks.

"Just a piece," I say. "That right there—" I point to the lintel over the door, and Thomas's eyes widen "—is pirate wood. It's for good luck. We're going to put a piece of pirate wood in each of the houses we build along the shore. But it's a family secret. You can't tell anybody else." When Helen gets home, I'll have to tell her about the pirate wood.

Victor, it turned out, had been buying up parcels of land along this beach for years. "Build," he told Helen and me from his hospital bed. "One for yourself, then more, for vacationers. I made a mistake with the dunes, but I'm right about building on the ocean. Don't be afraid. Sell the diner and build."

✺ ✺ ✺

Secrets. I lie in bed next to Helen—she's pregnant with our second, and she's snoring lightly under the weight of her big belly. The mounded blanket reminds me of my castle under the dunes. I look for it whenever we pass Jockey's Ridge. There hasn't been a sighting in years, but I find it hard to believe it will be buried forever. Sometimes I think I'll tell Helen about the German my father and I left to drown. I picture myself sharing the story with Thomas when he's older—he'll be long and lean, taller than me, and there'll be a curious but sympathetic look in his green eyes. We'll be building another house on this beach, maybe sneaking a piece of pirate wood under a joist, and I'll stop him. With our hammers at our sides, we'll look out over the breakers toward the horizon. I'll begin by describing the way the U-boat rose out of nowhere.

I've been to my dad's grave in Arlington. Helen's thinking about trying to find her father, but she doesn't know where to begin. "I've probably got siblings I don't know," she says, "maybe way over in Japan. That's something, isn't it? Thomas has Japanese cousins. It's an amazing notion."

When I'm on the edge of sleep, like tonight, I think of another secret I discovered only recently. It's a crazy one: I understand German now. I was in the lumberyard outside of Kitty Hawk, and two men stood waiting for a stack of two by fours to be cut. Their blue eyes flashed from side to side while they conversed in a language I'm sure was German. I listened to their foreign syllables, and, to my surprise, heard my own voice telling me what they were saying. *Do they still hate us here?* one asked. *I don't know*, the other answered. *Maybe we should pretend to be Swiss.* Their soft laughter sounded like yodeling.

I hear this laughter when I'm nearly asleep, and then I see ten-year-old me, kneeling in a motorboat, watching a man splash in the water almost within reach. He shouts in German, but I hear English: "Hold on!" he calls, and I don't know if he's crying to himself or to me. Then I'm wrapped tightly in blankets in a bunk deep within a U-boat. From behind a steel corner I hear my father's voice. He's begging for a life. German voices answer him, and I understand. But when the dream-child-me nods off, I drift away, too. By morning, we'll have forgotten what we heard.

NUZZI
GREAT-GRANDPA

As Jesse stoops to kiss his mother good-bye, his lips compress her waxy hair and melt to the shape of her skull. He resists the odor of crayons that tugs him toward childhood. He's shut his eyes. If he doesn't, he'll see the woman's mouth pop open for food like a baby jay's. Her eyes have been closed for years, though once in a while there's movement under her lids like puppies squirming beneath a blanket.

"Take it easy, Mom," he says and sweeps out of her room, leaving a nod for one attendant, a wave for a second he passes in the hallway. And he's out on the pavement, splashed with a bucketful of sunlight. He squints against the glare of windshields in the parking lot. His car waits in the third row, where there's always a spot. On a usual Thursday, Jesse would rush from the nursing home back to school for his post-lunch classes.

But today Sally Barnes will cover Jesse's American History sections while he keeps an appointment with Ms. Jackson, the principal of the elementary school on the other side of the Wampanoag District campus.

"Please see me about Greta," Ms. Jackson's e-mail said. *"We need to discuss an issue."*

All the schools on the Wampanoag campus share the same vast lot, and Jesse parks in it every day—but the "visitor" space he fills across from the elementary school feels like it's in a different country. He's nervous. He doesn't know what Ms. Jackson wants to discuss about his daughter, but he's been listing excuses since he left his mother's nursing home: *I know it's been two years, but Greta still hasn't gotten over her mother's death. And she's been lonely at home—my little brother, her uncle— he'd always been around to help me take care of her, but I encouraged him to go away to college because he needed to establish some independence. And this is my tenure year—you know what that's like. And her grandmother's rotting in a nursing home.*

Jesse recognizes the security guard seated at the desk in the school's lobby. The guards shift buildings, and Rita is often in the high school.

"You got a kid here, Mr. C," Rita says, and Jesse smiles in confirmation. Has the "issue" he's been summoned for been the subject of break-room gossip? He takes the clipboard Rita offers and prints his name, records the time, and writes "see Ms. Jackson" under "reason for visit."

"Everything seems little here compared to the high school, doesn't it?" the guard asks, gesturing at the low water fountain down the hall. She glances at the clipboard Jesse returns. "Principal is down to the left."

Jesse nods and turns away, stopping short as a group of three children, younger than Greta, maybe first graders, pop in front of him from around a corner. Each of the three has a hand on a Frisbee-sized wooden disc with "BATHROOM PASS" printed across its face.

"Watch the kids," Rita calls as the children scamper away. "They're little, too, Mr. C."

Jesse waves limply, but he's back to reviewing his list of excuses—*dead mother, beloved uncle gone, dad's too busy, rotting grandma.* Including that last would be a stretch. His daughter barely knows her Grandma Janet—his mother has been institutionalized since Greta was a toddler. The woman bears so little resemblance to any idea of "Grandma" that Jesse wouldn't think of exposing his child to her. "*It's not Alzheimer's, it's Pick's disease,*" Jesse will explain to Ms. Jackson if the topic arises. "*The symptoms are similar in their early onset versions, but the diseases have different causes. Not that it matters. She should be dead by now, but, bless us, she's a tough one. She won't stop eating.*"

He's at the main office, where a secretary sits behind a computer. The principal's shut door is tucked into a corner next to the teachers' mail cubbies. A fresh excuse boils up, and Jesse rehearses it, breaking into a sweat: *She was bitten by her dog. It was a rescue. We got rid of it.* "I'm here to see Ms. Jackson," he tells the secretary. "I'm Greta's father. I teach at the high school."

The secretary leads Jesse to Ms. Jackson's door and opens it after a double rap. The principal, a woman about his age, stands behind her desk. He recognizes her from school district events, including his daughter's Back to School Night. Ms. Jackson's lips move, and he exchanges greetings with her that he doesn't hear. He's slipped into a memory as dense as fog. Sound first: growling and screams. Then his heart pounding as he rushes into the kitchen, where Greta's on her back, shrieking silently while a yellow flash of a dog shakes the leg in its clamped jaws as if the limb is a small animal with a neck that needs snapping. Jesse's brother

Austin, slight as a reed, hollers and kicks ineffectually at the dog's ribs. Jesse straddles the snarling animal, Pirate they'd named it, grips it by the scruff, and pounds its head with his fist.

"—a seat," Ms. Jackson is saying, her hand extended.

"Yes," Jesse says. *Greta had tried to take away the dog's bone*, he wants to explain, but the words buzz in his head as he hovers before the principal. *I'd told her never to try to take a dog's bone. Her knee needed stitches. The dog was what they call a "sato," a Puerto Rican street mutt, shipped in from San Juan where they don't have animal control measures— dogs run wild in the streets. When we got back from the hospital I brought the dog to the vet's and had it euthanized. Did you know Greta's dead mother was a famous zoo veterinarian? She used to sing Swiss lullabies to pandas so they wouldn't reject their babies. She was even on TV. And she's on Youtube, yodeling a lullaby to a panda.*

Jesse knows he doesn't have to tell the principal about Briggie. A children's picture book had been published about his wife's exploits. Jesse had seen a copy in Greta's classroom on Back to School Night. Briggie sang Swiss lullabies to Greta, too. Greta had spent the first few days they'd had Pirate cuddling the dog while humming her mother's melodies. "I'm trying to get him to nurse," she'd said, half-seriously, pulling the dog's muzzle to her eight-year-old chest.

"Hi, Daddy." Behind Jesse, sitting in a plastic seat, is Greta. She gives a small, circular wave, as if she's polishing a pane of glass between them.

Jesse meets his daughter's blue-eyed gaze. He tries not to see Briggie's face there—that wouldn't be fair to Greta—he must see her for herself. But there are his wife's features, superimposed in ghostly outline on the little girl's—the cheekbones, the ears, the flaring nostrils are as striking as scars. Those blue eyes, a shade lighter than his wife's, but no less deep—the sky instead of a lake. The smile that says all is right with the world, if only you'll let it be.

"Please have a seat," Ms. Jackson repeats. "There, next to Greta."

Everyone sits. Jesse, careful of his posture, leans forward, then slouches back. The faces of the girl and principal follow him like flowers seeking the sun. Are they waiting for the first excuse? But what will he be trying to excuse?

"Greta," Ms. Jackson says, "please show your father your knee." The hem of the seated child's plaid skirt falls just above her kneecaps. As she bows to look at her leg, a pink ear sticks out of her sheaf of bobbed, yellow hair. Jesse's eyes follow his daughter's gaze, and he sucks in a breath—the knee is horribly bruised. Hadn't it been over a year since the dog had torn it open? His cheeks and forehead burn. Is he being accused of something? Does Ms. Jackson suspect that some dark secret blights his and Greta's home? He stares at the black knee, afraid to look up. Then he sees—the knee isn't bruised—it's *too* black. There's no purpling or yellowing. It's just black. Ink black.

"It's ink," Ms. Jackson corroborates. "The children were using ink in art class. Tell your father what you did with the ink, Greta."

"I painted my knee with it," Greta says. Her voice is higher, breathier than Briggie's, but, though she's never been out of the country, his daughter speaks with a trace of an accent. So this meeting is only about a dirty knee? Jesse sighs, light-headed with relief. But—why is Greta blacking her damaged knee? Is she ashamed of the scar? It's not much more than a crease, is it? And she insists on wearing skirts.

"She was badly bitten by a dog," Jesse says. "There's a scar. The doctor says she can have it removed with plastic surgery when she stops growing."

Ms. Jackson is shaking her head, her eyes closed, her lips crimped in a frown. The principal's short dark hair fits her like a helmet. She picks up a white sheet of paper from her desk and extends it toward Greta.

"Why don't you show your father, Greta. Here, take the paper and show him what you've been up to."

Without hesitation Greta rises and plucks the blank sheet of copy paper from the principal's hand. She retakes her seat, flattens the paper against her inked knee, and rubs it hard with the heel of her fist, finishing with a few firm blows. She peels the paper off, and, gripping it top and bottom as if it's an unfurled scroll, displays the result to her father.

"See?" Ms. Jackson asks.

But Jesse sees only a gray smudge the size of a man's palm. He peeks at Ms. Jackson, lifting a brow.

"Look closely," she says. "When the ink was fresher the print was much more visible."

Jesse squints at the paper—and chokes. Emerging from the center of the smudge are the dim but definite perpendiculars of a swastika.

"It's my scar-print," Greta says.

"Her 'scar-print,'" Ms. Jackson repeats. "And this morning she left her scar-prints in quite a few places, didn't you, Greta? The classroom. The girls' room. Walls, desks, notebooks. Who knows where else?" The principal's face is calm, but her exasperation hisses from her like steam.

"Nowhere else." Greta says. She offers the paper to Jesse, who takes it and looks at it. There it is: a swastika.

"Well, the custodian cleaned up all we could find. As best as we can tell there are no Jewish-affiliated children in her class. But we can't know which students were offended. Or which parents might be. I'll be expecting phone calls this evening." Ms. Jackson's hand crawls toward her desk telephone in anticipation.

Jesse clears his throat. He looks from the faint swastika nestled in the gray cloud to his daughter. "You know what this is, don't you, honey?" He *knows* she knows. Children are aware of such things by the time they're nine. But why hadn't *he* known that the scar on her knee was swastika shaped?

"It's a tribute," Greta says. Her eyes are blue slashes. Her lips shift as if to accommodate an expression she's never tried—there's an unfamiliar dimple in her cheek.

"A *tri*-bute?" Ms. Jackson asks.

"To my mother's Nuzzi grandpa. My great-grandfather. I didn't know him. He died in Switzerland." Greta reaches for the paper Jesse holds, and he surrenders it. His daughter folds it in half and pats it down on her lap.

Ms. Jackson winces. Her hand jerks from the telephone to her mouth. This complication has stung her like a slap, and Jesse feels it too, though his wife's family history is no surprise. Briggie's grandfather had been a minor Nazi official. His wife had confessed this to him ten years ago, moments after announcing she was pregnant with Greta. "We must cleanse our closets," she told him, crying. He'd reacted poorly to the news about her family tree, declaring, to his later regret, that she'd "stolen the joy from the moment." What Jesse can't recall is how Greta came to know about her ancestry.

"Your mother was a great, brave woman," Ms. Jackson says, attempting to regain some footing.

"A panda killed her," Greta says. Her hands lie flat on the folded paper, and Jesse notes that his daughter's nails are neatly trimmed. "She was singing to it so it would take its own baby, and it bit her."

"An infection no one diagnosed until it was too late," Jesse says. "It went straight to her heart. Massive doses of antibiotics did no good." The children's book about Briggie was written before his wife's death. It hadn't been set on display on Greta's Back to School Night, but Jesse had recognized its black and white spine on the lower shelf of a bookcase. Did his daughter's teacher realize it was there?

"Right. So very sad. Tragic. I'm sorry." Ms. Jackson's face clenches with sympathy. "That was before you moved here?"

"Just before," Jesse says. "We were about to move into our house. I'd already started teaching here at the high school. My little brother, he lives with us, took a gap year after he graduated so he could help care for Greta. Austin's my half-brother, actually, from my mother's first marriage. I'm quite a bit older than he is —he's much closer to Greta's age than mine. He's finally off to college. I think Greta misses him very much. You miss having Austin around, don't you, sweetheart?" Jesse asks, watching the principal out of the corner of his eye. *Excuses*, he's thinking.

Greta shrugs and scratches her black knee. "I pretend he's still home," she says. "At night I make believe he's telling me stories. While you're busy grading papers." She blinks at Jesse before shifting her attention to Ms. Jackson. "Daddy was a lawyer, then a house-husband, then a lawyer again before he decided to be a teacher." Her tone is the same she'd used to declare her swastika-fest a "tribute." This is what family means to her.

Ms. Jackson's head bobs slightly. Her eyes shift to the door: muffled sounds of a class in transit—shuffling feet, children's giggles, a teacher's warning.

"We killed Pirate," Greta says.

"Pirate was the rescue dog that bit her. The one responsible for the scar. I had him euthanized after the attack, of course." Ms. Jackson has settled back into her seat. Jesse tries to decipher her expression—is she juror or witness?

"Nuzzi Great-Grandpa helped take care of *Hitler's*

dog. Blondi was its name. It was a German Shepherd," Greta says. Her gaze drops to the folded paper on her lap as if it's a document proving her statement. "Austin told me," she adds. "He said we wouldn't have had to kill Pirate if Nuzzi Great-Grandpa had been around to do the training. I wouldn't have been bit and I wouldn't have a scar-stika on my knee."

"I thought a dog would be good for the children after my wife died. My little brother was very close to her," Jesse explains. He takes a deep breath and releases it slowly through lips pursed like a kiss. "Austin makes up stories sometimes." Or is this one of the stories Greta invented for her *imaginary* Austin to tell? "The children in my family have vivid imaginations. I didn't know about this Hitler dog-training." He turns to Greta. "Mommy only told me one thing about her grandfather—that he gave her a gingerbread cookie once at Christmas."

"Austin says Nuzzi Great-Grandpa helped train Blondi," Greta says firmly. "He knows what he's talking about." She inclines her head confidentially toward Ms. Jackson. "Austin was in a mental hospital. After he stopped talking—after Grandma forgot who he was."

"That was years ago. Not a mental hospital," Jesse corrects. "A 'wellness camp,' just for the summer, for kids with problems. It's in Nag's Head, you know, on North Carolina's Outer Banks. Austin lost his dad when he was just a little younger than Greta. Then he grew close to *my* dad, and then my dad died, too. Then, yes, our mother started deteriorating from Pick's Disease—it's a lot like Alzheimer's. All of a sudden Mom stopped acknowledging Austin—he was twelve. She thought he was me at a younger age. It was as if he wasn't there. It was all too much for him, and he had a bit of a breakdown."

"He didn't talk," Greta says. "I don't remember, but that's what he says now."

"We—I—worried about him having a relapse when Briggie—my wife—Greta's mother, you know, passed. But Austin was okay. He *is* okay. Like Greta and me, he accepts what has to be accepted. Maybe he learned that at his wellness camp. He was cured—he started talking again. Now all he does is tell stories. Apparently."

"I remember his camp at Nag's Head," Greta says.

Jesse frowns and shakes his head. "I think you were too young, honey. You weren't even three yet."

"I *do* remember. Mommy took me to Nag's Head to see Austin one weekend. When you couldn't go. We flew on a jet. Austin reminded me, and I remember. I remember the dunes—the big sand dunes. I remember seeing the ocean from the sand dunes. I remember being in mommy's arms on top of the world, and she showed me the ocean. Just the little bit of it we could see from the dunes. Austin says that before Nuzzi Great-Grandpa helped train Blondi he visited America. On a submarine. And he was right there in the ocean at Nag's Head. He looked at America through a periscope, and he thought it was the most beautiful place he'd ever seen, and he thought it would be nice if his children and his great-grandchildren lived here. That's what Austin said."

One of Ms. Jackson's eyebrows rises and falls like an insect about to launch itself. Her hand is back at her mouth, and she bites a knuckle. Jesse's own brows converge. "There *were* U-Boats off the North Carolina Coast," he says. "Dozens of them. At the beginning of World War II. They used to rise up right in the middle of the fishing boats. The locals knew they were there, but our government kept the information classified because they didn't want to create a panic all across the country. The U-Boats destroyed so many American and British oil tankers that no one could use the beaches along the Outer Banks for the whole summer of '42—

they were covered with oil."

"I want to put my ashes in the ocean at Nag's Head," Greta says.

Something ice cold flips in Jesse's gut. "*Your* ashes?"

"Not *my* ashes. I didn't say *my* ashes." Greta shakes her head violently, her blond hair a spinning halo. "I said *Mommy's* ashes. Mommy loved Nag's Head."

"Mommy doesn't have ashes, honey. Remember, she donated herself—her parts—to help others get better. And to help train new doctors." Jesse's cheeks ache from grinning or frowning—he's not sure which. Greta taps a slow beat on the tiled floor with her sneaker tips. "And your mother was only at Nag's Head that time you said, baby, when the two of you visited Austin."

"Austin says she loved Nag's Head." Tears well in Greta's eyes. "He says that if we could scatter her ashes there then they'd get mixed up with the oily beach, and it would be like she was with her grandpa."

Jesse shrugs. His neck is stiff. He stretches it, turning from side to side. "It's funny, the name 'Nag's Head,'" he says finally to Ms. Jackson. "I was just telling my history class about it. There used to be land pirates along the coast of the Outer Banks. They marched ponies with lanterns hanging from their heads along the shore on moonless nights so that incoming ships would think they were the lights of safely harbored boats. The lured ships would crash on reefs like the land pirates planned. Plunder and murder would ensue."

"Austin says that story's only a legend," Greta says. "A tall tale."

"Oh—" the hollowness of his own laugh surprises Jesse "—*that's* a legend, but the 'tall tales' about your Nazi grandpa—*great*-grandpa—those you believe? Hitler's dogs? Submarines?"

"Austin says the oil and mommy's ashes would mix into a '*grew-some* paste,'" Greta murmurs.

"Mmm—" Ms. Jackson hums, as if something's caught in her throat. "Do you think Greta would like to call her brother at college? Has she spoken to him recently? Greta, would you like to talk to your brother?"

Jesse's cheeks throb. "I guess it's been a couple of weeks. We're all adjusting to not having Austin around. It's a good thing, learning to be apart. Independence, right? And it's *uncle*. Austin's Greta's *uncle*. He's *my* brother. Half." Jesse shakes his head, too fast—it feels empty as a gourd. Why doesn't anybody know who anybody is?

"Yes," Greta says. Her head dips over the paper bearing her knee-print, threatening it with tears. When she blinks up at Jesse, all he sees is Briggie, a Briggie he never knew, the Swiss-child Briggie. *Lake Geneva*, he'd call his wife sometimes, after the color of her eyes. But the blue of all lakes is only a reflection of the sky. "Yes," Greta repeats. "Austin."

Jesse sniffs a long breath. "You want to talk to Austin? Okay, honey. When we get home. We'll call him right up." He looks at Ms. Jackson. "I'm going to take Greta home now, is that okay? Her day is almost over, right?"

The principal nods. Greta tilts toward Jesse, and, seeing she's about to slip from her chair, he leans into her and loops an arm over her shoulder. Her head burns through his shirt, and he wonders if she's fighting an infection. His free hand drops to her inked knee.

"And Grandma," Greta says. "I want to see Grandma. You'll take me there."

But she won't know who you are, Jesse doesn't say, and he doesn't add, *she forgot who you were when you were still a baby—she hasn't even been able to dream about you. And the ugliness that you'll see is unimaginable.*

"Sure, of course," he says instead. Because bodies have to be identified, don't they? When a body dies, it knows nothing, not even itself. A body needs someone else to tell it who it is, or it belongs to nobody. That's why names are chiseled into headstones. "Of course I'll take you to see Grandma," Jesse repeats, aware that in a moment he'll be walking out the principal's door, then down the hall, out of the school, and into the parking lot. He pictures Greta beside him, hurrying to match his pace. He sees the two of them holding hands. But his empty hand, the one he'd rested on his daughter's knee, is balled into a fist. What he can't imagine is when he'll have the courage to see if it's been marked.

IOTA

This is to be the final day at the old house: the deal had been struck, the walk-through is tomorrow, the closing the day after. As Gifford exits the front door to give Iota the Dachshund her last walk on the property, he floats in a thin slice of time between nostalgia and the exhilarating potential of a new life. He and the dog will be the last of the family to vacate the house. Val awaits her husband in a condo minutes away from their daughter's home in the suburbs of a grand city two hundred miles east. Few of their friends remain in the old neighborhood, and Gifford and Val are eager to follow their daughter and assume the roles of doting grandparents.

Iota's belly drags on the grass Gifford is no longer responsible for mowing. Usually, there's no need to leash her: even with Gifford's achy knees, she can't out-waddle him. But the new condo has strict rules about dogs being leashed at all times, and Val has insisted that Iota practice. Gifford studies the thirteen-year-old dog. She'll probably be their last pet. He can't imagine himself training a frisky pup, and he and Val have plans to travel.

"Say goodbye to the yard, kiddo," Gifford says, but near-sighted Iota stares up at her master instead, as if she senses he's considering life without her. Gifford looks away, letting his own gaze sweep unsentimentally across the grass, through the oak trees to the sparkle of the river. Preparing to move has been exhausting, and all his nostalgia has been sacrificed to Lance the Junk Man or packed away in RubberMaid tubs.

"It's all over but the shouting," Gifford tells the dog. He turns his back, closing this chapter of his life. They amble back toward the front porch. The flowers their broker suggested bloom along the side of the house, and honeybees rise and fall among the blossoms. Crows nag from the neighbor's roof and white cabbage butterflies dance raggedly across the driveway. A bee zips by his face, as startling as a bullet, and Gifford sniffs, then smirks. *Float like a butterfly, sting like a bee.* "Come on, Ali," he says to Iota.

But after a few more steps another bee shoots by, and this time Gifford ducks. Then three more honeybees, then dozens, streaming toward his house. And there they gather, a mass of bubbling gold on the freshly stained cedar shakes. He leans forward for a closer look, a few late-arriving bees circling him like tiny planets. One by one the insects wriggle into a tiny hole between the shingles. Panic flushes Gifford's cheeks and temples: this is a swarm. These bees have followed a queen that's probably already in the walls of the house establishing a hive. *Now?* With buyers set to examine the house in the morning?

※ ※ ※

At the hardware store Gifford asks the young woman assisting him for the most powerful wasp-killing spray on the market, afraid that if he mentions endangered honeybees, she'll insist he contact an agency that will safely remove the swarm from his house—an option he would gladly take if he had the time. But this is an emergency. He'd already risked being stung when he plugged the hole between shingles with a stick. And in his basement he'd discovered dozens of bees crawling over the cinderblock walls and concrete floors. How many more were burrowed in the insulation?

In a sixty-minute mad rush, Gifford purchases, transports, and empties ten cans of spray and one container of quick-dry hole-plugging cement. Sweeping up the carcasses of a hundred bees occupies another quarter of an hour. Five more minutes to set up fans that blow the fumes out the basement windows. All told, in less time than it takes to watch a movie, Gifford eradicates a new queen's empire.

※ ※ ※

Amazing, Gifford thinks, driving eastward toward his new home, his wife, his daughter, and his grandchild: amazing that the walk-through and closing are done. The bee issue has wrung the last bit of sentiment from him—the future is all. If the honeybees return, they're not his problem. Iota snoozes beside him on the passenger seat. It's mid-morning and the highway is practically empty. He lowers his visor—it's the glare of the sun off the hood of his car that gets Gifford thinking about the green ray.

The green ray: a wink of green light at sunset, appearing for no more than a second or two at the precise moment the sun dips below the horizon. The rare phenomenon, requiring perfect atmospheric conditions, is said to possess mysterious powers—at least in literature and film. According to legend, the green ray bestows on its witnesses deep insight into their own hearts and the hearts of whoever they're with.

It's pure whimsy, Gifford knows, that inspires his and Val's pursuit of the green ray. But isn't that what retirement is for? They've tried once, lingering for a week at a Key West resort that advertised "green ray sunsets." But the experience had been a dud—clouds and mist obscured the horizon every night. Gifford catches his smiling eyes in the rearview mirror. He gives Iota's sun-warmed hide a pat. After they get their new lives settled, he and Val will try again, maybe Scotland's western islands or the coast of southern France, sites famous in fiction and film for green ray moments. Val has suggested Maui, which the internet praises for its glorious South Pacific sunsets.

Gifford passes a sign for a rest area, but they're just an hour from his new home, and neither he nor Iota needs the break. The truth, he admits, is that the search for the green ray has already taught him something about himself— he's discovered that he's colorblind. Val saw the flash of green in the French movie along with the lovers, but he hadn't, though he'd pretended to. After his wife went to bed, he rewound the film to the key moment ten times and saw nothing but reddish sky and blue sea. Then he sought out Youtube videos of the phenomenon on his laptop: where others gasped and applauded, he saw nothing.

A connecting link led him to Ishihara colorblindness tests—the kind where numbers are hidden among multicolored bubbles. Again he saw nothing— it was as unnerving as staring at a mirror that didn't show his reflection. What else had he missed in life? How would he even know?

So, he acknowledges while he steers, the odds are not great that he'll ever see a green ray. Could it be that simply being in its presence is enough? Faint hope. But he would never spoil Val's happiness by confessing his deficiency. A green ray sunset is meant for sharing.

"Can't let the juice run out, right, Iota?" Gifford says when he notices his cell phone is low on power. However, the instant he tries to plug in the charger, a pain explodes in his thumb, and he jerks his hand away. The car slides in and out of its lane, and a passing eighteen-wheeler blasts a warning. Gifford eyes his thumb: a honeybee is still there, its stinger stuck in his flesh. He closes his fist around it, squeezing until he feels a tiny pop, then flings the crushed body to the floor under Iota's nose. She doesn't react. She's lying on her side, exposing twin rows of tiny nipples she's never used.

Gifford's thumb hurts. Was the bee alone? In the engine's hum he hears the buzz of a thousand bees—has the swarm he thought he'd slaughtered taken refuge under the hood of his car? An attack *en masse* might block out the sun. Hadn't that happened with locusts a long time ago out West? Or was he thinking of the plague in the Bible? He switches the windshield wipers on for a few swipes, then flicks them off. No, he concludes, his attacker was a lone wolf, a sole survivor.

This injury is something else to hide from Val. If he tells her about the sting, he'll wind up spilling the beans about the invading swarm, and she'll worry that the house sale will somehow retroactively fall through. His left hand at 9 o'clock on the wheel, Gifford sets the heel of his wounded right hand at 12. He sticks up his swollen thumb, targeting the white dashes dividing the lanes. "Ouch-ouch-ouch—" he mutters with each strike.

The glare off the hood stabs his eyes. The cloud-free conditions are perfect for a green ray—except it's morning. But somewhere in the world the sun is setting. For those equipped to experience them, mysterious phenomena are as available as low hanging fruit.

❧ ❧ ❧

How long to establish a new home, to settle a routine, to grow comfortable with a fresh life? For Gifford, it's been three months—one season. His granddaughter Emma, barely a year old, is the catalyst of his rebirth. She can't say "Pops" yet, but squeals "Dah" for dog when she sees Iota, who sniffs her toes before licking them.

It's a Thursday, one week before Gifford and Val's first Christmas in their new home. Thursdays are Gifford's mornings to babysit, and he and little Emma are in the car on their way to the library for Book Babies. There, Gifford sits every week on the carpeted floor, Emma on his lap, in the middle of maybe a dozen other toddlers with their moms or nannies. He's the only grandpa ("the elephant in the room," he tells Val), but no one sings or claps with more gusto when following the lead of the young librarian in charge of the session.

On this morning's ride, Gifford's attention, as always, shifts from the road to the rearview mirror, though he can't see his granddaughter because her seat faces backward. What is she looking at—the gloomy sky? Squirrels on leafless branches? Iota is asleep on the passenger seat, where she'll wait under a blanket during the half hour Gifford and Emma will be in the library.

Gifford wishes he could see the child's face. He doesn't like the silence. "How's little Emma," he sing-songs. "Keeping busy?"

Silence. For all he can tell, the car seat might be

empty. He double checks the floor in front of Iota for Emma's diaper bag, which contains extra diapers and wipes, a water bottle, and, most importantly, the baby's EpiPen. The poor kid tests allergic to everything from nuts to milk—including dog dander. Iota has been blamed for rashes on Emma's tummy, and just this morning his daughter suggested that Gifford limit their interaction.

"Your daddy has lousy genes," he says to the baby. "None of us on your mommy's side have allergies." He waits for a response, but none comes. Of course the baby is asleep—but shouldn't he pull over and check? And why did he say that nasty thing about his son-in-law?

"I don't mean you should blame your father—nobody's genes are perfect. I mean, I hope you don't inherit my colorblindness. I don't think girls are as prone to it, though. So you should be able to see the green ray. I'm at best a 'maybe.' Have I told you about the green ray?"

Emma lets loose a cry, startling Gifford, as well as Iota, who lifts her head. Of course the baby's fine, Gifford thinks with relief—but now she's sobbing.

"Shhh, baby. Everything's okay. Most people don't even know green rays exist. Have you got a poopy diaper?" He sniffs—yup. Better to take care of it now— the library bathroom might be too crowded. They drive past a sign for the state park, and Gifford recalls a lot near the entrance that would be perfect for a pit stop. It's by a pond where there were ducks and swans last summer. Gifford turns into the park.

"Want to see swans, baby? And ducks? Quack-quack-quack."

The sobs cease. "Kak," Emma murmurs. "Kak-kak."

"Quack-quack-quack," Gifford replies. There's no guard in the booth at the entrance, but the gate is open, and he heads down a narrow road that cuts through a thick pine forest. They pass a trailhead.

"Not the time of year for a walk in the woods. What do swans say, Emma?" What *do* they say, Gifford wonders.

"Kak-kak," his granddaughter answers.

"Maybe. Maybe swans talk duck. The ugly duckling was really a swan, and he understood duck-talk. We can look for that story in the library sometime. But now we've got to change your poopy-doopy diaper. Where's that parking lot?"

Gifford wonders if he's got his state parks wrong. If the lot doesn't turn up soon, he'll pull off the road at the next trailhead and tend to Emma. For a moment the scent of pine covers the poop smell. Gifford takes a deep breath and releases it in a shuddery sigh. He could be in a fairy tale—lost in a dark forest, protecting a princess. *Green ray-shmeen ray*—this is enchantment enough.

The parking lot finally appears, and, behind it, like a black mirror, the pond. "Here we go," Gifford says, and, because he can't see Emma, he pats Iota, who looks up at him. When did her muzzle get so gray?

"Who needs a sunset, right, pup? Dogs are colorblind anyway."

"Kak-kak—" the words come loaded with the diaper's smell, and it occurs to Gifford that his granddaughter hasn't been "talking duck." She's been telling him that she's sitting in poop and he'd better do something about it.

"You mean 'kaka', baby. Don't fret, Pops is on it." He checks the rearview for a glimpse of the baby, but she's still nestled too deeply in her car seat. "Let's get it toasty warm in here," he says, reaching for the heater knob. A low, unfamiliar grinding stops him—it's Iota, her nubby teeth bared, growling at the dashboard.

"Girl?" Gifford follows his dog's stare—there, right on the knob he was about to touch, is a bee. He swats at the insect, which sails over Iota, hits the passenger window, and, flying now under its own power, bounces back toward Gifford. When he twists away, the wheel slips from his hands. The car bumps over the curb and skids to the edge of a ditch that parallels the park road.

"Whoa—" In slow motion, Gifford's view turns counter-clockwise as the car tips sideways into the ditch. Out of the corner of his eye he sees Iota slide against the passenger door, then scramble atop the window glass before the car bumps to a stop, upside down, leaving the dog crouched with flattened ears on a ceiling that's become a floor. Gifford, inverted, is caught in his seatbelt and harness, his legs tangled in the steering column. His own weight crushes down on him, bending his neck and wedging his cheek against the vinyl ceiling fabric. Is he hurt? Every body part he can think to move moves, but he can't orient himself. Then the baby's whimper slices through him like a cold razor.

"Emma—" he wheezes. "It's okay, honey. Everything's okay."

"Kak," the toddler sighs. Wincing at the windshield, Gifford has to acknowledge the truth—he's flipped the car, which lies in this ditch like a turtle on its back. Who will find them in this empty park? A pale flash in the rearview mirror— the baby's hand. Emma must be suspended by her seat straps, belly down, as if she's flying. And she's waving.

Gifford tries to see more of her, but can't. "Super baby," he pants. "Quack- quack. Flying ducky?"

For a few moments he hears only creaks and squelches, the sounds of the car settling. Then Emma starts to coo. Gifford feels a gust of chilly air and discovers that the passenger door popped open during their tumble. Through it he sees a swath of the grass-covered ditch wall. But where's Iota? Outside? She must be okay if she can walk. She couldn't have wandered too far; she'd never be able to climb out of this ditch.

Iota, get help, girl, he thinks. But his old Dachsund isn't Lassie.

Emma babbles to herself. Gifford reassesses his physical condition. He's still pinned down by his own bulk, and there's a dull ache in his neck and shoulder. But he believes that with maximum effort he'll be able to free himself, though he's a little dizzy from the blood collecting in his head. First he'll take care of the baby, then look for Iota —and find his phone, which was on the passenger seat with the dog, but now is nowhere to be seen. He's never had to dial 911 before—what will he tell them? An accident—started by a bee.

For a moment, he thinks he must have been mistaken, that he was hallucinating or suffering from a flashback: bees don't pop out of nowhere in December. But no, he definitely slapped at something— a honeybee — where did it go? Hopefully out the door. Everything is still, the only sound the baby's prattling. A bead of sweat slides down Gifford's cheek—then it reverses direction and trickles back up. It's not a sweat droplet— the bee is on his face. Gifford shallows his breath. The trickle stops, and he pictures the insect lowering its stinger, hunched like a shitting dog.

Maybe it's a cold breath of wind that brushes the bee from Gifford's cheek. The insect buzzes forward, skips off the windshield, and swerves past him into the back of the car. Gifford panics—with Emma's allergies, a sting could be fatal. He spots the bag with her EpiPen half out the open door. Rocking his hips, he frees a leg, but in spite of his contortions, can't extend his reach. He squints into the rearview and blinks to clear his vision. Is that the bee on Emma's hand or just a shadow? The tiny spot creeps onto the underside of his granddaughter's wrist, pausing on a pulse point. *Don't move*, he thinks, afraid that if he speaks, she'll flinch and be stung. Emma's nonsense syllables rise and fall like an incantation, and the bee, as if shot from a pistol, flies straight out the door. Emma points a finger after it as if she's conducting an orchestra.

Gifford shudders—there's a change in the light; maybe the sun has burst through the clouds. "You okay, baby?" he asks over and over. "Of course you are." *Unbuckle*, he thinks. *Find the phone. Find the dog. Get the EpiPen in case the bee comes back.* It's cold—is the baby warm enough? He fumbles with the clasp of his harness.

Movement at the door. Iota—one item to check off his list. But when he glances over, Gifford sees that it's not his fat little pet. A different dog, lanky, and raggedly furred, stands at the opening. Maybe it belongs to a hiker—are they about to be rescued?

"Hello?" Gifford calls. "We're here. We're okay."

The canine studies him with honey-colored eyes. A coyote: the paper has mentioned sightings. Ribby, triangular head, pointed ears. The coyote yawns, exposing jagged teeth. Determining Gifford is a non-threat, it looks to see what's behind him. Emma is silent. Asleep? No—in the rearview Gifford sees her fingers wiggling like little white bait worms. The coyote's rank odor is worse than any diaper. Gifford's eyes fill with tears.

The coyote takes a step into the car, and Gifford screams, thrashing his arms and kicking his legs. He hits the horn, and the coyote pauses and cocks its head back. Those honey eyes. Gifford meets them—is that right for coyotes? Stare them down? Or is it the opposite? The coyote shifts its attention back to the rear of the car. Gifford bangs on his window, blasts the horn again and again, hollering until he's faint. The coyote ignores him.

What happens next will forever be a blur. The coyote

advances, until Gifford can only see its hindquarters. Whether or not Emma whispers "Dah," will never be confirmed. But Iota appears at the passenger door. She hesitates, perhaps confused by the discovery that she could enter the car without being lifted.

"Iota—" Gifford croaks, not sure if he's summoning his dog or warning her off. The old Dachshund teeters, then waddles into the car, where her nose pokes the black tip of an unexpected tail. The coyote whirls, plucks up Iota by the back of her neck, dives out of the car, and trots up the embankment, leaving nothing to see but a wall of grass.

❧ ❧ ❧

Years later, Gifford will stand with Val on the western beach of Maui, watching the sun sink beneath the horizon. Conditions will be perfect for the sighting of the green ray. At the climactic moment, he will shut his eyes and will hear his wife utter, "Oh—oh, my God, Gifford!" Her fingers will tighten around his wrist, while he replays for the ten thousandth time the image of Iota being carried off by the coyote. She resisted no more than if she were a kitten being moved to a safer place by a doting mother. As if it was the way things had to be. This is what Gifford vows to tell Emma some day before he dies.

BALANCE

You feel the girls cowering behind you, but you don't turn. The rusted tracks lead through the trestle's steel frame: it looks like the entrance to a giant Have-a-Heart trap. Thirty feet below, the river is slate blue, except for the trestle's skeletal shadow. The day is breezeless, the water without a ripple. Though it's October cool, you're all sweating—you've been running for almost an hour. Across the river the curving tracks disappear into a forest of scrub oak.

"Cross or don't," you say. "It's two miles back if you do, five if you don't."

"What if a train comes?" a nervous voice asks.

"They don't use these tracks anymore," you say, though you're not one hundred percent sure. "Look how rusty they are. I run this trail all the time." This is a lie. You have never crossed the trestle before. But you can see that there are wooden planks on either side of the tracks all the way to the other side. Your heart is pumping. You're sure the girls' fifteen, sixteen, seventeen-year-old hearts are pumping, too. This is something new, something to break the monotony of training. Something inspirational.

"The Wellington girls do this kind of thing every day," you say. "That's why they're champions. Who's first?" You know who'll be first, Mary, determined as a pit bull, likely to qualify for states. Of the dozen members of your cross-country team, her name is one of the two you'll always remember.

"It's empty between the wooden things," somebody says.

"Railroad ties. Stay off of those," you warn. "Stay on the side boards, like I said."

"Is there room if a train comes?"

"I told you, don't worry about trains." You're challenging their trust. "Just go slow and be careful. Jog. Hold the side rail if you have to. If the boards don't look right, if they're rotten or have a hole or something, just stop. And don't bunch up. String out, spread the weight. I'll follow you. Just keep your eyes forward—down on the boards in front of you." You disallow second thoughts, theirs and yours. This crossing will be the stuff of legends.

Mary dashes past you. Her running shoes thud on the boards, and she slows, but keeps going. The twins, the skinny seniors, follow. The hoods of their blue team sweatshirts flounce on their backs. Then they're all out there, all twelve girls stretched out like a blue caterpillar. The last pair of feet belongs to Cherise, a lanky JV sophomore, who's directly in front of you. Cherise has talent—you'd run her varsity if she didn't miss too many practices because of her lead role in the school play. "World of potential," you told her mother last week after watching her win her JV race. "She tries to do too much," her mother said, shaking her head with poorly disguised pride. "Sometimes we worry that she's spreading herself too thin. We hope she learns to balance things. She's going to have to make choices." "Balance is important," you agreed. The two of you gazed at the girl, who sat on the grass, tugging on her sweatpants, sharing a post-race laugh with her teammates. At that moment you'd had a premonition that Cherise would not be remembered for running.

There's a shout up ahead, Mary's: "Stop—hole!" and the caterpillar bunches up and halts. Cherise, directly in front of you, looks up from her feet and veers to her right to avoid bumping into the girl ahead of her. She trips, grunts, lunges to her left for the side rail, misses, stumbles, and slips between ties.

What? you wonder. *Is she melting?* But you know Cherise is falling. Her hair flaps for an instant at your feet. Then there's only an arm, a hand, spread fingers. You bend over the space between ties and see nothing but shadowed water ten yards down, and only then do you shout her name. Eleven heads jerk around, mouths gaping. When they understand why you're stooping, they bleat like frightened sheep.

Your team shuffles back to you, their knuckles white on the side rail. Your jaw moves, but no words come out. All eyes are on the water.

"There—Cherise!" Mary yells, pointing at a spot downriver. "She's okay, look, she's moving. Cherise!"

Where? She's okay, she's moving! Che-riiiiise! Is she climbing on shore? She's trying to climb on shore! Che-riiiiise!

Faces flash towards yours, each pair of eyes a slap: *Coach? Coach? Coach? Coach?*

You watch the twisted figure bob in place just off-shore, less than a hundred yards away: just a waterlogged bundle of clothes, snagged on something unseen.

⁂

Waking or sleeping, you relive versions of her fall. Images shift randomly, like a television with a fitful remote: you see yourself save Cherise with a steadying hand on her elbow; once, you snatch her hood at the last second, and as she sways in space between the ties, her eyes bulge up at you with confused gratitude; another time, you stand on shore, watching from a distance as she plunges toward the water like a stone.

Sometimes you slip between the ties with her, and there's a thrill in your gut as the dull water rushes toward you. You fall beside her for what seems like hours, both of you squinting and grinning against the updraft. Her hair streams skyward. She's asking you a question, but you can't make it out. Is she rehearsing lines from her play?

⁂

Your senior girls take action: the twins sprint off the trestle with tear-streaked faces, looking for a house from which to call 911; Mary and another slide down the embankment beneath the trestle and make their way toward the spot where Cherise bobs; you herd the remaining girls off the trestle and tracks. They huddle together, trembling and crying silently. One vomits behind a bush. Your challenge to cross the trestle hangs in the air like burning sulfur.

Ankle deep mud prevents Mary and the other girl from reaching Cherise. Their teammates and you watch them flounder. Police cars, fire trucks, ambulances arrive. Stony faces ask question after question and you answer in a numb-lipped monotone. EMTs wrap the girls in foil blankets. An hour passes before firemen in a rescue boat reach Cherise.

❧ ❧ ❧

Once, the hair disappearing through the ties is nothing but light that stains your fingers yellow. Once, the hair pours through your cupped hands like cold, hard coins. Another time Cherise's hair turns into a waterfall of tiny goldfish as it spills through the gap at your feet. One fish misses and lies quivering on the wooden tie. You squat, flick it off, and watch it drop like a golden tear.

❧ ❧ ❧

You are never criminally charged because town records list the trestle as a "pedestrian bridge." Crossing it was perfectly legal, though now yellow barricade tape blocks the plank walkways. Your union would have been obliged to support you in a criminal case. There is talk of a civil suit brought by Cherise's parents, but it never materializes. Regardless, you resign. You don't impose yourself on friends, colleagues, acquaintances. Apparently relieved at the distance you keep, none of these seeks you out. You will never coach or teach again.

You leave town the night of the final performance of Cherise's play. Her understudy performs in her place. As you drive across the state line heading west, you picture a curtain call dedication to Cherise: actors and audience offer a tearful ovation to the auditorium ceiling.

You leave behind rumors, launched, you suspect, by your ever-faithful runners: Cherise at the time of her fall was teetering emotionally, they whisper, working too hard, in despair; she wrote "LIFE HURTS 2 MUCH" on an Etch-a Sketch at a team sleepover, then shook the message away. They hint that the incident on the trestle was less a horrible accident than a seized opportunity. No one believes them, and these girls, your team, will eventually forget that they love you. When they grow older, marry, have children of their own, their sympathies will change. *Poor Cherise*, they will sigh as they rock their babies, *how could he have let her fall?*

❧ ❧ ❧

You punish yourself with exile to another coast, but Cherise fills the vacuum inside you: in the corner of your eye there is always a girl slipping between railroad ties, a flap of hair, a waving hand. What if you offered her fear: if you found work as a firefighter, a coal miner, a deep sea fisherman? Might risking your life daily against earth, fire or water free you from the girl you let fall? Maybe, but you lack the qualifications or opportunities for these dangerous jobs. Instead, you lie about your janitorial experience and find employment as a nightshift custodian in a nursing home.

You find a sparsely furnished flat and swear yourself to monkish isolation, but the nursing home's night security guard foils your efforts at friendlessness. He synchs his rounds to yours and follows you like a puppy from waste basket to waste basket, toilet to toilet. Jeff thinks you're intelligent because you speak in polysyllables. He pries at your history, but his own guesses bore him, and his questions are always self-referential.

"Do you have any sisters?" Jeff asks. "I don't"

"Nope," you answer. "Only child." You don't tell him that your parents are dead, that you're glad they are, because what you let happen to Cherise would have been impossible to explain to them.

"If I had a sister, I bet I'd have better luck with

women," Jeff muses. "You get used to talking to girls if you have a sister. I only have a brother."

"What about your mother?" you ask as you follow your push-broom down one of the facility's many long, brightly lit hallways.

"What about her?" Jeff scurries to keep pace, an edge to his voice, wary of an insult a smart guy like you might try to sneak by him. He is an army veteran, though he survived his enlistment without leaving the country.

"Your mother's a woman, isn't she? Don't you talk to her?" As you ask this, familiar female faces appear in the gleam of the floor you're sweeping; your broom chases them away.

"Oh." Jeff ponders. "But a mom is different. Some guys have sisters, you know, who are, you know, *hot*, right?" He pauses, struggling to organize his thoughts.

"Yup," you reassure. "I get it." Did Jeff see your head snap as if you'd whiffed the undiluted ammonia you use for toilets? Had you ever thought of Cherise as *hot*? You increase your pace with the broom. The click of Jeff's heels on the linoleum behind you speeds up. You reframe your memory: *Cherise might have been hot someday* —if you hadn't let her fall.

Jeff leaves to check on the other wings. He will ogle the night duty nurses without speaking to them. After mopping, dusting, and scouring, you doze on one of the love seats in the common room. You hear your runners' feet echoing on wooden boards. Where is Cherise? Tracks and trestle emerge from a bright fog. You glance down between your legs, thinking of hair being spun into gold. *Rumpelstiltskin* , someone whispers in your ear, but in the fairytale it's not hair being spun, it's straw. A shove in the back jolts you awake.

"Caught you," Jeff chuckles, "red-handed." Your heart pounds.

The security guard stares into space, suddenly attuned to the snores growling from every open doorway. "Listen to that racquet," he mutters. "Good thing they're all too deaf to hear each other."

You hold up a finger, as if testing the wind. "Room 107," you announce, nodding down the hall. "Mr. Johnson has stopped snoring."

Jeff cocks his head, listens, then squints at you. "Bet?"

"Five dollars," you say.

Jeff hooks his thumbs in his belt, strolls to room 107, and ducks his head inside the door. When he pulls it out, he's shaking it. "You got great ears," he concedes when he rejoins you. "That's a beer on me."

You lick your finger and mark a one in the air. What you don't tell the security guard is that Mr. Johnson never snores.

❧ ❧ ❧

You take your first run in your new town, and you have a plan. You jog past apartment buildings like your own, noting trees with unfamiliar bark and leaves. Soon you turn onto the main drag: a mile stretch of small businesses, coffee shops and convenience stores. It's been a long time since you've run in place at a red light. The first bridge you come to crosses the Interstate. The bridge is part of your plan.

The sidewalks on both sides of this overpass are empty of pedestrians. The guardrails are hip-high, metal, the top rail flat, the approximate width of a gymnastics balance beam. Once on the bridge, you discover that the highway below is traffic-free: there's not a car, truck or bus heading in either direction. There doesn't appear to be any construction underway, and the six lanes seem fine; it's their emptiness that's disconcerting. At work you'll ask Jeff about it. But the absence of witnesses is probably better for your plan.

It should be simple: you will take a deep breath, and, without breaking stride, leap atop the guardrail and balance yourself. Then you'll jog a few steps along the rail and hop back down to the sidewalk. You'll commit yourself to this risk on every run. You'll test the rails of every bridge and overpass in the city, come rain, snow, or wind. Every precarious step will be dedicated to Cherise.

But at this moment, on this overpass, you hesitate—you jog back and forth half a dozen times. You rehearsed for this last night by jumping on and off the back of your sofa for ten minutes. A city bus pauses beside you, and you wave the driver on. You stare through the windows as the vehicle glides by; none of the passengers looks back.

You grasp the railing and, releasing a deep breath, peer down at the vacant highway. Cherise fell no further, though you'd strike pavement instead of water. You don't trust the Interstate's emptiness: what if you survive a fall only to be crushed by a truck? But the contemplation of such consequences—this is exactly what you're offering Cherise, isn't it? You turn and lean against the top rail, which cuts across the small of your back. You find the rail with your hands, hoist yourself up, and set your bottom on the steel. Your feet hover six inches above the sidewalk. Behind you, nothing.

You grit your teeth and pivot. Your feet dangle out in space, and you resist looking down. You focus on a tall uptown building you think is a hotel. When you pull up your legs so that your feet are under you on the top rail, you fight an impulse to sob. Awkwardly perched, chin on knees, you look up at a chalky blue sky.

You remind yourself that when you rise you must keep your center of gravity back. And just when it seems like you'll never pull the trigger, *you are up!* One-two-three, chest pressed against space, arms spread... and then something yanks you from behind like an invisible hand. You pretend it's Cherise, but you know it's your fear. You're on your knees on the sidewalk, but you're not praying. Caught between triumph and terror, you reject both: you can't do this again, even for Cherise.

❧ ❧ ❧

It's been weeks, and you haven't laced on your running shoes since the day you mounted the railing. You're gaining weight. On this Saturday evening you sit on a tall chair at a high table in a popular neighborhood bar. It's your first night out with Jeff, and under the table you pinch your soft belly. He's paid off his beer debt and then some for your correct call on Mr. Johnson's snoring.

"We're night workers," he hoots over the din of juke box music and chatter. "The later it is, the sharper we get." He sloshes beer from a third pitcher into his glass and yours. "It's science." He burps and lifts an eyebrow. "Physics?"

You're only half listening. "English, not physics. I taught English. I told you that." You're still not drunk enough to tell him that you also coached. Then you reconstruct his question. "Yes, physics. F=MA: Force equals Mass times Acceleration. I'm in training for the midnight toilet cleaning Olympics."

Jeff, glassy-eyed, nods and glances around the bar. Four laughing young women crowd into a booth across from your table, and he smiles toward them as if he's in on their joke. He takes a swallow of beer and blinks at you with heavy lids. "If I had a sister—" he starts, and you expect him to repeat himself about knowing how to talk to women, but he doesn't, "she'd be smarter than me. Like you."

You raise your glass to toast the compliment. Jeff thrusts out his jaw.

"What's the shittiest thing you ever did?" he asks.

"What?" The question knocks you off balance, and you look away. One of the young women catches your expression, rolls her eyes, and turns back to her friends.

"The worst thing," Jeff repeats. "I'll tell you mine, then it's your turn." He rubs his chin. You notice for the first time that he's missing the last inch of his pinky finger, and you try not to stare. Did something bite it off, or was he born that way? Your brain feels like a snowball being squeezed into a ball of ice—your worst thing? Really?

"So listen," Jeff whispers gruffly, peeking around like he wants to be overheard. "When I was a kid, I was playing in the backyard with my brother. He's not too bright, and even though he's a year older than me, I kind of always bossed him around. He still lives with my parents. Anyway, we were throwing around a ball or something when a little bird shot between us, and bang! —it hit the house—the window—it must have been fooled by the reflection." He pauses, checks to see if you're following, and you bow your head.

"The bird was on the ground. It was bright blue, a bluebird, I guess, bluer than any bird I ever saw. The color of that bird's feathers is what I picture when I think of 'blue.' The little thing was quivering. 'It broke its neck,' my brother said, and *I* said, 'We've got to put it out of its misery.' I'd heard that from somewhere, about putting suffering animals out of their misery. It seemed very important, like a religious law or something. The bird stopped quivering, but its tiny beady eyes were flicking around. Neither of us wanted to touch it, but I had an idea. It was my job to mow the lawn, so I knew we had a full gas can in the garage—I figured we could soak the bird in gasoline and light it on fire. I guess I'd seen it in a movie, where some foreign people in white robes build a pyre and burn up a body. We could put the thing out of its misery and give it a funeral all at once."

You keep nodding. *Like a phoenix*, you think, but don't say, because Jeff probably wouldn't get it.

"So we do it. I get the gas can, and my brother gets a box of matches from the kitchen. Now the bird's eyes aren't moving around anymore, but they're still open. We thought maybe it was dead, but neither of us knew if a little bird like this one had eyelids. I mean, how small can eyelids be?" Jeff frowns at you like he expects you to know, but all you do is wink. "Dead or not," he continues, "we'd already made up our minds to burn it up, so I tipped the can over it and soaked it good. The bird didn't move, but its wet feathers turned almost black. We both wanted to drop the match, but my brother said he was older, so he should." Jeff sucks in his lips, eases back in his chair, and lets his gaze fall on the young women, who are showing each other pictures on their phones. He finishes off his beer and sets the glass down.

"Then things got hairy," he says. "My brother dropped the match, and floom, the flame jumped up right in our faces, and we fell back on our asses." He laces his fingers around his glass, and you pour the rest of the pitcher into it. The pinky stump reminds you of a bald man's head. "That bird was on fire," Jeff says, "but it suddenly started flapping its wings, and then it took off, like a little fireball. It flew about ten feet past us, then dropped to the grass. By the time we got to it, the fire was out, but the bird was scorched black, still smoking. It couldn't have been alive, but who knew?" He reaches across the table and gives your forearm a squeeze; the stubby pinky pokes the knob of your wrist and you shiver. "So I stomped on it," he says. "Put out the fire, put it out of its misery, ended the funeral." He releases you, runs his hand through his hair, and sits back. "I'll never forget the squish of that charred little body under my foot. I still get jumpy in the dark when I step on stuff I don't expect."

Jeff closes his eyes and folds his arms across his chest. The women at the nearby table are quiet. They stare at their drinks—two hold beer bottles, the other two have twined their fingers around the stems of big cocktail glasses. Maybe they heard the story, maybe they didn't. Jeff's eyes pop open, and the way he's smirking makes your stomach churn, because you know what he's going to say next. A waitress comes by, picks up the empty pitcher. She shifts a look between the two of you. "Another?" she asks, and Jeff nods without looking at her.

"Your turn," he says. "What's the shittiest think you've done?"

And then you're talking, too fast at first, until you get into the rhythm of the story you've chosen to tell. There are facts in it, enough to hide behind, but it isn't really the truth.

You tell Jeff you were an early reader— you practically taught yourself, you say, by looking at the comics in the newspaper. Then one day you found the obituary section, and you asked your mom who all the people with little pictures next to their names were.

"Dead people," she said. She told you to skip that section, but you didn't.

"After that," you say, "I turned to the obituaries every day after the comics. It was the little photos I liked, the headshots: new photos with old faces, old photos with new faces, once in a while a new photo with a young face. So, I'd look at each face, and then I would decide who was going to go to Heaven and who was going to Hell."

"*You* decided?"

"Absolutely. Most of people got sent to Hell. I guess I

was a mean little kid, but that's where I put most of them. One or two a day got to go to Heaven."

The waitress drops off your pitcher. You top off Jeff's glass and your own. He seems to be buying your story.

"So you got to be like God."

"Exactly. I marked Xs with a pencil over the eyes of everybody I sent to Hell."

"And the ones going to Heaven?"

"Their eyes got stars." You think of telling him that Jews got Stars of David, but that seems too sophisticated for a little kid just learning to read. "When my dad got mad at me for messing up the paper, I quit, which I was ready to do. At some point it struck me that all the people I'd doomed to Hell were stuck there forever, and I felt guilty that I hadn't thought more about the selection process."

"You couldn't change where you sent them?"

You look aslant at the security guard, as if he's missing the point. "How?"

He frowns. He slides back in his seat. Then he shakes his head. "Nah," he says, "Your story doesn't count. Not shitty enough."

You pull your glass from your mouth—beer runs down your chin. "What? Why not? Sure it's shitty."

"God can't be shitty," he says. "God's all-mighty. Whatever God decides goes." He leans forward on his elbows. "You're not getting off that easy," he hisses, and you feel like your skin is melting off your face. "What the hell are you doing out here really? What are you running from? Got to be the shittiest thing ever."

❧❧ ❧❧ ❧❧

There's only an inch of beer left in the pitcher— did you drink the rest over the last twenty minutes while Jeff listened without interrupting to your trestle story? His face is a jigsaw of shadows in the dim light, and you guess yours is, too. He's let you go on for so long you half-hope he's fallen asleep with his eyes open. Maybe he hasn't retained a single word of the "shitty truth" you just shared. Most of the tables in the bar are empty now, including the booth where the young women sat. Nobody's fed the juke box, and rain patters on the pavement outside the open front door.

"Shit," your companion mutters. He smacks his forehead with the heel of his hand. "What—so—did she have something on you? Is that why you pushed her? You pushed her, right? The whole thing, running across the bridge—the trestle, whatever—that was just a set up so you could shut her up, right? What'd you, fuck her? The kid? Make the moves at least—and she was going to tell?"

You feel like a knife's twisting between your ribs. "No," you protest. "Nothing like that. I was just irresponsible, that's all. I shouldn't have sent the girls across the bridge. Not criminal—I said, there were boards to walk on next to the tracks. It was on the records as a pedestrian bridge—"

"You said you could have grabbed her."

"I said I *felt like* I should have grabbed her." In your mind's eye you see a golden braid slithering down a hole —stepping on it would stop, maybe save whatever it's attached to, but you can't move your foot.

"You said you loved her."

"No I didn't."

"You said all the girls loved you."

"I said they *trusted* me. That's what I meant."

"You said love. You said you loved her."

You shrug twice, three times; you're shaking. "Maybe I said I loved them, like all of them loved me. I didn't say I was *in* love with any of them. With her. If I loved her, why would I push her?" You feel the thread of your argument slipping through your fingers. What *had* you said about love, exactly? You'd told Jeff you thought about Cherise every hour of every day. Is that love? Or is it more than love?

Jeff holds up his hands. "No worries," he says. "Your secret's safe with me." His eyes look closed, but there's the slightest glitter between his lids. "I don't know if I could have coached a team of girls. I wouldn't have known how to talk to them. But I tell you what—if she was my sister, I'd be after your ass. She have a brother?"

Your head flops from side to side. You feel hollowed out, like you're made of papier mache. "Don't know. I don't think so."

"Hm. You're probably okay then." Jeff clears his throat. "So it's late, even for us night owls. Time to settle up. Who wins? I think I do."

"Wins what?"

Jeff's grin warps into a leer. "Whose story is shittiest? Mine, right? Yours was an accident, right? You didn't 'push' anybody." His half-pinky mars his finger quotes. "But I set a bird on fire. I stomped on it. I made *choices*. All you did was panic. Anybody can freeze up. Even God, right?"

"But you had good intentions. You wanted to put the bird out of its misery. You did what you did out of kindness."

Jeff looks down at the table, then back at you. "Mostly," he says, "I wanted to torch a little bird. And that, my friend, makes me tonight's champion."

Champion. The word rises like smoke. Your eyes sting. You once told your team that running across a trestle was what champions did. And then one of them fell and died. You lost everything you had, moved as far away as you could—and the truth of it can't even win you a "shitty story" contest? You try to pour the rest of the beer into Jeff's glass, but he covers it. "Whoa," he chuckles. "Party's over." So you refill your own, and gulp the beer like you're trying to put out a fire in your heart. But your heart isn't on fire at all—it's a cold, hard stone, and the beer splashes over it and trickles down, down, into a terrible darkness.

"Okay," you say to your newest, closest friend, slitting your eyes to match his. "Okay, you're right. I *was* in love. I pushed the girl because she had something on me." You lift your glass like it's a trophy. You imagine cheers. "So *I* win, right?"

GLORIOUS VESSEL

My seven-year-old son Aaron sits coloring at the back of the conference room in the Mobile, Alabama, Hampton Inn. Aaron adds red to Jesus' flashing robes as He throws the moneylenders out of the temple while I stack my official Awake and Aware relaxation recordings on the table in front of him. You'd think a twenty-first century kid would be involved with a game on his smart phone instead of with a Bible coloring book, but Aaron's fundamentalist mother and new stepfather don't allow him electronics. *No electronics, including TV* is first on the list of rules I signed off on a week ago so they'd trust me to watch over my own son for the summer. Shelley and Rodney are on an "Evangelical Inspiration Cruise" along the coasts of Central and South America. By the time I return Aaron to his home in Pensacola, he'll have witnessed my Awake and Aware group hypnosis sessions in nearly two dozen Southern cities.

The first nine rules I've sworn to uphold include keeping the Word of God holy, making sure Aaron says his prayers, and refraining from carnal activity. But Shelley and Rodney left a blank space after the number for a tenth rule.

"We've left you room to create a rule of your own, as needed," Shelley said when I questioned the omission. "We trust in the Lord to guide you with His wisdom."

Shelley and I met in Alabama twelve years ago. I noticed her first at a continental breakfast at the Best Western outside of Mobile, caught her eye a week later at the omelet station in the Montgomery Sheraton, and three days after that introduced myself at the make-your-own waffle griddle at the Holiday Inn off Interstate 85 in Birmingham. She was conducting sessions for a company that packaged educational programs for parents who wanted to home school their kids.

"Mostly for religious people who are afraid public schools don't provide good Christian values," she said. "It's a job. I don't trouble myself much with the content." Shelley giggled when I told her that I hypnotized people to stop overeating and smoking. I invited her to attend my morning session for free, but she declined.

"I'll be busy right next door, Conference Room C. And I don't smoke," she said. "Do I look overweight to you?"

"No," I said, because she wasn't at the time, though I should have noticed her heavy hand with the syrup. "But maybe you look different to yourself. And maybe you're white-knuckling through an urge to smoke."

Mistaking coincidence for fate and lust for love, we

slept together for the first time a week later at the Hilton in Tuscaloosa, and two months after that we were married. Shelley quit her job and moved into my cottage in Pensacola. I'd return from the road every few weeks because we were trying, without much luck, to have a child. Shelley's failure to become pregnant left her terribly depressed, and she spent the lonely hours I was away eating and poring over the Christian home school materials she formerly sold. When I returned after a month-long stint in Mississippi, she met me with a gleam in her eye. I patted the belly swelling over the elastic waistband of her stretch pants.

"This is it, right?" I grinned. But the gleam had been fired up by Jesus, not a baby, and the big belly was nothing but extra flesh.

"The Lord is testing us," she said. So we kept trying. We barely left the bedroom whenever I was home. Shelley got bigger and bigger and more and more devout, but not at all pregnant. After another evening's struggle with "baby-making" (we'd stopped calling it "lovemaking"), I thought she was asleep and tried to plant a whispered hypnotic suggestion that she eat less.

"Close your eyes and retreat to the pure silence you felt in the womb," I began. But it turned out she wasn't asleep. She was praying.

"Don't start your hypno-tricks with me," she snapped. "Not while I'm talking to Jesus."

It was Shelley's dream that got us to a fertility specialist. She phoned me at four AM at the Hampton Inn in Biloxi, Mississippi, to tell me about the beautiful, slender woman in a flowing white robe: "She had streaming hair, dark as midnight, and eyes that glittered like a Fourth of July sparkler. And her lips looked so red and soft even a woman would want to kiss them—and still feel guiltless."

Coincidentally, there was a woman with long, dark

hair and kissable lips asleep in bed next to me, an attendee from the day's session. It was not unusual for one of my subjects to require free "extra attention" for a particularly noxious tobacco addiction. My bedmate lay with her back to me while Shelley continued.

"The beautiful woman pulled out the most precious baby boy, all swaddled up, from the folds of her robe. He had my blue eyes and little dab of a nose, but your mouth. 'Go see a doctor,' the woman said, displaying the baby, 'See a doctor, and this will be your prize.'"

So Shelley flew into Shreveport, Louisiana, my next stop, where we visited the Center for Fertility and Reproductive Health. For her own reasons, she wanted the testing done as far from Pensacola as possible. The conclusion of our visit? Though neither of us was sterile, Shelley had "anatomical peculiarities" that made conceiving and carrying a child impossible.

Shelley had prepared herself for all eventualities: "But Jimmy and I can make a baby in a dish, can't we?" she asked. "And have an angel carry it who'll pass it on to us the second after Jesus brings it into this world?"

The answer to both questions was "Yes," and so it went: while an anonymous surrogate in Louisiana carried our baby, Shelley pretended to be pregnant back home in Pensacola. Shelley believed it was part of our private miracle—hers, mine, the dream-woman's, and Jesus'—that she "feel" pregnant. Her size permitted the subterfuge. She donned maternity clothes, "ate for two," and "glowed," according to her church friends.

When the time came, we flew back to Shreveport, where we took care of the necessary paperwork and the hospital staff handed over Aaron. Holding him to her bosom in her non-maternity dress, Shelley looked particularly stout—I guess I half-expected her weight to melt away with the birth of our child. We never met the surrogate, and no such encounter was planned. "It would spoil the miracle," Shelley said.

After a week back in Pensacola enjoying my new family, I needed to get back on the road. A year and a dozen trips later, after I came home without a believable explanation for the mingled scents of tobacco and perfume that saturated my flesh, Shelley filed for divorce. Until this summer road trip, my time with my son consisted of the occasional weekends I'd hole up with him at the Pensacola Motel 6.

And now my boy gets to see his daddy at work. He looks up from his coloring book and stares out over the registration table at the rows of chairs and the podium where my lectern stands. "This is like church, isn't it Daddy?"

"A little," I say as I appraise the Awake and Aware recordings display, then lay out the registration materials, including the cashbox. "But it's not." I stride down the center aisle and mount the podium. I test the microphone.

"Hello, there, young fellow." My amplified voice crackles before achieving perfect modulation. Aaron waves. I expect a good crowd. There are eighteen pre-registrants—ten smokers, eight overeaters—and I estimate at least a dozen walk-ins. I move back to the registration table to await my flock. As usual, they slink or waddle through the conference room doors one at a time, slouching under individual clouds of failure. They register, pay what's due, and take their seats. Before the day is over, most, motivated by a host of strategically dropped suggestions, will purchase an Awake and Aware Relaxation Re-enforcement Recording at the special reduced price of $49.99.

I leave my son and make my way to the podium, from which I smile down upon the attendees. "Look around at your fellow health-seekers," I say, and neighbors blink into each other's faces. I see hope and resentment in their tobacco-stained teeth and double chins—and shame, always shame. "These are your brothers and sisters," I say. "Though you've taken your own routes, you've all been on the same pilgrimage, and that pilgrimage has brought you here. Check your watches—your new lives start *now*."

Aaron colors away as I summarize the basis of hypnotherapy to those who've placed themselves in my hands: synapses will be rewired; unwanted desires will be purged. Surrender through relaxation is the key. I remind my listeners that I've been certified by the American Board of Neuro-Linguistic Learning as a Master Hypnotherapist and Master Success Coach. If my titles impress my son, he doesn't show it—his crayon work is all he's got eyes for.

I ask my subjects to inhale deeply, to hold their breath while I count to five, and to release. Wheezes and gasps—a familiar odor of burnt paraffin washes over me. "Close your eyes," I say, and I begin the entrancement.

"Imagine that you're asleep and dreaming. All parts of you melt toward your center and form a single weight, a soft heaviness. You're a baby in the womb, floating; you have no memories because you've only breathed in darkness."

Now Aaron lifts his head, his mouth open and crayon poised. I wink and blow him a kiss over my shut-eyed subjects. He bows back to his coloring.

"After I instruct you to open your eyes," I say, "I will ask you how it felt to travel back to the womb, and some of you will describe the experience. But then I will say a sentence with the word "dog," in it, and when you hear that word, "dog," you will think it's funny and you will laugh. I'll say the word "dog" several times, and each time it will seem funnier and funnier, until you won't be able to control your laughter."

I clap and direct my subjects to open their eyes. "What did you see?" I ask. They are shy and hesitate. "Who saw darkness?" A few raise their hands. "Who saw light?" More hands. A woman volunteers that she saw her child-self in a crib clutching a teddy bear.

"Very good, yes." I nod. "And did anybody see a dog?" There are chuckles. I look perplexed. "Nobody saw a little puppy dog?" There's increased laughter, and puzzled participants glance at each other, unable to explain their merriment. "It's not unusual for hypnotized subjects to picture a *dog*," I say, raising my voice as guffaws crescendo.

"What if I told you that I hypnotized you to visualize a *big, shaggy dog*?" The room rocks with spasmodic laughter. Arms akimbo, I smile a knowing smile.

"And perhaps you recall," I say after waiting for the hilarity to subside—my audience becomes rapt—"that I *told* you—I planted the thought in your minds—that you would find the word d-o-g irresistibly humorous."

There's an electric silence. Faces close like fists. Then, as my subjects accept that surrendering to my will is a good thing, that it's what they paid for, foreheads uncrease and frowns relax. For the first time, they allow themselves hope. I snap my fingers. "You are now free," I say. "'Dog' is no longer funny. And now we can begin."

At the back of the room, Aaron is waving his hand. His legs dance under the table.

"Yes?" I call back to him with a stiff grin.

"Daddy," he pipes, "I have to go the bathroom."

It's too early for a break, but I have no choice, and I release my subjects for five minutes, assuring them we'll get to the heart of the program when we all return. Aaron waits for me at the table and takes my hand. The women who file past beam at us with puckered smiles, while the men in the hall and in the restroom avoid eye contact. Aaron and I take care of business and wash up, my boy carefully mimicking me as I rub my hands under the blower.

"I didn't laugh when you said 'dog.'" He forgets to stop shouting when the blower stops, and his fluty voice bounces off the tiled walls.

"You did fine," I say.

"Why didn't you make the word 'Jesus' instead of 'dog'? You could make your people rejoice in His name every time they hear it."

"But that wouldn't be fair, would it? They should rejoice because they want to, not because I make them. And remember," I say, "what I do isn't church. Zip up your fly."

Our father-son summer passes quickly. Between cities and hotels, Aaron and I float along Interstates as if they're rivers: I-10 through Mobile, then I-65 through Montgomery and on to Birmingham. We take notice of road signs, bridges, and water towers. Sometimes we observe the travelers we pass or who pass us, and we guess if they're smokers or if they're Christians. Sometimes we decide they're both. The overeaters are obvious. When we reach our next city, we check-in, and there's dinner at Denny's or Applebee's, unless the hotel restaurant is having a special. If we find a playground nearby with a swing, we'll stop, and I'll push Aaron. I'll feel his fleeing, returning weight in the pit of my stomach as if I'm the one riding. I grab him only to shove him away, his body compact as a yo-yo, his blond hair flapping.

Some days, usually at sunset, whether we're in the car or in a park or enjoying dishes of plain vanilla ice cream at an outdoor stand, my son will lecture me about the Rapture. He'll stare toward the flood of colors at the horizon, orange and lavender, and describe how the sky will open wide and Jesus will descend amid the blare of trumpets and the fluttering wings of golden angels. "We're all to have glorified bodies like Jesus," Aaron says. "We'll be like ghosts who can walk through walls." He'll become so steeped in the narrative his face will flush pink, and he'll stammer. His enthusiasm is so visceral, I wonder if such vividness is healthy for someone his age.

Back in our hotel room, I'll read with him from his Bible comic books, or he'll color or work on one of the Bible word searches in his home school workbook. While I lie on one of our pair of queen beds making notes for the next morning's session, he'll stretch out on his, circling the names of ancient Bible places he finds in the big block of letters. "Thessalonia," he might murmur with the slightest of lisps, or "Jerusalem." Finally, when it's time for lights out, I'll heed the rules I agreed to and listen to Aaron recite his prayers. If I can't sleep, I'll listen in the dark to one of my Awake and Aware recordings through my ear buds: my own mellifluent voice merges with the sizzle of a summer rain shower and the heave and suck of ocean waves on a pebbled shore, and I'm soon asleep.

One August evening after we've settled into our room at the Embassy Suites Hotel in downtown Birmingham, the air conditioner gives a long, desperate shriek and quits. It's declared "unfixable," and, because the hotel's regular rooms are jam-packed with a hundred-plus nurses and midwives for a weekend conference on "Birthing in the 21st Century," management resituates Aaron and me "at no extra charge" in one of their honeymoon suites. Our suite features two rooms: a bedroom with a king-sized, heart-shaped bed and an "entertainment area" with a foldout sofa. I give him his choice, and Aaron picks the foldout.

It's past midnight when I look into the neighboring room and see that my boy is still awake. He's coloring on his made-up bed. We haven't been this far apart all summer. I invite him up to my giant heart, and he climbs aboard with the coloring book and a fistful of crayons. He shows me the picture he's working on: a huge dinosaur with a spiny back and dagger teeth. Aaron's coloring the dinosaur blue. It towers over a half-dozen bearded cavemen with raised spears. A few spears already pierce the beast's hide, and blood that Aaron has colored yellow drips from the wounds. Little dinosaurs spy on the battle from behind the trunks of coconut-laden palm trees. The baby dinosaurs sit in half-shells like Easter chicks. A caveman with his back to the central struggle waves his spear at the babies. Aaron has colored the palm fronds purple. The picture reminds me that one of Shelley's irrefutable rules sets the age of the world at six thousand years.

"There's a life-sized dinosaur and caveman fight just like this at Creation World," Aaron says, as if eavesdropping on my thoughts. "Rodney took us there. The dinosaur moves its head and roars, and the cavemen shake their spears. Rodney knows the names of all kinds of dinosaurs."

"Rodney's a smart man," I say, though there's no rule dictating that I compliment my son's stepfather.

Aaron stops coloring and winces at me. "Daddy, what's a 'woom'?"

"A 'woom'?"

"You know—you tell the people to close their eyes and picture that they're back floating inside the 'woom'."

"Oh—'womb.' It's got a 'b' on the end that you can barely hear." I pause. What does Aaron know about babies? How much does any seven-year-old know? Have I got a rule for this? Could this be a call for Rule Ten—the blank one that Shelley says the Lord is supposed to help me with? I sniff a deep breath and wait, but there's no divine intervention. I exhale.

"A womb is where a baby grows," I say.

"Like my *bed*-room?"

I look at the dinosaur picture, at the spears in the blue dinosaur's side, and I bite the side of my cheek. Aaron is my son, too. He isn't kin to Rodney at all. I deserve some say in my boy's upbringing; Rule Ten should state that it's a father's right and responsibility to see that his child understands *something* true about life.

"Wom-*b*," I say, exaggerating the final letter. "Has your mom talked to you yet about where babies come from?"

Aaron shrugs. "Babies are miracles. They're Jesus' gifts."

"Yes," I nod. "That's true. But Jesus has to work at the miracle, and miracles aren't easy. That's why Jesus had to suffer for us, right? Okay, so—you know how there are lots of fat ladies in the world? Like a lot of the ones who come to see me? Well there are other fat ladies who get that way not because they eat too much, but because they have a baby inside—in their womb."

Aaron grins, but his brows knit. "Nobody eats babies," he says.

"Of course not. But Jesus makes it interesting. He's fixed things so a mom and a dad make a baby together. He gave dads something like a key to open up a mom. And a mom's got an egg inside of her, a little tiny one—in her *womb*, which is a big space behind her belly button that's got room enough for the baby to grow into." I hear myself purring, just like my voice on my recordings. "The dad uses his key to 'anoint' the mom's egg, or it won't start growing into a baby. That's how Jesus works it out. Once the egg is anointed, it starts to grow in the womb, bigger and bigger until it's ready to come out. It takes a long time—about nine months."

Aaron's scowling with concentration. He might be

puzzling over any of a thousand particulars. *Key? Anoint?* What was I thinking?

"How's the baby get out?" he asks.

I choose retreat over graphicness. "Usually a doctor in the hospital keeps an eye on things. A doctor or a midwife."

"I bet Jesus touches the baby just like He'll touch us at the Rapture," Aaron speculates. "Babies get glorified bodies just like His, for just a while, and they pass right through the mom's skin. I bet that's the miracle."

"Something like that," I say.

Aaron puffs his cheeks, then lets them go slack. "So — I grew in Mom's womb. She was my glorious vessel, and then I passed through her and into the world."

I start to agree, but something stops me. Maybe it's the way Aaron lisped "glorious vessel." Maybe I'm mad about the rules I'm forced to follow—and maybe I'm mad at myself for promising to follow them. But I don't waste a lot of time looking for a rationale for telling the truth—I just tell it. I clear my throat.

"Your mom wasn't actually your 'glorious vessel,'" I say. "Your miracle was a little bit different." The heat of Aaron's gaze singes my cheeks. My eyes drop to the coloring book and the standoff between the cavemen and the dinosaur. "Your mother's womb—there was something wrong with it. It was broken. She had a good egg, though. Jesus helped the doctor take the good egg out of your mom. I 'anointed' it in a special dish, it turned into you, and then the doctor put you inside a very generous woman who volunteered her womb for you to grow up in. With Jesus' help, of course. It was that special woman's flesh you passed through when you were born."

Aaron's mouth is an O: he's trying to make a word— maybe "womb."

"Who?" he asks. He's as white as the bed sheets.

"Who was my glorious vessel?"

I shake my head. "We don't know. Jesus has kept it a mystery. When you were ripe, you passed through the special woman's womb, and the doctor called us and told us to come get you." I wonder if Rodney knows that his new bride has fertility problems. Does he know that a dozen of Shelley's eggs—fertilized by me—wait in a Shreveport freezer? "We've got zero information. Either the woman or Jesus must want it a secret. She could be anyone. Maybe she's an angel," I add, admiring my tone. But have I gone too far? These revelations will bear consequences. "It's really late," I fake yawn. "We'd better get to sleep."

"My glorious vessel," Aaron whispers. He squirms down under the covers of the giant heart-bed. His coloring book and crayons slide into the valley between us. It would be cruel to send him back to his foldout, so I turn out the light and listen for a while to my boy breathing before I plug myself into one of my recordings.

The breakfast buffet is packed, and I seat Aaron before waiting on line to fill a plate with blueberry muffins for us to share. My son barely registers my return. He's jerking glances from table to table.

"I'll know her, right?" he asks. "The lady I was born from?"

Something in my belly squirms. My gaze follows Aaron's: women of all ages, shapes, and sizes fill the dining room. They sip coffee, fork up slices of melon, nibble toast and chat with tablemates. "I'm not so sure," I say. "You're made up of part your mom and part me. The woman who carried you was like a Fedex driver who's got nothing to do with the package she delivers. You're not part of her."

"Didn't I share her body and her blood?"

"I guess," I frown. "But finding her will be like looking for a needle in a haystack." I look at my watch. It's time to go—my session begins in half an hour. I lead Aaron between tables. Woman after woman flinches as we pass, each face stung by my boy's sudden glance.

There's chaos in Conference Room B. Eager nurses and midwives crowd the registration table, while my smokers and overeaters shrink into the background. Who would have believed that there are two unrelated hypnotherapy sessions occurring simultaneously in the same hotel? Exasperated, I direct everyone to find a seat. The multitude surges forward as if I've started the world's largest game of musical chairs. I stand behind Aaron, my hands on his shoulders. His head wags as he sifts through the woman rushing by. His home school manual is open to a word search: "Women of the Bible." "H-A-G-A-R," circled as an example, spills diagonally through the block of letters.

The crowd quiets as I stride up the center aisle and take the podium. I fasten my microphone to my lapel. There are two sessions, I explain, unrelated. The one for nurses and midwives on "hypnosis techniques for childbirth" meets in suite 201 and begins in fifteen minutes. Awake and Aware attendees are in the right place. "So let's all get where we belong," I smile.

Two-thirds of the mob rises, mostly women; they shuffle out the door past my son's keen-eyed squint. About thirty remain in what might be the largest room I've worked this summer. It's definitely got the highest ceiling. My voice, as I get the ball rolling, shimmers with authority.

"You're dreaming of yourself deep in the womb," I intone. At "womb" I look back at Aaron—he's bent over his word search, framed by twin towers of Awake and Aware recordings. My subjects sit, some with lifted chins, others with lowered foreheads, all with eyes shut. But then there's another face—it belongs to a woman who sits in an otherwise empty back row. Her orange hair glows like a sunrise over her red track suit. She's straight-backed and bites her lower lip. She seems to feel me observing her and shakes her hair. One of her eyes pops open, then shuts. She twitches a smile. My chest feels light, as if I'm breathing helium. When I plant the suggestion that "dog" is an irresistibly funny word, my throat feels rusty.

As the induced laughter begins, the woman laughs along, but without the perplexity of her session-mates. And, after I instruct the group to listen to the sounds of their bodies, she opens her eyes and pins me with a green-eyed gaze so intense that my skin prickles.

"*Jesus loves me, this I know—*" Aaron's voice is like a little bird's. He's on his feet now behind the registration table, his attention fixed on the orange-haired woman between us. Hers is the only head that turns to find the singer. Everyone else has focused inward, mesmerized by his or her own body sounds. The woman waves at my son. He waves back and sits.

At the break, the woman lingers near the exit while I process registrations. *She knows me*, I think, but I can't place her. Is she someone I saved? Someone who's shed a hundred pounds or sworn off cigarettes and now sparkles with good health? As the others leave for the restrooms, she steps forward. She's about my age, but has freckles like a kid.

"This is your boy," she says, smiling at Aaron, whose blue eyes glisten. "He favors you in the chin and mouth. I'm Megan." It turns out she's one of the midwives who'd come to Awake and Aware by mistake. But, unlike the others, she decided to stick around. "Your session seemed like fun. You're so *earnest*." She waves at Aaron again, and his arm rises and sinks as if he's underwater. "I'll be glad to pay. It wasn't right for me to intrude. I'm sorry if I made it hard for you."

"No charge," I say. "We'll call it an introductory special. You don't have to leave."

"Oh, but I do," she says. "I'm afraid I'm spoiling your magic. Maybe I can treat you and your son—" she pauses.

"'Aaron,'" I say. "And I'm Jimmy."

"'James,' yes, it's all over your materials." She nods at my recordings—my picture is on the cases. "So—can I treat you two to dinner?"

I accept, and a few long strides carry Megan through the door and into the hotel lobby. Aaron appears at my side.

"You let her go—" He's staring into the vacated space.

"It's okay. We'll see her at supper."

"*Megan.*" Aaron weighs the name in his mouth as if it's a gold coin.

We meet in the hotel restaurant. I wear a fresh shirt under my session suit, and Aaron has tugged on his favorite John 3:16 T. Megan's green dress turns her eyes into emeralds and sets her hair aflame. She's driven in for the conference from west of the Mississippi, she says, looking for a vacation. When she describes her last few months as "rough," a shadow falls over her face that discourages pursuit of the subject. I tell her about Aaron's mom's honeymoon by way of explaining our "summer bonding tour," and she makes a face at the idea of a cruise.

"They're like prison islands, those cruise ships, aren't they?" she asks. "Like Alcatraz? And they force feed you." She cocks her head "Though I guess that's good for your business?" She asks Aaron what grade he's in, and he tells her he's home-schooled. He asks if her name is from the Bible.

"I don't know." She looks at me with a raised eyebrow, and I shake my head.

"His mom has become *very* religious since we split up," I say. "Aaron's been filling me in about the Rapture."

"Really?" Megan leans toward my son, absorbing him in eyes as green and wide as any meadow Jesus blessed a lamb in. Aaron tells her all about Jesus' glorious body, and how the saved will have bodies made of air just like His when the Rapture comes. We just have to be prepared.

I'm sure my boy believes he's found his needle in a haystack—the "glorious vessel" whose flesh contained him until his miraculous birth. He might put his suspicion into words at any moment, and I should be planning an explanation. But there's a faint hum—a single lovely note—inhibiting forethought, and I've surrendered to it. I don't taste my steak, and the conversation passes into the ether, and I'm as happy as Megan and my son seem to be. When the waiter asks about dessert, I order Aaron his dish of plain vanilla ice cream. Megan wants only a coffee. "I'm not crazy about sweets," she says.

"Oh, but you'll like our suite, won't she Daddy," Aaron says. "We got a special one because the air conditioner in our first room broke. Megan can come up to see our suite, can't she?"

"How did you come to do what you're doing?" Megan's voice surprises me—she's been breathing so gently beside me I've assumed she's been asleep. I've only been awake myself for a few minutes. I drifted off for the first night in a long time without listening to myself on an Awake and Aware recording. Is it Rule 6 or Rule 7 that forbids "carnal activity"? My hip presses against Megan's. "Carnal" implies a guilt I don't feel. "Carnal" reeks of stale cigarettes and perfume, of greasy sweat. What I feel is cleansed.

"Daddy's bed is a heart," Aaron murmured after Megan and I had tucked him into his sofa bed. He fell asleep before the end of the Christian movie about righteous cartoon vegetables we found on the Gospel Network—our first television of the summer.

"A heart-shaped bed," Megan responded without inflection while I dimmed the light in Aaron's room.

I close my eyes and imagine Megan's freckles glowing under the sheets like trapped fireflies. My skin tingles as if it's been scoured. Has she just asked about my history? I'm afraid I'll compromise the present if I speak. But thinking about the past implies the future: what will we say to Aaron when Megan exits this room with me in the morning?

A muffled commotion from behind the closed door jars the silence and I half sit up. Megan stiffens beside me. "My phone," I whisper. "I left it on the table out there. That was my ringtone." We hear a high-pitched voice, indecipherable. "Aaron answered it," I say. I switch on the bedside lamp. Megan, her eyes slits, pulls the sheet under her chin. Her hair is a blazing nest, her freckles spatter her cheeks like dried blood. We hunch shoulder to shoulder, trapped by the child's voice.

"It must be his mother," I say.

"At two in the morning? What about her cruise?"

We listen. Aaron's voice drones short and long. What questions is he answering? What is he volunteering? Then his words grow more distinct—he's approached the door.

"—right here. Daddy has his own room—no, no it's okay—we have a *suite*! I'll wake him up."

As the knocks sound there's a blur, a snapped necklace of bouncing images: I jump out of bed and throw the door forward while using it to hide my nakedness; I feel a concussion through the knob and curse doors that open outward. Aaron sits on the floor, stunned, one hand to his nose, the other gripping the phone, from which a voice buzzes like a bee in a jar. *He's going to cry*, I think, but before I process what this might mean, Megan, who's yanked on her dress, rushes past me, a burst of green. She scoops my boy from the floor and hands me the phone. I pull the door shut. The last thing I see is my son's face: he's caught up in Megan's arms, and our gazes lock over her shoulder. He presses his cheek into her wild hair. Blood dribbles from his nose, but he's smiling.

I press the phone against my temple as if it's an icepack. "Hello," I gasp. "Hello, Shelley?"

"What's going on there?" my ex-wife demands.

"Nothing," I say. "Aaron dropped the phone while he was knocking. We have a suite."

"You shut your door on him?"

"He slept with me the first night. But tonight I needed to listen to some new Awake and Aware recordings, and I couldn't find my ear buds. So—you're calling from your cruise?"

"Don't you pay attention to the news? We've been on the news. I know you had the TV on—Aaron said you watched a movie."

"On the Gospel Network. It was about vegetables. But that was all. We kept to the rules. What happened?"

"Some kind of bacteria got on the ship. In the food. Half of the passengers got sick. Not me, thank Jesus, but Rodney got so dehydrated they had to hook him up to an IV. They had to helicopter in medical supplies while we made our way back. I thought sure you would have called to check on us, but nope, not a single message."

"Because we didn't know," I say. "But that's horrible. You deserve better."

"Rodney says the Lord must have had His reasons, and I guess he's right. Who are we to question?" I pull on my khakis while we speak as if Shelley's about to walk through the door. "So," she continues. "Aaron's okay?" There's something coming, and I gird myself.

"He's fine," I say. "He's a good boy. He keeps himself occupied with his Bible stuff. I promise, except for tonight with the TV, we've been following the rules." I button my pants and contemplate my bare-chested reflection in the dresser mirror.

"Hm. Maybe you have been and maybe you haven't. I had a long talk with Aaron just now." Shelley's so wound up her voice shakes. "You had that blank spot for a tenth rule—for the Lord to guide you—and it sounds like you must have ignored Him. You went and told Aaron the facts of life? He's only *seven*. He's got to be twelve for that. There'll be pastor-talks and workbooks—but not until he's twelve."

If this is all she's got, I can defend myself. "A father has a right—"

But Shelley's not done. "You told Aaron that I didn't carry him?" She's struggling so hard to control her voice she must be beet purple. "You told him that he grew inside a woman that wasn't me for nine months? A 'miraculous vessel'?"

"'Glorious vessel,'" I correct. "He got the idea from the Rapture."

"So-he-tells-me—" Shelley hisses. "You know what you've got to do now, don't you? There's only one way to make this right. You know what that is?"

"No."

"You've got to get him right this second. You're going to put your phone on speaker, and I'm going to listen to you tell him that everything you said about that 'miraculous vessel' was a lie. My boy's not going to think that his mother didn't carry him. You're going to tell him that you were trying out some new kind of hypno-something, or whatever. But you will make it clear to him that

I'm one hundred percent his mother in every single way!"

I hesitate, reflecting on the circumstances. If I'm going to trade the truth I've shared with Aaron for the lie his mother demands, I've got to pry him from the arms of the woman who's got him—and me— enthralled. And I've got to accomplish that without revealing Megan's presence to Shelley.

"Okay," I say. "I'll tell him."

"Yes you will," Shelley huffs. I picture her gripping her landline receiver as if she's choking Satan's serpent into silence so it can't offer the apple of knowledge to Eve.

"I'm putting the phone on speaker," I say and push the button. I drop to my knees. "Aaron," I call under the bed so my voice is smothered, "your mother wants me to tell you something." I count to three. *"Okay,"* I squeak, holding the phone at arm's length. "He's tired," I say to Shelley in my own voice, "but he's here."

"Daddy's got something to tell you, honey," Shelley says.

"Un-hunh," I squeak.

"Aaron," I say, "remember the other night when I told you about how moms and dads and Jesus work together to make a baby? About how the father anoints the mother's egg, and parts of both parents join, and a child starts to grow inside the mother's womb?'

"Yes—" My "Aaron" voice cracks, but I lisp the "s".

"—And I said something about Mommy's womb being broken—" I hear a groan from Shelley's end— "Well, I was wrong about that. I was wrong about somebody else carrying you for nine months. There was only your Mom. She was your only 'glorious vessel.' There was never another."

"No?" I squeak. *"But why—"*

"Why did I tell you that? I don't know, son. I guess I

was trying a new kind of hypnosis. For Awake and Aware. I used it on you because there wasn't anyone else around. It was mind control—like the way I make people laugh when they hear the word 'dog.' But let me make it clear: what I did was wrong. None of what I told you is true."

"*Not the 'anointing' either?*" The words I speak for Aaron are sticky on my lips, and the silence on Shelley's end looms like an iceberg. She hasn't bought a word of my subterfuge—she's pretending, too.

"There's a little truth to the 'anointing,'" I say, because what else can I do but keep going? "But I should have waited until you're older to tell you about that. The part about your 'glorious vessel' not being your mother, though, that's a complete and total fib. You understand?"

"*Okay*," I squeak, without much conviction. The bedroom door swings open. Megan is holding Aaron in one arm. They're cheek to cheek. She presses a washcloth to his nose. They're looking down at me where I'm kneeling next to the bed.

"Time to sleep now, Aaron," I say. "It's late. Tomorrow morning we drive all the way to New Orleans." I lift the phone up to my son. "Say good night to your mother."

"Goodnight, Mommy." The washcloth muffles Aaron's voice.

"Goodnight, precious," Shelley says and makes kissing noises. "We'll see you soon, okay. You said your prayers?" He doesn't answer because Megan has backed out of the doorway.

"He's gone," I say. "I'll make sure he says them." I take Shelley off speaker. There's a curtain closed over a window of truth, and neither my ex-wife nor I touch it.

"Jimmy," she says, "You ought to bring Aaron home. Right now, this weekend. New Orleans is a sinful city."

"Can't afford to miss New Orleans," I say. "Those will be my two biggest days."

"Well," Shelley sighs, "I've got to wash the germs out of all our clothes and take Rodney some soup and crackers. He still can't keep anything inside himself." Shelley's tone is flat—she's given up something important, but she's not sure what. How much truth and how much falseness are we going to let stand? "You keep to your word," she says. "Don't confuse real life with Awake and Aware. Jesus loves you."

"Yes He does. Goodnight," I say into a phone that's already dead.

That's how we leave it, Shelley and I. After New Orleans, my summer with Aaron will be drawing to a close, and I don't know if the time we've got left with Megan is only a matter of minutes or days, or if our glorious vessel will carry us toward some permanent transcendence. But there's a reckoning to come, of that you can be sure. However I phrase it, Rule Ten will require at least one reckoning.

BLUE MADELINE'S VERSION

Eric pulls up short of his driveway. It's 11AM on what had begun as a work day, and his house doesn't look right. He's seen it catching the mid-morning sun on weekends, but this is different. Everything else on the block of modest homes seems switched off—no cars or hum of mowers, no kids on bikes. He doesn't see a squirrel or a sparrow—and if he had seen a bird overhead, frozen in mid-flight as in a museum diorama, it wouldn't have surprised him. But Eric's Cape Cod glows: the bricks seem kiln fresh, the red door and shutters blaze. The hedges swell with vibrant green. His home seems lit from within, like a poorly timed holiday display.

Three hours earlier, he'd left for the office, passing his jogging neighbor, Larry Feldstein, the bachelor retiree. "DMJ," Eric called—Dead Man Jogging. Twelve times around the block for Larry, like clockwork since his triple bypass five years ago. "DMW," Larry responded, pointing at Eric. Dead Man Working. They share this exchange most mornings. DMW no longer, Eric hopes Larry hasn't noticed his early return.

At 9:30, Eric had been called into the third-floor conference room and sacked. *We recognize your contribution*—the director of human resources said, smirking, as if the firing was a preliminary reading for an absurd play. Eric had never heard her voice until that moment. Kurt, his boss, didn't lift his eyes from a document that could have been a script. *But you haven't met the agreed upon goals set at your last performance review.* Performance review? Eric couldn't recall such a meeting. At the water cooler a few months earlier Kurt had asked about Eric's family, nodded, and encouraged him to *get those numbers up.* That had been a performance review? *Up* was a goal? He'd had thirty minutes to clean out his desk, then was paraded by security past his former colleagues.

Now Eric stands on the stoop of his empty home—Celia is at a three-day button convention in Buffalo. Nothing is familiar. He fumbles for his keys before finding them in the hand grasping his briefcase. He might as well have left that behind. All he'd shoveled into it was a staple remover, a box of ballpoint pens, and the photograph of Celia and his children, David and Eva, taken a dozen years ago on a Lake George beach. He's thinking of that white beach and the deep blue water behind, the green Adirondacks humped in the distance when he stumbles over a package on the welcome mat.

Returning home to a package is a first. Celia would usually have claimed a delivery by the afternoon, and nothing ever came on weekends. Is this something from work? *Recognition for his contribution.* A gold watch? Or something, he can't imagine what, acknowledging that a mistake had been made— *please accept this token of apology and return to work tomorrow morning.*

The package is the size of half a shoebox and weighs almost nothing—no gold watch. Eric's name isn't on the label: "Training Facility, 232 Van Curler Road." His address is 232 Verona. The police training facility is two blocks south. There'd been a mix up once before. On a Saturday afternoon, an officer had stepped out of his cruiser and presented Eric, who was wondering if he was about to be cited for an unmuffled lawnmower, with what turned out to be a box of copper buttons addressed to Celia. Never before, however, has something intended for the police been left at the door.

The return address on this package is for Atlantic Chemicals in Union, New Jersey. Clamping the box under his arm and sweeping the street with a wary glance, Eric unlocks his front door and steps in, calling, "Hello!" out of habit. A man should accept his dismissal stoically. He wouldn't interrupt Celia's pleasure trip with his bad news—she'd leave her convention to offer her unnecessary support. He can afford to retire, if they're frugal. There'll be severance pay, then unemployment, and before long his pension and Social Security. They're mortgage free, and the kids are responsible for their own graduate school loans.

No one will expect him to complain; he's gruff, not much of a talker. He'd run out of things to say to his children years ago, and, unlike Celia, who bemoans their absence, he can celebrate memories without a *corpus delecti*. Children move on; it's the way of the world, and silence needn't imply the washing of hands.

And Celia lives blissfully in her world of antique buttons. "Imagine the hearts that beat behind these bits of bone and horn and metal," she mused once, stirring a cookie tin filled with her favorites. Eric woodworks, a pastime both physical and practical. It looks to the future. His wish for more time to pursue his hobby has been granted.

The couple has faced life placidly for years. Only once had Celia's mask loosened: ten years past, when a beloved younger cousin died tragically of an aneurism. No father in the picture, her orphaned five-year-old had only her grandmother, Celia's aunt, who, Celia fretted, was "nearly deranged, possibly an alcoholic. If we offer, she'll let us have Madeline. We've got the guestroom."

Romantic fantasies about buttons were one thing. Raising a stranger probably damaged by both nature *and* nurture was something else entirely. Eric and Celia had the one boy and one girl of the perfect family. A new, unplanned child would have subverted the mathematics. No noble gestures, he'd declared. The fire in Celia's eyes flickered and died. "Impulse buying has messy consequences," he concluded. His wife whispered her final accusation: "You are a hollow man." They never spoke directly of the little girl again, though somehow Eric knew the grandmother had proven unsuitable, and the child had ended up in foster care.

❧ ❧ ❧

From the folding chair beside his basement worktable, Eric contemplates the mis-delivered package. If the police come looking, he'll deny knowledge of it. He cuts the packing tape and opens the flaps. Nestled in shredded green paper is an ampoule of golden liquid. When he plucks it out and holds it up to the fluorescent light, a yellow streak runs down his wrist, as if the ampoule is leaking color. An invoice lists a single item: "Cadaver scent." Neither the price nor directions are included, though a bold-faced statement cautions, "Simulated cadaver smells are available only to certified training facilities."

Eric grimaces—on this of all days to have the smell of death delivered to his home. Artificial, yes, but death nevertheless. He's seen "cadaver dogs" featured on TV—German shepherds digging through the smoldering ruins of the Twin Towers or the rubble left by an earthquake in a South American city. He's seen them bounding through marshes on taut leashes, their nasal receptors stimulated by the smell of decaying human meat. What draws a dog so powerfully to a scent, Eric wonders. Does instinct feel like an emotion?

Eric sets the ampoule on his worktable, where it stands like a golden bullet. There are laboratories, he's read, that concoct artificial scents and flavors: luncheon meats, French fries, and even the essence of death. When had they known they'd perfected "cadaver"? The ampoule glows with cloudless purity. Would the essence be considered artificial if it had been distilled from a dead heart?

"Uncle Irk—" Because the voice is feather light, it doesn't shock Eric. He turns to find a young woman—a girl?—sitting midway up the open basement steps. She's thin, her arms and legs sprawling from her black tank top and cut off shorts, every inch of her visible flesh a silvery blue. Her face is lost in the shadows, but when she pushes back dark bangs, her eyes gleam. "That's what I would have called you, when you lectured me about, I don't know, not doing my homework, or spending too much time on the phone, or not helping Aunt Celia with the dishes. I'd have pretended to be miffed, but it would have been playful. 'Uncle Irk.' It probably wouldn't have stuck. Maybe I would have left it at 'Eric' and 'Celia.'" She pauses, as if counting breaths. "Surprise! I'm Madeline!"

No surprise. Given the unsettled state of his thoughts after the morning's firing, it's no wonder he'd forgotten to lock the front door. If not the police looking for their cadaver scent, why not this girl? He's been thinking about her, hasn't he? "Of course," he says. It's Celia who would have been shocked. She would have cried with joy to see her cousin's child. But the idea of hosting is exhausting; he gestures toward the floors above them.

"The guest room is the second door on your right after the kitchen. The bathroom is the room before that. Towels in the bathroom closet, and take anything you want from the refrigerator. Have a glass of milk."

"Un-huh." Madeline's voice tickles his ears. "What's that you've got there? Is that a pee-sample? You don't need one for work anymore, right? You would have threatened me with one, and we would have had a fight about it, but you'd have believed that I was clean, I think."

Eric picks up the ampoule. An air bubble shifts through it. "It's scent," he says, "for training dogs—it smells like cadavers. So they can rescue dead bodies."

Silence. Across the basement the hot water heater ticks. If he closes his eyes, he might be alone, the stairs unoccupied. A giggle: "You don't 'rescue' dead bodies. I mean, it's a little late for a rescue once you're a body, isn't it?"

"Not 'rescue.' I meant 'recover.' Sorry—tough day." Eric suddenly sees himself as his coworkers must have, trailing the security guard past their cubicles. Had he really held his briefcase like a lunch tray?

"And what are you going to do with it?"

"I don't know. It was delivered by accident."

"Are you sure it was an accident?"

"It had the wrong address. It was supposed to go to the place where they train the dogs."

"Mmm—" A thoughtful pause. "Maybe it got there. Maybe one of the dogs brought it over. He thought you needed it. Did you check the box it came in for teeth marks? Saliva?" The girl shifts on the steps, crosses her legs, and there's a shimmer like bubbles released underwater.

"Maybe." Conversation and concentration are impossible to maintain. He feels the weight of his house on his shoulders.

"So—what are you going to *do* with it?"

"Tomorrow," he murmurs as his eyes close. "I'll think of something tomorrow."

"Okay if I look at it?" the blue girl might have asked.

❧ ❧ ❧

It's morning, and Eric sits at his kitchen table with a mug of coffee he doesn't recall brewing. "Late for work," he mutters, then remembers, as if stepping into a cold rain, that there isn't any work. Routines will change. Time will unfold differently. He can read the paper now instead of waiting for the evening. It had been his daily custom to pull it from the box at the end of his driveway and toss it toward the front door for Celia, giving himself a mental fist pump if it reached the stoop. If Larry was jogging by, Eric would wave: "*DMJ!*" "*DMW!*"

But what if Larry passes by this morning when Eric—who still wears a sweatshirt and flannel pajama bottoms—is fetching the paper? He leaves his coffee and hurries to the front door, where he squints through the small, chin high window. His eyes rove the street and adjacent lawns, alert for movement—if not Larry, maybe a dog, a trotting German shepherd with a lolling tongue. He remembers the package, the cadaver scent, and Madeline.

How odd, he thinks. On his way back to the kitchen, he checks the guestroom. The door is shut. He peers into the hall bathroom, and there's a rumpled towel on the rack. The faucet drips, and he tightens it. His reflection in the medicine cabinet mirror startles him: his cheeks are raw red, frosted with silver stubble; brown stains pollute the whites of his eyes. His thin hair is pasted over his crown, and his lower lip sags. There's a new toothbrush in the holder, wet.

On his way back to the kitchen, he pauses outside the guestroom door, but hears nothing. He's about to sit back down to his coffee when he notices the blink of the answering machine. It's a message from Celia he's somehow missed: "Hello, Eric. Everything's fine, the convention is fine, I'm fine. Lots of networking and trading. I've got a bid in for a Czech unicorn turquoise. And Eric, unless there's a problem, I won't be coming home Sunday. Some of us are going to Toronto. There's an exhibition there, too. International buttons. Three more days. So carry on without me—I'll call again soon."

❧ ❧ ❧

Eric is in the basement, where he's spent most of the day, forgoing lunch. He's been measuring and sawing long white pine boards for a built-in storage bench for his work area. He doesn't remember when he bought the wood, but the pine smell reminds him of the camping trips the family had taken in the Adirondacks. Now and then he catches a golden wink from his worktable—the cadaver scent—and he listens for footsteps overhead. Taking a break from sawing, he picks up the ampoule, shakes it, and watches the froth of bubbles fizz out until the liquid is again clear and golden. It's only half full. Is this all there was?

"I'd have shared a tent with Eva when we camped." Blue Madeline has returned to the shadowy basement steps. "David would have shoved toads and newts under the flaps, and we girls would have screamed and held each other's hands, even though we weren't really scared. Eva's how much older than me, Eric?"

"I don't know—how old are you?"

"Fifteen."

"Then ten. Ten years older." Eric has been staring at the white pine so long his focus won't adjust; the figure on the steps wavers like a blue flame.

"So she would have been like I am now. We would have gotten David back, though—maybe we'd have stolen his shorts from the shower building. Swimming in the lake would have been good enough for the rest of us, but David always wanted a shower. Celia would have said he was 'preening for the ladies.'"

"He was older—"

"—And used to drink beer with the boys down at the boathouse when he thought everybody was asleep. But Eva and I would have sneaked down and watched from behind the trees. The boys would be swimming without their suits. I would have thought their bare bottoms were as white as the moon, and I'd giggle—and the boys would have pulled their shorts on and called us out— mostly for Eva, she was so pretty. And we'd have toasted marshmallows at a campfire while the boys drank more beer and Eva tried some. When we all got back to our campsite just before dawn, we'd hear you snoring, and it would have made you seem harmless. Oh—I took care of things for you."

Harmless? "Took care of things?" Before Madeline's last words, Eric had retreated with her to the Adiron- dacks—crisp air and sunshine, campfires and boggy soil, mildew waft of camping equipment used once a year. The kids—just his boy and girl, younger than Madeline's version, slick and wet, slipping through black inner tubes into the blue lake. And Celia, in cuffed jeans over her swimsuit, her face unavailable to his memory—as featureless as one of her copper buttons.

While he's listened, Eric has framed his bench and measured the seven-foot planks he'll use for its top. He'll fix it to the wall perpendicular to his worktable. The top will be hinged for storage. Why had she said 'harmless'?"

"You took care of what?" he asks again.

Madeline's voice floats like a gull in an empty sky. "You'd have said, 'This isn't real camping—showers and RVs and paved roads.'" When the girl imitates his voice, Eric feels the weight of each word in his throat. "What I took care of is that lady from your office—the one who had the pig-faced grin when she fired you. Did you know she just finished putting in a pool?"

"I didn't, no."

"Um-hmm. Hadn't filled it yet. I guess they were waiting for it to set. But imagine all the work..."

"Work?"

"To dig it up. Underneath it, when they're looking for the body."

Eric wipes sweat from his brow with his wrist. The girl shimmers like a leaping fish. She drops her hand from her smile, and her teeth shine.

"You'd have gotten me braces when you saw the big space between my front teeth. I imagine the police are still at that lady's. A little of that cadaver stuff down the pool drain, and a call to the police—not from here, don't worry. An 'anonymous tip.' You know that kidnapped baby they've been looking for? From Pittsfield? Missing a few months? Imagine if someone told them it was buried under that pool. They'd have to dig the whole thing up, just to check it out, wouldn't they? Especially when a cadaver dog sniffed out something down that brand new drain. It would sure make a mess for that lady. Lots of questions, and, well, she won't be using that new pool for a while after they chop out the whole bottom. Can't you just see it? It only took a few drops of that scent."

Eric looked over at the half-empty ampoule.

"That'll be a headline story," Madeline says. She sighs. "I'd have been so close to Eva. Would she have been in college when I had my first period? She'd have been a comfort. Maybe she would have been home on vacation. Celia would have given me 'the talk,' though. Is this embarrassing you, Eric? Girl talk?"

He doesn't answer. He's envisioning a swarm of police invading the backyard of a suburban mini-mansion, scrambling over the manicured lawn and draping the coiffed shrubberies and ornamental trees with yellow tape. Shovel and pick ax wielding workers attack a swimming pool. Chunks of aquamarine concrete and fresh red dirt pile up, and police officers surround a woman who clasps her pink robe to her throat—the human resources director. All stare at a gaping hole at the bottom of the destroyed pool. A police dog strains against a leash, barking into that void, where a hip-deep officer sifts blindly with gloved hands.

"Do you think I could have convinced you to get a puppy after Eva left?" Madeline asks. "A dog would have filled a pretty big gap. What're you making there? That's quite a box."

"It's a storage bench," Eric says.

❋ ❋ ❋

The next morning already? Eric, half-hidden by a drape, stands at the living room window, staring at the street. If he chances a dash to the mailbox, he'll find the morning paper, flush with the details of the "Search for Lost Baby under Suburban Pool." But if Larry Feldstein jogs by, Eric will have to explain about his lost job. Curiously, papers are piled under the box, as if someone thought he'd want souvenir copies. But if anybody knew, then wouldn't the police? Madeline suggested that a cadaver dog might have brought the package to his stoop. Maybe a German shepherd would trot up his driveway right now. And here's Larry—*DMJ*! His neighbor stops at the pile of papers, glances at Eric's house, then kicks the extra copies onto the curb. He keeps jogging.

The guestroom door is shut. Eric doesn't check the bathroom. Confusing messages flood the kitchen answering machine. Eric listens twice, then a third time. First is David—it's been two years since he's heard his son's voice, though Celia keeps in contact: "Dad, we should talk. I'll try again."

Next is Eva; he doesn't understand her message at all: "Sorry we missed you, Mom and Dad. Stephanie wants to show you where her tooth fell out. I think she's hoping her grandpa is the Tooth Fairy. It'd be nice if she were right. Ryan says, 'Go Yankees,' Dad. I forgot—Mom is away, isn't she? Okay, we'll talk soon."

Stephanie and Ryan? Who are they? The names are familiar, but placing them is like thumbing through a book written with a foreign alphabet. There are two more messages from Celia: "Toronto was great. Buttons galore. But now the gang is heading to Ohio for Button Week, if you can believe it, and I figure I've only got this one chance, so off I go. Defrost something for yourself, there's plenty in the freezer." His wife's second message, the last on the machine: "Don't ever let anyone disparage Cleveland. We had loads of fun, although I have to admit, I haven't much use for that rock music hall of fame. But the word's out about a private exhibit just outside of Denver. My friend Dierdre knows somebody who knows somebody, and we think we'll be able to get a peek. This could be the experience of a lifetime! I'll let you know how it works out."

Certain he's missed something, Eric is about to listen to the messages for a fourth time when the doorbell rings, and he freezes. The doorbell rings again. He isn't dressed for company—he still wears a sweatshirt and pajama bottoms. And for how long has he been barefoot? He could step on something on the basement floor if he's not careful. The doorbell rings a third time. Eric hunches and shuffles down the hall to the living room's second archway, where he might be able to glimpse a visitor. There's an elbow—yellow reflective fabric—Larry's running suit. Both men hold still for nearly a minute. When Larry finally leaves, Eric exhales and drifts away.

❧ ❧ ❧

That evening, Eric is sanding the pine bench when Madeline arrives.

"I'd have been a Girl Scout, like Eva," she says from her usual perch on the steps. "Our projects never involved woodworking and race cars and things you made for a while when David was in the Cub Scouts. It was the Pinewood Derby car that made him hate you, wasn't it? When he wanted to glue Eva's Barbie to the top, and you hit him? I think it was Ballerina Barbie—she had a pink tutu."

There's a flap of torn skin on Eric's knuckle, oozing blood—has he sanded through his flesh while lost in thought? But when he looks closer, there's nothing there. Then he sees himself reaching toward young David. Blood drips from the boy's nose onto his lip; the boy flinches from his father's hand. His eyes shine with defiant tears.

"Just a slap—he moved into it—he wouldn't stop whining about the doll. Like a broken record. A doll on a race car? We'd made such a beautiful car, and he wanted to ruin it."

"That was the end of projects, wasn't it? Did Celia even know? But you did sell Girl Scout cookies for Eva at your office. She was afraid to go door to door. You would have done that for me, right? But if I was still selling cookies, how would you get them into your office for my customers?"

Mention of doors reminds Eric of Larry at his. His neighbor will be back.

"That Mr. Feldstein must have run a million miles by now," Madeline says, dipping into Eric's thoughts. "Do you remember how Eva and David switched rooms because Eva thought Mr. Feldstein stared into her window? 'Like I'm supposed to wave,' she said. It was nice the way David always tried to protect her. Wasn't that why she stopped selling cookies in the neighborhood? Didn't Mr. Feldstein invite her in and 'try something'? You said she had quite an imagination. I'm glad my room doesn't face the street. Celia said you had to go over to Mr. Feldstein's right away and get to the bottom of it. You said you didn't know what to say. Your solution was to sell her cookies at work. Eva cried, and David switched bedrooms with her. Hey—how do you want to use up your cadaver scent?"

Eric squints at the ampoule. Not much is left. His throat is scratchy—sawdust clings to his lashes and covers his forearms. "You girls were always safe," he croaks.

"Of course," Madeline says. "You know what we could do? We could find some real killers, and we could use your fake scent to lead the police to them. Maybe make a trail from the perp to the hidden body. There are crimes everywhere, right? And bodies. You could be like Robin Hood, and I could be your sidekick. Robin Hood had a sidekick, right?"

"He had Merry Men."

"I thought he had a sidekick in a red outfit and mask

that matched his green one. A kid. Both of them had bows and arrows—"

"That's The Green Arrow and Speedy. From a comic book I read when I was a boy."

"Un-huh. Well, David would have read it to me. You saved your old comic books—that's your legacy. With Eva I would have read *Archie*. The paper would have been musty and flaky. Do you think I'm more like Betty or Veronica?"

"Veronica," Eric says without thinking.

"Probably. She's a little bitchy, right? Eva's more like Betty—a girl next door. Hey, you know, wouldn't it be something if Mr. Feldstein was ringing your doorbell before because there was something wrong with him? Didn't he have a heart transplant or something?"

"A triple bypass."

"Wow—that sounds worse than a transplant. Maybe he came over because he was having chest pains and didn't want to keel over alone in his house where nobody would find him. What if you'd let him in, and he'd sat down at the kitchen table, and you'd brought him a glass of water, but he slumped over and died right there —at the kitchen table."

Eric pictures Larry, who'd never been in his house, lifting a glass of water toward worm-colored lips, then dropping it, the glass shattering on the table. The jogger's eyes roll back, and he slips to the floor like shifting freight and lies spread-eagled. Does Eric dare call 911? Won't the police find the mis-delivered scent? When Eric looks up from his fallen neighbor, he sees the blinking answering machine. He steps over Larry to play them back.

David: "Dad?"

Eva: "Dad?"

Celia: "The Pacific Ocean is beautiful, Eric—we should have made that cross-country trip with the kids.

I have no idea what the time difference is here in Honolulu, but I guess you're asleep. The buttons are spectacular—coral and shell, like nothing I've ever seen."

"I think they'll look for Larry at his place first, when somebody figures out he's missing," Madeline says. "Too bad about him. It's a question whether he really deserved what he got."

Somehow, the girl and Eric have switched places, and he's on the steps. Madeline scintillates under the fluorescent light, poised over his pine bench with his hammer in her hand. She's so bright, so silvery blue, it hurts as much to look at her as it does the white boards of his project. What evening is it?

"Eventually, they'll start poking around the neighborhood, and before long, they'll be here. A dog will catch his scent. Or maybe the dogs will catch *your* scent—oh, but wasn't yours *theirs* in the first place? It's hard to keep track." Blue Madeline pauses. Eric, wincing, sees that she's pointing his hammer at the worktable. "But all of your scent is gone!" From the stairs, Eric can't make out the ampoule. "Now how are we going to be Robin Hood and Speedy?" She slides a pine plank into place, sets a nail down, and the hammer drops. The sound echoes from the concrete walls and floor. She sets another nail. How thin she is. Translucently thin. She pounds the second nail.

The lights dim, but Madeline is impossible to watch. Eric wants to tell her to hinge the bench top, not nail it. If it's nailed, who will find whatever's inside? But his tongue is thick, and she's working so diligently he doesn't dare stop her.

"But your scent was artificial, right? Now we've got the real thing, right here in storage. We'll figure out a way to use it sooner or later—you know, for leading police to the bodies criminals have hidden." Her words are hard to decipher. She might be holding nails in the corner of her mouth. But it sounds like she's slipping into a different language. She keeps pounding away, and each concussion hurts Eric's ears. He wraps his arms around his head, but the sound grows louder. He's smothered himself in total darkness.

"You know—" the voice penetrates from above, the pounding now more like knuckles on a wooden door—only every few words are audible because of the knocking, "—it would have been... to have grown up... family... Spectacular!"

Pinocchio in
New Hampshire, 1993

The iconic author ushered Raymond Walchuk and his son Carl to his writing bunker, a healthy walk from the main house. At its wooden door, which he unlocked with a brass key on a short leather strap, he pointed to a bench that overlooked a valley. The two men and the boy squinted in the morning sun. "Would you wait for us, please," the writer asked Raymond. "I'd like to speak to your boy alone."

"Of course," Raymond said, and the old man lay his hand on Carl's shoulder and guided the child into the squat building. The wide-eyed gaze his son tossed back as the door shut clutched Raymond's heart. To any inclined to suspicion, the situation might have seemed questionable, even dangerous—a stranger disappearing into locked solitude with a nine-year-old boy. And was Raymond, the procurer, a neglectful parent?

But this was *Salinger*; he was obviously interested in Raymond's "Teddy" screenplay. Raymond had been careful to submit it through the writer's agent—at all costs he'd wanted to avoid the appearance of intruding on the author's privacy. And he'd been summoned! A nine AM appointment at the New Hampshire residence. Father and son had flown from the West Coast into Boston on the redeye, slept in a hotel near the airport, and had risen before dawn for the long drive through the New England countryside in their rented car.

Raymond had brought the boy along for luck and company. And his kid had a budding career of his own to promote. He had a hunch the author would fall into the depths of his son's dark eyes, find his black curl's irresistible, mark the child's fragile sturdiness. Or was it the boy's sturdy fragility?

"We'll get it into the conversation that you're an actor," he told Carl. They rehearsed their meeting while they dipped over the hills and rounded the curves en route. "We'll plant that seed. "Tell him you 'grew yourself' if he asks your age," Raymond said, quoting his screenplay's paraphrase of Salinger's story. "Then we'll make sure to turn the conversation to my screenplay. And then to my credits as a director."

"I don't want him to think I'm a phony," Carl had yawned. He'd read the story and the script, and while Raymond thought his fourth grader a little young to understand everything, he trusted the boy's intuition. "I'll be okay with him. He likes children. I can tell by the way he writes."

The first words Salinger had spoken as he shook Raymond's hand on the front porch of his home were directed at Carl. There'd been a Norman Rockwell beauty to the scene, without the sentimentality.

"So, you think you can be my Teddy," he'd guessed, taking in the child without releasing Raymond's hand. "We'll talk out back."

❧ ❧ ❧

Raymond checked his watch and squirmed on the bench. A large, broad-winged bird, maybe an eagle, circled over the valley beneath him, oaks and pines descending toward an invisible river. The big bird's focus would soon rivet on some unsuspecting thing scavenging through the wildflowers. Was there anything watching Raymond with such intensity? He peeked at the sun, then his gaze dropped to the bunker. It was low, maybe fifteen feet square, without windows on either of the sides he could see. He thought about walking around its perimeter. But Salinger had told him to wait on the bench. What could the old man and the boy be talking about? The hawk was gone, which probably meant it had streaked out of the sky and snatched the life out of something when Raymond wasn't looking.

The bunker door finally opened, and the author guided Carl out. The sunlight rinsed the color from the scene. The exit of old man and boy had the look of an important event captured by chance on an 8mm film—like overexposed clips of dignitaries descending from an aircraft, of a passing motorcade, of children running from waves on a beach. Carl winced a smile. Salinger seemed more stooped than he'd been when he'd greeted the Walchuks; his weathered face was impossible to read. Raymond stood and waited for them at the bench.

"This is some boy you've got here," Salinger pronounced. "The two of you will make "Teddy" a remarkable film. Thank you. I promised the boy a bowl of ice cream." He'd looked down at Carl, back to Raymond, and back to Carl. "Unless your father thinks it's too early for sweets."

❧❧❧

Raymond quizzed his son in a whisper while the famous author was in his kitchen dishing out the desert. "What was it like in there? What did he say? What did you do?"

"It was dark except for two lamps," Carl said. "One standing up behind an armchair, the other on his desk next to a typewriter. He told me to sit in the big chair, and he pulled his desk chair around to talk to me. There were stacks of paper on the desk and on a table, and against the walls were those old-fashioned gray metal file cabinets. Tall ones. Three or four. There were stacks of paper on those, too. The place smelled like old newspapers and socks."

Raymond nodded. He was trembling, as if something momentous had, or was about to, occur.

"Would you like a glass of iced tea?" the author called.

"Please," Raymond shouted. "If it's not any trouble." There wasn't an answer.

"Did you give him the line about growing yourself?" Raymond asked, but Carl bugged his eyes to let his father know that the author had returned. Salinger handed Carl a blue bowl of vanilla ice cream and perched on the edge of a chair across from the boy and his father. He seemed to have forgotten his offer of tea.

"I loved the old *Son of Kong*," he said. His eyes reminded Raymond of those gag glasses that blink when the person wearing them shifts his head a little. "I wasn't much older than your boy when I saw it. It was more poignant than the first *Kong*—that was just a big ape causing trouble. And I have to say, Mr. Walchuk, your remake captured the essence, the charm, the vigor of the original *Son*—yet you produced something unique and beautiful. That's why you're here. I don't see many movies. Yours is a gift. A jewel. I felt like a child again watching it. Where, may I ask, was it filmed? The landscape was stunning."

"Kiriwina Island. It's a stone's throw from Papua New Guinea. My father was stationed there during the war—World War II."

The author frowned. Or it might have been a smile. He craned his vulture neck; his hands hung from his wrists. He didn't say anything for a while. Then he braced himself on the armrests and pushed himself to his feet, stretching with some effort to his full height. "It was a delight meeting you both. Maybe we'll see each other again. But, please let's communicate through my agent." He made a wave, as if imitating royalty. "I grant full permission for you to move ahead with the "Teddy" project." He turned to Carl. "And you'll be wonderful, Pinocchio," he said, and winked. "You can put your bowl in the sink when you're done. Don't gobble, or you'll get one of those headaches. Now if you'll excuse me, I've got some work to do. Let yourselves out." And he shuffled past them and through the back door. Raymond and Carl watched him make his way down the path back to his bunker.

❧ ❧ ❧

"'Pinocchio?'" Raymond asked a few minutes later. It wasn't yet noon, but they were already in the car on their way back to Logan Airport. "What was that about?"

Carl slouched against the passenger door. "He said most people were wooden puppets, but I had what it took to be 'a real boy.' He said it was a tribute to you. The ice cream was chewy, Dad. I don't think ice cream's supposed to be chewy."

"Probably old," Raymond said. "So—did you talk about the screenplay? Did he say what he liked about it?"

The boy shook his head. "No. We sat down, and he gave me a quiz. He reached over to one of the piles of paper and pulled off the top sheet and handed it to me. He asked,'What do you see there, boy?'"

"What was it? A story?"

"I just glanced at it. There was a title: 'Edna's Daughter,' or something."

"'Esme's'? 'Esme's Daughter'?"

"Ed-nay?"

"*ESS*-may."

"Something like that. Do you know who he reminded me of? Remember when we watched *Plan 9 from Outer Space*? You told me that halfway through making it Bela Lugosi died. He was playing some kind of weird space vampire, right? So Ed Wood got his dentist to play the part. He kept his arm up to hide his face behind his cape. That's who Mr. Salinger reminded me of—the dentist-vampire. I felt like he was hiding his face the whole time we were with him, didn't you?"

"So what did you do? Did you read him the title of his story? You didn't say 'Ed-nay,' did you?"

"My stomach hurts. No, I didn't read it at all. I turned the paper over and looked at the blank side. Then I tore it up. In half, then in quarters, then in eighths. I dropped the pieces on the floor."

Raymond lifted his foot from the accelerator. He turned to his son, who had closed his eyes, his cheek against the window glass. He was rubbing his belly. The car coasted down the country road. "You did *what*?"

Carl lifted the shoulder closest to his father, turning away. "I tore it up. He stared at me and kind of tilted his head. 'You need to tear up one of these a day,' I said. He was quiet a minute. Then he asked, 'Just one page a day?' I told him one would be a day's work if he did it right. 'Think of how many days you've got left until you're done.' There were lots of pages. It'll take him a really. really long time."

For a moment Raymond couldn't see—he'd had dreams in which he'd been driving a car and his vision had suddenly become obscured and he'd found himself heading over the edge of a cliff. But he was wide awake now, and the shadow passed. He fixed his eye on the double yellow line and pressed on the gas. "And then?"

"And then he called me Pinocchio. Dad, is there a place to pull over? I think I have to throw up."

Amabel's Children

From up here on the ceiling, I see three scalps beneath me. The fluorescent lights illuminate a shaved and gleaming head. It has an indentation in the center that looks like a sunken grave. One of the heads has a hairline that recedes into dark curls, and the third has a comb-over that fails to cover skin the color and texture of butterscotch pudding. This head and the head with curls belong to men I knew when I was alive.

I've been dead for days and days, and this is the first time I've recognized anyone. I don't know if my presence in this room is by coincidence or design. Being dead has been a completely passive experience. Every morning I wake up attached to something that's living, something different each day, no repeats, at least not so far. Yesterday I was with a Goldendoodle, the day before a Starbucks barista. Today, it's this spider on the ceiling. I've got no will of my own, no physical essence. Where my host goes, I go. And though I share my partner's space, I'm neither seen nor felt. So far I've had no appetites at all. I recognize emotions, but I don't seem to feel them. Like when you fall out of love. I have fallen out of love with everyone. I have fallen out of fear of anyone. I have extraordinary patience. Have you ever spent a day connected to a clam?

This morning the men down at the conference table are talking about me and the eggs harvested from my ovaries before I lost my battle with acute myelogenous leukemia. Carl, the one with the curls, was almost my husband. The comb-over guy is P. P. Frederico, the filmmaker who gave me my big break after my last stint in rehab, years before my death. The shaved pate belongs to a stranger. The three are discussing an idea for a reality TV show—*Amabel's Children*, one of them called it.

"You say you've got full legal rights to Amabel's eggs?" asks the man with the shaved head.

Carl clears his throat. "Zygotes," he says, "not eggs. Amabel and I were told that fertilized eggs would survive the freezing better. I supplied the sperm. The zygotes are legally mine."

Carl's right. My eggs were harvested because aggressive chemotherapy and radiation were going to sterilize me. His sperm fertilized the salvaged eggs *in vitro*, and the zygotes were frozen so we could have our own biological children when I recovered. But I didn't.

Light reflects off the stranger's polished head. He must be a network executive. His fingers drum the table. "I don't know. Isn't the point of this show that each couple—each husband of the couple—will fertilize one of Amabel's eggs himself? The way I understood it is you have the competitive stuff first—the sports and the trivia contests and whatever—singing, if you want—with the usual up-close-and-personals, followed by the audience vote. Then the winning dads would fertilize the eggs, which get implanted in their wives."

"We plan at least one show on the science of it all," P. P. says. "Doctors, test tubes, petri dishes. Footage of sperm penetrating eggs. We stagger the implantations so we get about eight weeks' worth of births at the end of the season. Twelve couples is the target."

"Hunh," says the network guy, "But Amabel is the attraction. People want to be connected to *her*! No offense, but what's the appeal of kids that are half Carl's?"

"Didn't you read the market research we sent?" P. P. asks. "Focus groups couldn't differentiate between "egg" and "zygote." We just de-emphasize Carl. We lose him in the scientific mumbo-jumbo, as far as the TV audience is concerned. For potential competitor-parents —ninety-five percent of those polled deemed the father's biological involvement 'unimportant.' This *is* about Amabel and nothing else, Larry."

"If we include episodes on the impact of environment on child development, it'll be better scientifically if all the kids had the same biological mother and father," says Carl quietly.

"But," P. P. says, "what we're selling is Amabel and her children."

Carl's head has flushed pink, but he's silent. Is he angry? An *in vitro* conception and surrogate delivery are part of his family history—his little brother Wray is somewhere among the dead. The men with him know this, of course. P. P. was with Carl when Wray died. It seems this bargaining with my eggs would have disturbed me once. Was it Carl or P. P. who cooked up this reality show idea? They'd collaborated on the cartoon-horror remake of *The Island of Doctor Moreau* that resurrected the career I'd done my best to trash, an idea that originated with Carl's dead father Raymond. I am no longer afraid of Raymond, wherever he is. The animated *Moreau* tanked at the box office, but the voice I gave to the wretched dog-man M'ling found empathetic ears among the lonely and miserable, and my performance drew raves. With P. P. to vouch for my rejuvenated work ethic, offers poured in. Broadway called, and I won a Tony playing a young mother. Even illness couldn't keep me down—when work became impossible, I became a role model, a leading advocate for cancer research. Those *Thrive* awareness anklets, the magenta ones you see everywhere? Inspired by my tribulations.

"Amabel Hadley is a classic American story of redemption, Larry." P. P. slaps the table. "*Amabel's Children* will immortalize her!" He pauses. "From porn star to angel."

"I don't know about 'porn star'," Carl murmurs.

I don't deny it could have happened. Prior to my final visit to rehab, while promoting my Scaredy Cat line of clothing in a Walmart, I'd made lewd gestures with my microphone before propositioning the store manager. Then I spit up.

"We wouldn't go there," Larry says, "But I'll admit, she had a hell of a life." And I know he's sold on my show.

"Right," P. P. says. "We start with a documentary. Two hours, Carl?"

"Two parts, one hour each."

"M-hmm. Two hours on Amabel's roller coaster life. We'll show the couples competing for the zygotes weeping over the highs and lows, the final tragedy. But the winners will have the chance to bear Amabel's children!"

"The couples' demographics?" Larry asks.

"Like any other reality show: rich, poor, minorities—hey, Carl, gay men would need their own surrogate wouldn't they?"

My husband shakes his head. "Too complicated. It would be easier to go with a lesbian couple."

There's silence, and P. P. looks up toward the fluorescent lights. His dark glasses are impenetrable. The other men follow his gaze. Carl's brown eyes look sad. I think Larry might see my spider, but he doesn't say anything.

"She was beautiful, wasn't she?" P. P. says. Carl and Larry mumble assent.

Larry's indentation reminds me of an infant's soft spot—I could swear something's pulsing in it. Maybe Carl should have been the one to bring up my beauty. Being dead, I don't dwell on it, but somewhere between party-girl bloat and dying-woman desiccation there *was* beauty. And in the beginning, too, when I was an innocent child with Hollywood dreams.

"Reunion shows," Larry says dreamily.

"And guaranteed spin-offs." P. P. adds. "Maybe decades of programming. Amabel's children will be the biggest entertainment phenomenon we've ever seen. Think of the merchandising opportunities. It's like we're breeding our own celebrities."

"We *will* be breeding our own celebrities," Carl says. I look down at the curls I used to run my fingers through. I remember that Wray is dead. What does Carl hope to find?

A cell-phone chimes, and all three men reach for a pocket. My host spider dashes into a gap in the dropped ceiling. It's dark. Today is about to end. If death holds form, tomorrow I'll wake up with a new partner. I've got forever to find out what happens to my children. As far as I know.

※ ※ ※

I'm attached to a pet ferret. Its nose and eyes are tiny and black, and it wears a blue collar as thin as a rubber band. We curl around a pink bunny slipper and peek out from beneath a sofa. Running shoes flank our sides like the walls of a fortress. Two adults and two children sit above us. From time to time a popcorn kernel drops, and the ferret darts forward and nips it up, then retreats. Sounds of nibbling accompany the TV voices like static. The television's flickering light paints every surface.

The children are young—a boy and a girl. Nothing has been familiar since Carl and P. P.'s meeting. I suppose my presence above that table was just a coincidence and not part of any plan. I can only guess that my experience is the same as everyone who's dead—we're all attached to a living thing. Wouldn't it be something if the entire universe of the dead was attached to the same body—my ferret, for instance? We're a weightless and volume-less population, we overlap, and, in our perpetually increasing numbers, maybe we all switch to a new body together every night. Who can say?

My ferret's family is watching a documentary about me, the prelude to *Amabel's Children*. There are clips from some of my earliest movies. When I was a child, my eyes were wide and green and impish. My hair fell over my shoulders in auburn waves.

"She looks like Cindy, doesn't she look like Cindy?" the mother on the sofa says. No one answers. On screen my child-self makes a sassy quip, and above me the children and mother giggle. Another popcorn kernel falls and my ferret grabs it. A solemn voice narrates over photographs of me. I'm not so cute here—makeup distorts my features, and I wear short skirts and low-cut blouses that show my developing breasts. When I smile my mouth is open and my tongue shows. Pose after pose in gown after gown on miles of red carpet. How many packs a day was I smoking? When did I develop a taste for Jack Daniels? I'm in a courtroom. My hair is tied back, and I look sorry. A judge speaks without making eye contact. Police officers usher me away, their hands floating beside my elbows without touching them. Then I'm dancing wildly, my eyes raking across space as I twirl. There's my little red Porsche—and there it is again with its front crumpled. The dad sitting above me on the sofa laughs, low and guttural.

"*Rehab*" punctuates every other sentence.

Things were to get much worse before they got better.

There's a grainy video on the screen— a security tape. That's me in sweatpants and a hoody. I'm at a gas pump next to the Porsche, which has either been repaired or has yet to be damaged. Gasoline gushes from a hose dangling from the car—a puddle expands on the pavement. I've wrapped an arm around the pump, and I'm waving a cigarette lighter and howling. Next, an officer protects my head as I'm plugged into the back of a police cruiser: I grin as if I'm listening to a private joke.

There's M'ling—the vivisected cartoon dog-man from *The Island of Doctor Moreau* who led me back to a righteous path.

"Did we see that cartoon? Can we see it?" asks one of the children.

"It's a horror movie. It's R rated," the mother says. My dog-man cowers in the midnight shadows of tropical trees. The narrator mentions P. P. and Carl. I stand between them in a photograph. All three of us are smiling. I'd forgotten that I'd buzzed off all my hair while recording *Moreau*. I knew what baldness was like before chemotherapy.

A *PLAYBILL* cover—I'm wearing an apron. My hair is shoulder length. I'm playing a mother. Then I'm standing at a podium, displaying an award.

Part two tomorrow! Recovery and triumph.

I don't know where I'll be tomorrow. My host may not be near a television, and I'll miss seeing my final chapter among the living. They'll say I "*battled bravely.*" This documentary won't show Carl, though he surely helped make it. He held my skeletal hand as I shuffled in loose pajamas to the rooms of doomed children. In my last days I bowed over them, my head as hairless as theirs, and offered what I could. There'd soon be nothing left for Carl. Maybe I owed him *Amabel's Children.*

🙦🙤 🙦🙤 🙦🙤

Try to imagine an existence without expectations. Without surprise. Without impatience.

Season One of *Amabel's Children* is about to conclude: the twelve couples who have won my fertilized eggs will be named. Implantations are to take place during the summer hiatus, and Season Two's opening episode will reveal the successful pregnancies. Viewers are teased by the prospect of a dozen mothers swelling to term with babies due in the spring.

I gather this information while in the company of a speckled catfish. We're suctioned to the glass of an aquarium. Algae and dust obscure the television across the small, dim room. It's a struggle to hear over the pump's hum and filter's bubbling. Other fish waft above, beneath, and behind us. A young man, alone, slouches on the futon beside the table that supports our tank. He's wearing shorts and a t-shirt. One hand is down his pants, the other is holding a beer. The pillow and blanket on the futon suggest it's his bed. I see a sink, a mini-fridge and a counter full of dirty plates. An open door exposes a toilet.

Also on the table with our aquarium is a framed photograph of a young couple, which I study during commercial breaks. The man in the picture is the person on the couch. The woman is... me. I glance away again and again, but each time I look back there's no question that I'm looking at myself. I've been photoshopped into the picture—I'm almost twice the young man's size. I recognize the silver gown I wore at the Tony Awards. I suspect I'm replacing another woman, someone the young man wants to exclude from his home. He continues watching television, unaware that he's been found out. Is this what "haunting" means?

Amabel's Children highlights the months of competition that will earn the winning couples my eggs: a young African-American couple stagger through calf deep mud—the man is heavy, stumbles, and pulls his wife down face first into the muck; another couple, tan and blond, argue over a quiz question I can't hear—the woman offers an answer with a furrowed brow, the couple embraces joyfully, and the number of points displayed in front of them grows by a hundred; a pair of young women struggle across a rope bridge over surging rapids while carrying a life size baby doll.

The couples who have competed fill an auditorium. The camera sweeps over eager, anxious faces as all await the outcome of their trials. My catfish dislodges from the aquarium glass, drops to the blue gravel, and wriggles and sucks its way behind a scummy rock. Fish cruise over us like spaceships. Time passes.

We're back on the glass. A dozen smiling couples stand on the stage—the winners. The host introduces profiles of the last few: here is the blond couple. Their ages, jobs, state of residence (Massachusetts), and income are posted over a video of the pair frolicking with a Husky in their suburban yard. The next couple, a black man and his Asian wife, sit on the stoop of a modest Indiana home. Their posted income is a tenth of the blond couple's. The last duo, a pair of healthy-looking young women, is doing as well financially as the blonds —one is a financial analyst, the other a photographer. They live in an oceanfront condo in San Diego. I wonder which of the two will carry my baby. I missed the profiles of the other winning couples while the catfish was foraging. The closing credits roll over a cartoon picture of a red-haired woman in an apron holding a basket of eggs aloft. I assume that's supposed to be me. Carl's and P. P.'s names slide over me and disappear.

❧ ❧ ❧

"Get to bed!" insists the robed mother to my host, a little girl of about seven who lingers barefooted on the linoleum floor of a narrow hallway. Her mother's lounging on a couch. Ashes from the cigarette pinched in the woman's lips threaten the face of the infant she is holding like a loaf of bread.

"But the babies are on. I want to see the babies."

"Then you shouldn't have back-talked about your homework."

"But I don't *have* any homework."

"Your teacher says she gives homework every night. That's what she said."

"But I did it in school. I promise! There was time to do it in school today. Can't I see the babies?"

If my host goes to bed, it will be dark, and tomorrow I'll be elsewhere.

"You got your sister Brittany. That should be baby enough." The mother stuffs her cigarette into a soda can on the table by her elbow. "Get me another Diet Pepsi, and you can stay up," she says to my partner, and the little girl scampers into the kitchen. There are dishes in the sink and bottles in a pot on the stove. A crayon drawing of a pony with a rainbow mane and tail decorates the refrigerator, and inside it there are cartons of milk and juice, Tupperware of different sizes, and a dozen or so cans of soda. We return to the living room, and my little girl hops onto the sofa after handing the beverage to her mom. She stretches her heels to the coffee table. Grime rims her toenails. The baby mews and snuggles into her mother's belly.

"Will Shana be on this one? I like it when Shana's on."

"Shh. How do I know? Keep quiet or you're going to bed."

Shana is three, as are all nine of my children. Ten of the couples winning my eggs had successful, full-term pregnancies. One of my babies, Harrison, died with his mother in a car crash last season. I missed the special memorial program, though I saw the commercial for it: Harrison was shoveling Spaghetti-o's into his mouth, but most of the pasta was on his cheeks and chin. He had red hair, like many of my children. His mother laughed in the background as she recorded her son's messy eating. If the deaths of Harrison and his mother are like mine, maybe they've seen themselves on *Amabel's Children*. I doubt Harrison would know what he is watching.

The first segment of tonight's show features little Veronica. Her parents have separated and share custody of their daughter. Veronica's dad is a construction foreman, and he brings her to work, where she wears a miniature hard hat. She has curls like Carl's. According to the show's host, Veronica *"was the first of the children to walk,"* but there's no video to document the event. I've seen other of my babies' first words and steps, birthday parties, and Disneyland vacations.

No Shana yet for my little host. Her dirty feet waggle impatiently on the coffee table during the show's second segment, which features the "scientific" aspects of *Amabel's Children*. There are statistics and numbers. How many hours are spent in daycare? Who was nursed and who given bottles? Hours of television? Hours read to? Nutritional choices? Doctors in white coats discuss the "likelihoods" of this or that, but no conclusions are reached.

"Shana!" my little girl cries when her favorite appears, briefly, stacking blocks while an analyst marks down her progress on a clipboard. My host has tied her pigtails in rainbow ribbons that match the bow in Shana's red hair.

I don't know what I am to these children. I'm not their birth mother, but their skin and hair and feet, their faces and their heart, have grown from my cells. I'm their First Cause.

The last segment features Simon. His parents are lawyers. He looks a lot like Shana, and seems to have an eye for the camera—he poses in ways that remind me of photographs of myself in fan magazines. Tonight, while bouncing Simon on their laps, his mother and father discuss "transgendering."

The *Amabel's Children* theme song plays while the credits roll. It's a version of my one hit from the two albums I recorded. "Who's your mother? Where's your mother?" I'd rasped and ranted punkishly. A children's chorus sings the TV show's rendition, accompanied by a harp. Unless I missed his name, Carl is no longer listed as a "Creative Consultant."

Baby Brittany wails, her mother swears under her breath, and my host rises, pats her little sister's head, and we're off to bed. My TV children have no siblings in their families. Did I miss a rule prohibiting them? I've seen no signs of a male in this house. It's hard for a single mother to care for more than her infant. Since I've been dead, I've seen the truth of that again and again.

I've been hosted by countless dogs, but this is the smallest. It must be some kind of Chihuahua. We're tucked between the knees of an old woman. She wears stretch pants and gray slippers that might once have been as purple as the burst veins mottling her swollen ankles. When the dog whimpers to pee, its owner's sagging face tightens into a fist.

"Jingles, can't you hold it?" she whines in a pitch that matches her dog's. She struggles with the lever to her easy chair, and Jingles and I hop to the floor of their double-wide. When she pushes open the aluminum door, we skip from a cinder block to the hardpan, and Jingles squats. The woman clings to the door handle while she waits and looks back over her shoulder at her small television. I can't see much in the dark, but from neighboring trailers I hear quarreling TV show voices.

Back between the bony knees, Jingles gnaws on a huge biscuit. It's been many nights since I've seen *Amabel's Children*. They're calling this special show a "reunion," but the kids have never met. When their parents won my eggs, they'd agreed to keep the children apart, "for the purpose of scientific observation." The boys and girls are eight years old now. Everyone is dressed nicely; children and adults sit at separate daises. Between them stands a microphone at which a tuxedoed host and several guests take turns reminiscing and joking mildly about *Amabel's Children*.

"The kids could have their own baseball team," a speaker quips. I anticipate other jokes about "nine," but all I can think of is that cats have nine lives, and "lives" don't seem appropriate to mention because of little Harrison. In all the time I've been dead, I've never been hosted by a cat. The children have seen their own TV show and understand its premise. They're awkward in the presence of so many biological brother and sister celebrities they don't know. They ignore the host and peek, mouths agape, at the familiar faces of strangers. No two are identical, and together they present a spectrum of resemblance that runs from Carl to me—dark curls to red hair, brown eyes to green. Looking at them is like looking into funhouse mirrors, and I suspect they feel the same way. Are they forming bonds or discovering them? Their parents squint toward the children with clenched smiles and seem to want to rush over and claim their own.

The kids, their parents, and the television audience watch a video montage that begins with swollen-bellied mothers, then shows the children as infants and toddlers, interspersed with clips of my childhood movies, then shots of me receiving my Tony. A final video shows me delivering a speech at a children's hospital shortly before I died. I am bald and hollow-eyed, but I say inspiring things about thinking positively and devoting oneself to a cause. When the video tribute is over, waiters roll out a grand sheet cake. "THANK YOU AMABEL" is printed across it. The host prepares to cut into it with a saber-sized knife and invites the children to gather around with their plates. There has been no mention of Carl.

Tears sparkle like jewels on the cheeks of Jingles' owner. Have I heard or am I guessing that this is the final episode of *Amabel's Children*? P. P. Frederico had predicted more than a single decade. While my anthem "Who's Your Mother?" plays, the camera pans one last time across the cake-smeared faces of my children. The song stops as the credits freeze on two names, little Harrison's and P. P.'s, followed by their birth and death years. Maybe P. P., wherever he is, has witnessed this memorial. Maybe he and Harrison are here. Maybe Wray. Maybe everyone's here.

🙖 🙖 🙖

If my death follows a pattern, I don't have the distance to interpret it. Frequently, I slide through the dark with nocturnal hosts I may or may not see. I have wheeled with bats and lain between crickets' whittling legs. I've experienced the speed and violence of hunting, the cries of power or fear. I have burrowed deep into loamy soil and rotting hearts.

When I am indoors, my hosts often dive for darkness, and I catch only winks of light. Tonight I hear whispered endearments and murmurs of pleasure: there's lovemaking, but I'm with neither partner. Too dark even for shadows—I must be attached to a dust mite between a mattress and box spring. We rock with the sex, and if by some chance Harrison is with us, maybe he remembers that rocking gave him comfort. One of the lovers cries out. Motion stops. Every moment is eternal patience.

🙖 🙖 🙖

I'm coupled with an infant—it seems like forever since I've been attached to a human. His face presses into his mother's breast. He gasps, exhausted and ecstatic from suckling. His mother watches television, but her embracing arms block the screen.

"Shh," the mother whispers.

Physics means pondering the imponderables, the TV voice says. All television voices sound like the announcer's from *Amabel's Children*. When I ponder time, I picture the lines a prisoner scratches on a cell wall—four lines and a cross hatch, four lines and a cross hatch—five and five and five and on and on, until everything is shaded into darkness.

My host-baby coos, frets, and reconnects to his mother's nipple.

His mother sighs.

Paul Dirac theorized that whether light is composed of waves or particles depends on whether you ask it a wave-like or particle-like question.

❧ ❧ ❧

On this endless day I can't tell to what or whom I'm attached; time no longer seems to be something that moves. There's light, but I don't ask it questions about particles or waves. The light illuminates the bookshelf I face and have been facing for what feels like forever. I focus on a book with a glossy paper cover; it's surrounded by dusty, title-less volumes. Studying the spine of this newer book is all I do.

I haven't lost the sense that I'm attached, but either the dynamics of connection have changed - were *due* to change? - or I'm hosted by something imperceptible to my understanding. What could be so small? A microbe?

The book I stare at is titled *My Life as Amabel's Child: The End of Reality TV*. The author's name is obscured by a low pile of books resting on the ledge. A sweep of auburn hair spreads over the book's spine from a hidden cover photo. It might be my hair. It could belong to one of my children. I've looked at this spine so long I can't imagine not seeing it. But does "End" mean "death," or does "End" mean "goal"?

THE DRY BOYS—PARIS, 1995

In Jean-Paul's film, Carl Walchuk played a juvenile Christ, and the young Jesus's Parisian tenement overlooked a black-topped schoolyard where adolescent Buddha and Mohammed played soccer without him every afternoon. But the tenement, the black-topped schoolyard, the soccer playing existed only in the filmmaker's imagination; in reality, the cast and crew were squeezed into a hotel suite. The furniture had been pushed against the walls to accommodate lights, cameras, and sound equipment. Two cameras focused on Carl as he sat on a metal radiator cover and gazed out the eighth floor window, supposedly at the holy boys playing soccer—"football," Jean-Paul called it. He strained to emote over what he didn't see—he stared at the late afternoon traffic clogging the rain-slicked avenue.

"You must look mournful, Charl," Jean-Paul insisted. "Mournful, but exultant. Your isolation is your triumph. I don't see it in your eyes. Do you see it in his eyes, anyone?"

No one answered, not any of the film crew, not Celeste, the pretty make-up woman who had been nice to Carl in small ways, or Raymond Walchuk, Carl's father, who had crammed himself into a corner chair and made notes in a paperback copy of *Crime and Punishment*. Giggles trickled from an adjoining room, Jean-Paul's bedroom, where Ernest and Phillipe—Mohammed and Buddha—played games while they waited for their scenes to be shot.

"When it stops raining, we do the football," Jean-Paul told the two teenagers each morning before shutting them in the bedroom. It had been raining for a week. "Now, you are the dry boys." Which was a joke, although Jean-Paul never smiled, because the working title of the film was "*Les Garcons Seches*"—"The Dry Boys." Carl didn't know whether or not Jesus was considered one of the dry boys. Not only didn't he speak French, the titles translated meaning had never been explained to him.

Everyone involved in the film was lodged on the eighth floor of the hotel. They'd been there for ten days, and Carl had seen nothing of Paris. Not a single frame had been shot outside of Jean-Paul's suite. Meals were brought in. At night Carl sat in the room he shared with his father and watched French television—football, plotless movies, and incomprehensible interview shows —while Raymond read Dostoesvsky's novel and jotted down ideas on a yellow legal pad.

❧ ❧ ❧

"I don't know what Jean-Paul's doing," Carl complained one evening after another unsuccessful round of filming. On the television two scruffy intellectuals, their voices hoarse from cigarette smoke Carl swore created a haze in their hotel room, droned on and on. "I don't know what he wants."

"It's because you don't understand French," Raymond said. He marked his page and looked at his son. "They should be tutoring you instead of having you memorize everything phonetically. Even though they're summarizing what you're supposed to be saying and feeling, there's a disconnect between the sounds coming out of your mouth and what's in your head."

"It's blah-blah-blah," Carl said. "But it's not just that I don't understand the language. It's the movie. I don't get it. Shouldn't I at least *get* it? Am I supposed to be one of the "dry boys"? And why is whatever that means a secret?"

Raymond shook his head and shrugged. "We all work differently. I like everything scripted with a story-board for everyone to see: a beginning, middle and an end. No improvisation. That's why we were so successful making *Teddy*—and why we could shoot so quickly. And you know if I hadn't provided Mr. Salinger with a detailed screenplay, he'd never have approved the project. Same thing with *Son of Kong.*"

"Jean-Paul calls Mr. Salinger 'the old Jew.'"

"I'm not sure he's Jewish. Maybe half. There's a lot of anti-semitism in France. And Mr. Salinger fought in World War II, like your grandpa, but here in Europe instead of in the Pacific. A lot of the French were happy but resentful when they were liberated. People get that way when they're saved. You're supposed to be Jesus, you should know all about saving. Some of the French hated Jews as much as the Nazis did. I would have thought somebody of Jean-Paul's generation would be over that, though. There—that's the history lesson you were supposed to have. When we filmed *Teddy*, you were required to have a tutor. But this is France. I'll have to do. 'Oo-lah-lah.'"

"Oo-lah-lah," Carl sighed. "Mrs. Abernathy smelled like cabbage dipped in vanilla perfume. She made me read Jane Austen and Dickens."

"Emma and Elizabeth Bennett and Oliver Twist and Fagin—that was good, right? It's awkward for Jean-Paul that we're here. We're something of a sensation, did you know that? The Paris newspapers are writing about us. *Son of Kong* was huge in France, and *Teddy*, too. Celeste says that reporters dressed as hotel staff have been trying to sneak up onto our floor. They're calling this hotel the Bastille. Like we're in prison here. The eighth floor is due for a storming. More history for you—that's the French Revolution.

"I know—'liberty, equality, fraternity'—1789, I knew that."

"They're camped out in the lobby. Photographers want to get a shot of you, Teddy-boy."

None of what his father spoke of was news, but Carl felt pressure building behind his eyes, as if his head was swelling. He'd grown accustomed to the attention he attracted back in the United States for playing Salinger's child genius in the movie his father had directed. He wished he had the freedom to enjoy his international fame firsthand. "We need to revolt, Dad."

"Yeah—I think our friend Jean-Paul is jealous."

"Is that why I'm not allowed out of here?"

"It probably has more to do with money. He doesn't have the budget to use too many locations. And it's cheaper to keep you under wraps—no bodyguards required for his little Christ. He's saving time and money."

"How's he saving time? We shoot the same thing all day long—me looking out the window. We never leave his hotel suite. And he's never satisfied. He's got to pay for the hotel, right? And we just sit around."

"He calls it 'interiorizing.' You're supposed to be an introspective Savior. In some ways his film is getting smaller and smaller. Maybe it would help if you spoke a little of the language," Raymond said.

Carl picked up a ceramic ashtray from the end table beside his chair. Tiny flower petals detailed the rim, and its bowl was stained ash-gray. "I don't like not knowing what I'm saying. It sounds fake."

"I'm sure Jean-Paul could give you a philosophical rationale. Like those guys—" Raymond nodded toward the gray men on TV. One rubbed at his tired eyes with the heels of his hands while the other gesticulated with the cigarette he held between his thumb and index finger. Neither stopped talking. Nothing indicated that they were listening to each other.

"Ernest and Phillipe speak perfect French."

"They *are* French," Raymond laughed. "And your Mohammed is a blond and your Buddha's a freckled redhead. And both are blue-eyed. I can't make up my mind if Jean-Paul's making some kind of ironic comment with his casting, or if he simply didn't try very hard. Maybe not trying *is* his ironic comment. Both kids are famous from French television, as I understand it. I think Buddha was in a vampire movie. Jean-Paul's probably exploiting them for their national box office appeal. Internationally, you're the big deal. Don't you talk to them?"

The ashtray slipped out of Carl's hand, struck the table, and wobbled loudly. He flattened it under his palm. "They're not nice to me. They stick together, and I think they make jokes about me." Carl found himself tearful. This trip to Paris had been nasty and claustrophobic, not the "once in a lifetime experience" he'd anticipated. He felt his father's gaze nibbling over his features, and he decided crying would be senseless.

"How about we order room service?" Raymond asked. "Anything you want. *Carte blanche*. See—now we're learning French. It's obvious those kids are overcome with envy. It's their national emotion. American stars shine the brightest, everyone knows that. Christ, you know what I feel like doing? I feel like smoking. Let's smoke. Everybody here smokes. We'll turn this French experience inside out. Just don't tell your mother. Maybe smoking's the secret way the French inhale their language." Raymond cocked his head at the television. "Look at those guys. It's got to be the more you smoke the more you can talk." He picked up the telephone and tucked it under his arm. "How about cigarettes and ice cream? French vanilla. And something to drink. Orange soda? It'll be an international sugar shock festival. We'll turn off the TV and I'll describe the characters in *Crime and Punishment*. You think French is tough, wait until you hear these names—try Raskolnikov—try Svidrigaylov. I'll tell you about the screenplay I'm working up, then you'll tell me about *Great Expectations*. Is that the one with Pip? And the little girl who never marries him? And the crazy old lady in the wedding dress? You know what? Tomorrow I'll demand that you and I be allowed to sneak out into the streets after you shoot. We'll slip out incognito. Jean-Paul owes us." Raymond slid the receiver out of his armpit and dialed the front desk.

❧ ❧ ❧

"You're watching the other boys play football," Jean-Paul said. The lights were rigged behind Carl so the cameras could capture the side of his face, the gray exterior, and the child's reflection in the glass. "Now say your line. It's your *thoughts*. There will be a close up of your lips later. Now speak."

"*Zhu-zhu, zhu-zhu-zhu, zhu-zhu*," Carl mumbled. The words fell from his mouth like pebbles— he had no idea what he was saying, and the ignorance made him tense beneath the tranquility he'd been instructed to project. Smoking with his dad hadn't helped him understand the language. His mouth and eyes were dry, and he felt feverish. He hadn't slept—his room had seemed full of large black birds that covered the chairs, the dresser, the floor, his bed. They were still and silent, except for an occasional preening rustle, but he could feel their collective mass. And the vanilla ice cream hadn't soothed his taste buds. After he'd choked through a few mouthfuls of smoke ("Don't inhale!" his father had warned) it had congealed in flavorless lumps on his tongue— like the ice cream J. D. Salinger had served him that had made him sick. He'd never seen Mr. Salinger after his one visit to New Hampshire. Carl fell asleep composing a letter of apology to the author.

"Who needs French? You're a born mimic!" his father had persuaded when the opportunity to appear in Jean-Paul's film arose. But, while it was true that Carl could reproduce his stepfather Klaus's German accent, his stomach ached as he listened to the French director's instructions—they were like the absurd courses of a meal he didn't understand, served at the wrong time of day. Like cold soup at dawn. Like the story he heard of someone drinking the water in a bowl meant for rinsing fingers.

"*Coupe!* Enough for now," Jean-Paul grumbled, and Carl turned toward the director a moment before the lights were extinguished, catching a painful instant of glare. "Go play with the other boys." Carl would rather have kept sitting at the window. It was quiet now in Jean-Paul's bedroom, where the "dry boys" waited, but an hour earlier there'd been laughter loud enough behind the closed door for the director to shout "*See-lans!*" The instant stillness had lasted for a ten count before titters resumed.

While he'd been locked in his through-the-window contemplation, attempting and failing to oblige his director's demands for shades of nuance he didn't grasp, Carl was certain that the boys had cracked open the bedroom door and watched him suffer. Maybe they'd peeked through the keyhole. He slid from the radiator cover on wobbly, bare legs—like all the children in the foreign films he'd watched with his father before coming to Europe, Carl wore short-shorts. He slunk toward Jean-Paul's bedroom.

❧ ❧ ❧

The French boys sprawled across Jean-Paul's king-sized bed, a deck of playing cards scattered between them. They made identical puckered smiles as Carl appeared, as if they'd been sucking on lemons. Both were blue-eyed, but Ernest-Mohammed's dilated pupils darkened his, and Philippe-Buddha's were the skim milk white of a February sky. Carl wondered when it would be their turn to act. Were the rain-delayed soccer scenes all they'd signed on for? They didn't seem to require parent chaperones—maybe things were different in Europe. Maybe their parents worked. Could they have been orphans? Why were they locked up all day?

Carl cleared his throat— the pseudo-French he'd been gibbering all day was stuck in it. During the hours he'd sat at the window he'd begun to wonder about the body he kept so still: soon he'd need to shave; patches of hair would surface at his crotch and under his armpits; the voice one reviewer of *Teddy* described as "sweet with truth" would change.

"What's '*moo-ton*'?" Carl asked as he entered, mostly for something to say. Jean-Paul had muttered that as Carl stepped away from his window.

"This," Philippe hissed. He poked the head of his

penis out of his shorts. He flicked the plump mushroom cap with his finger, giggled, and tucked himself away. Carl shivered as if he'd bitten into aluminum foil.

Ernest ignored the display. "'*Mouton*' is sheep, Teedy," he said with an exaggerated good-cop politeness that made him more frightening than his red-headed friend. He flashed mock-worried eyes. "Did someone call you a sheep? Jean-Paul said that?"

"Baaa!" Philippe rolled onto his back. "Baaa! That means that you are a very bad actor."

"I don't know." Carl tried to grin. "He might have said something else." Carl had grasped the character Teddy's transcendence; he'd assumed he'd *get* pre-adolescent Jesus—or at least that Jean-Paul would show him a path to understanding. But left in the hands of these boys, all he felt was foolish.

"*Mouton*! Baa-baa-baa!" Philippe bleated at the ceiling, flapping his arms and legs like he was trying to make a snow angel in the sheets.

"Jean-Paul should have called you '*agneau*,'—'lamb,'" Ernest said. "Jesus was the lamb, right? *Mouton* is not such a nice thing to say. It says you're dumb." He smoothed back his blond hair, sat up straight, and patted the edge of the bed beside him. "Sit."

Carl swayed forward, but his feet didn't move. He felt a little faint, and wished his father was with him. That morning before shooting began the senior Walchuk had pressed Jean-Paul for permission to leave the premises after filming.

"Go now, explore. The boy will be okay." Jean-Paul had shooed Raymond off with a back-handed wave. "I think maybe you distract him."

Raymond had hesitated, looked at Carl, who stared back impassively, though pleading inside for his father to *Stay, stay!* "I'd like to get to the museums," Raymond had mused, "and some of the galleries. Carl—Son of

Kong—*Fils de Kong*—what about it? Can you handle some independence? Your mom's been encouraging that. *Liberte, Egalite, Fraternite*, right?

Carl had bowed and smiled, even as he felt the blood drain from his face. "Get me a postcard of the Mona Lisa."

"Ah, *La Giaconda*," Jean-Paul had murmured, shifting his attention to the crewmen re-positioning the camera and lights.

"If I get to the Louvre." Raymond had given his son's shoulder a squeeze. Then he'd abandoned him to the French.

Carl looked at the boys on the bed. What, he wondered, was going on in the outer room now that he'd left? He thought of the last line he'd delivered: "*Zhu-zhu, zhu-zhu-zhu, zhu-zhu.*" If he asked Philippe and Ernest to translate it, they'd make fun of him. Their eyes danced over him as if they expected him to burst into song. They were panting, their mouths agape. Philippe sat up and crossed his legs in the middle of his nest of sheets and cards. He gripped his knees. A strange Buddha. But the Buddha hadn't been the Buddha when he was a kid. Had Mohammed been Mohammed? Carl didn't know. He was certain Jesus had always been Jesus.

"Teedy. Come over here, Teedy," Philippe wiggled a finger at Carl. "Show me your teeties, Teedy." The redhead pinched his own nipples through his striped polo shirt, elbows out as if he were doing the chicken dance. "*Teedy est un singe blanc,*" he trilled.

Carl wiped his nose with his shoulder.

"Philippe says you're a white monkey," Ernest smirked. "We liked your daddy's *Son of Kong*. We had Kiko monkey dolls in France. But they were made cheap in China—they leaked their insides."

Philippe stuck out his lower lip, spread his arms, and rocked from side to side, "*Maintenant, Je suis un singe-*

mouton blanc, comme Teedy! Baa-eee-eee!" he squealed.

"He says he's a white monkey-sheep. Like you." Ernest laughed. Carl had to pee, but didn't move. He was afraid these boys would stop him before he got to the en suite bathroom, and he'd piss himself. He looked longingly at its open door—he could see the white porcelain sink and the mirror reflecting shelves with folded towels. If he made it in there, he'd lock the door and wouldn't come back until he heard his father's voice. What, he wondered, if Jean-Paul had hidden a camera somewhere and was filming this scene? What if *this* was his movie? Carl wished he knew what the director was thinking. To Jean-Paul, he represented an idea, but since Carl had no clue what that idea was, he felt like nothing. Teddy he'd understood. Teddy had fit him like a glove. When Carl had been Teddy, he'd been the idea of Mr. Salinger and his father. But—and he felt the burn of tears he didn't dare release—even as Teddy he hadn't been himself.

"Teedy—" Ernest squinted one eye at Carl from his perch on the edge of the king-sized bed "Do you have a girlfriend?"

Carl shook his head no.

"Would you like to be *my* girlfriend, Teedy?" Ernest patted the bed again, and summoned Carl with a wave of his head. "Or—*I* can be *your* girlfriend. Come here, and I will give you a kiss." Philippe still rocked back and forth in the middle of the bed, but his hands lay in his lap, and he'd stopped screeching. His eyes were so white Carl thought they'd rolled back in his head.

Carl seemed to float, and he smelled something briny that reminded him of the sea. Had he peed himself? He looked at his crotch—his shorts appeared dry. Nothing ran down his smooth thighs.

Ernest rose from the bed and stood in front of him. The French boy was nearly a head taller. His knee brushed against Carl's thigh. "You're Jesus," Ernest whispered. "I'll taste you like a wafer, you see? The wafer is your body, yes? You pass yourself to me with your lips. Breathe like you're swimming. Do you like swimming?" He stooped slightly so that his head was level with Carl's. His breath smelled like peanut butter. Carl closed his eyes. He felt like he was wax melting through a grating into warm black space.

Pain and Philippe's screeching laughter bit into the darkness. Carl's lids lifted to Ernest's snarl as the French boy twisted his nipples through his T-shirt, back and forth. It took Carl a moment to realize that the pain belonged to him, and he cried out.

"*Kwa-kwa-kwa? Kwa-kwa?*" a voice boomed from behind and Ernest's hands dropped. From the French boy's eyes, Carl could tell that the bedroom door had opened behind him, but he couldn't look. In the instant before Ernest stepped back toward the bed, his lips brushed Carl's temple. "*Kiss-kiss,*" he might have whispered. Carl felt the side of his head, and it was wet. He rubbed his burning nipples. Tears rolled down his cheeks. He found himself staring at Philippe, who hadn't shifted his cross-legged position. His freckles rose and fell as he nodded at something Ernest was saying.

"Teedy asked us to teach him how to cry. It's a trick we use for sad scenes," Ernest explained with a look of patient intensity to whoever had opened the door. Carl finally turned, wiping away his tears with his wrist. Two men stood in the doorway, Jean-Paul and a thin man with a froth of platinum hair and dark glasses. The strange looking man spoke to him.

"You okay, kiddo?" The smiling faces of the film crew hovered in the background. Raymond Walchuk removed the bright wig and dark glasses. Phillipe giggled, and Raymond cracked a grin, though he kept an eyebrow raised while waiting for Carl's answer. "Incognito," he explained when his son said nothing, and he waved the wig and glasses. "And it worked. I wasn't recognized by a soul, even when I took the glasses off in the museums. I remembered your Mona Lisa post card—and I saw her live—what an expression! But you're okay?" he asked, confirming an answer his son had never given.

Carl opened his mouth, but nothing came out. His father nodded. "Remind me to tell you about an artist I saw—Balthus." He shook his head.

"Ah, Balthasar Klossowski de Rola," Jean-Paul said softly. The French director was studying Carl's tear-streaked face. "Innocence stolen with a voyeur's eye."

"Yes," Raymond said, "Yes!" He rested the heel of the hand holding his glasses and wig on Jean-Paul's shoulder, and though he still looked at his son, Carl felt his father's interest drift to the new subject. "Those little girls, yes. Can we talk about that?"

"*Oui*, later," Jean-Paul's focus was on Carl. "*Mon enfant*," he purred, "I think now would be a good time to film. Can you come back out here to your window, *s'il-vous plait*?"

Carl exhaled. He couldn't remember when he'd last taken a breath. Feeling was seeping back into his legs and feet. But he still had to pee, worse than ever, and knew sitting at the window would be impossible if he didn't.

"Tomorrow, you go out," Jean-Paul smiled. He ducked under Raymond's hand and backed into the suite. "You'll go see the Eiffel Tower and Notre Dame. We'll make you into somebody else, like we did with your papa."

An Evening with Willie Freeze

The Cubmaster introduces our guest speaker as George White Eagle. I don't recognize the name, but his face is familiar—it's a twist of rawhide, eyes hooded to a slit under bruise-purple lids. You'd think they were shut completely, except a gleam sneaks out now and then that reminds me of the husky dog we had when I was a kid. Wolfy slept with his eyes half open, and the dead look in them made me shiver, like he was watching us from some evil world. George White Eagle's black hair is tugged back into an inch of ponytail. New blue jeans cinch his waist, and his flannel shirt, rolled up at the sleeves, bags at the chest because he hunches.

"Mr. White Eagle is going to tell us some Indian lore and play his flute for us," the Cubmaster says. His face is ham red, as if his yellow neckerchief is too tight. "So let's quiet down, kids, okay?"

The scouts are sugared up on soda pop and cupcakes, unconcerned about whatever is happening on stage. They shout and bang folding chairs and play keep away with stolen caps or sneakers. The Cubmaster raises his hand and calls, "Akela." A ten count passes, and he repeats: "Akela!" The kids sag to the tiled floor in front of the cafeteria stage as if their bones have dissolved. Danny and I have been sitting for five minutes—sugar is not part of my nephew's diet. He rocks slowly, careful to stay on a black tile. He's fixed his attention on a heel mark on the white tile in front of him. The other kids keep their distance. Danny attends this school too, but he's in special classes. He doesn't meet eyes.

With all the kids and dads on the floor, the Cubmaster leads a recitation of their oath. Only Danny and I and Mr. White Eagle abstain.

The cub scout follows Akela.
The cub scout helps the pack go.
The pack helps the cub scout grow.
The cub scout gives good will.

After the oath, the chattering starts again. The adults don't help—two dads near me discuss creosote buildup in chimneys while one of their boys, his cheeks smudgy with chocolate, chokes his freckled pal.

My sister Tara thinks scouting is a good idea for her son. Her boss at the Walmart made it all the way to Eagle. As I see it, Danny will never be management material. Tara calls his autism "mild Asperger's." He's not a head banger yet—Tara doesn't need to hide his red curls under a helmet—but doctors warn that it's a possibility down the road.

Often at pack meetings a father will sidle over during refreshments, usually dragging his son, who'll be smirking around at his friends. As Danny presses against me, swaying to his own rhythm, the dad will say, "How's the boy—how ya doin', son?" Danny won't answer. Maybe he rocks harder. Maybe he makes a keening sound. To fill the awkward moment, I ask my default question: "So who's this Akela, anyway?" The dad will smile without answering. "We'll see you later," he'll nod, and shift away, while his son zips off like a released fish.

Tonight, I touch my nephew's shoulder, and he flinches. I think I hear him humming, and I slide my hand from his shoulder to his back, but I don't feel the purr I expect— only the ridge of his spine and the ladder of his ribs. The sound comes from the stage: Mr. White Eagle is chanting. The hubbub in the room subsides until everyone except my sister's son is staring at Mr. White Eagle.

"Respect," he whispers. His purple lids are squeezed shut, as if we're something he doesn't want to see. "My people use a special, holy word: *Blah-dee-blah*." The syllables melt together. "It is a tradition that passes from fathers to sons. Say it with me: *Blah-dee-blah*." We try. We watch each other's lips. "*Blah-dee-blah*" Mr. White Eagle repeats, and we catch on. "*Blah-dee-blah*." Our chorus echoes through us, as if we're in church. Danny's mouth is shut, and he's still staring at the heel mark.

"It is with respect we treat our elders, our parents, our guests, each other," Mr. White Eagle says. The Cubmaster bows. These are the values we hope to instill in our boys. Several dads nod, too. I'm still trying to figure out where I know George White Eagle from.

Respect hasn't been part of the formula with a lot of our Pack's guests: the young veteran of the Iraq war lost the kids to giggle fits when he couldn't keep from swearing and quit his speech in the middle; the professional football player who'd never made it off the Oakland

Raiders taxi squad only took questions. He said "yes" or "no" to a few, then stationed himself at a table where he signed autographs for two dollars each. After twenty minutes he stood and asked, "Who do I see about my fifty dollars?"

But Mr. White Eagle commands the kids' attention. He blows three long, sad notes into his wooden flute. We hear wide open plains and forests full of wildlife. "These are mourning songs," Mr. White Eagle tells us. "Songs of loss. Songs of death. Loss is part of the great circle of life, boys. Life begins with creation. Sex is creation. The mating of creatures. Of your mother and father. We have respect for sex—*Blah-de-Blah*." Our "*Blah-de-Blah*" is automatic, but "sex" has some fathers frowning. The Cubmaster's got a glazed look; his ears and neck are crimson.

"I'm going to tell you a story about respect." Mr. White Eagle speaks in a slow, measured beat, with his head still and his eyes closed like a blind man's. "It's an important story. It's about my people, the Creek. And America." I expect something about the world on the back of a big turtle, about brave warriors.

"Not too long ago, I was driving on a long stretch of Interstate 10," he begins, "just into New Mexico from Arizona, on my way to visit some people in Ohio. My car was borrowed from a friend in Bakersfield. The highway stretched far and wide in front of me, with great mountains in the distance. I was smoking— a cigarette—something you shouldn't do, boys. But when my people smoke, we're mourning our losses." Several adult heads bob, most likely the smokers. "It was a bright afternoon. No one else was on the road. Then, in my rearview mirror I saw a car, a state trooper, closing in quickly, and I said a prayer of welcoming. The trooper's lights started flashing, and I said another prayer to speed him safely to whatever emergency called him.

When he pulled up beside me, he looked over. I nodded at him through my open window, and when I smiled, my cigarette fell out of my mouth. I couldn't see his eyes behind his mirrored glasses, but I saw his lips curl with hatred. He pointed to the side of the road, and I pulled over."

Mr. White Eagle has been speaking in a prayerful monotone. From time to time there's a glint from between his shut lids, as if there are jewels hidden behind them. He continues his story: he's asked for his license and for the registration of the vehicle his Bakersfield friend apparently failed to renew; he's ordered to wait with his hands on the hood of the car while the trooper searches it; finally, he's handed citations for littering (the fallen cigarette) and the lapsed registration, and the trooper races off, lights still flashing.

"Do you see?" Mr. White Eagle asks the boys and their dads. "Shame—it sucks the warmth from the sun and the sparkle from the lakes; it steals the sweet scent from the pines. Do you see? It's this—" and he presents his profile: his hatchet nose, his high cheekbones and crag of a brow, the stump of the ponytail he waggled between his thumb and forefinger. There's a hush. Then Mr. White Eagle turns toward us and opens his eyes fully wide for the first time, and we gasp. His eyes have no whites—they're silvery irises set in absolute black— eyes that belonged only in nightmares. And I remember where I'd seen Mr. White Eagle before.

He's nearly whispering now. "What that officer showed was the ugliest thing in the world: prejudice. Against me. Against my people, for nothing more than a ponytail, and for skin a few shades too dark." He doesn't mention his eyes. He doesn't have to. "No respect. *Blah-dee-blah.*"

I'd seen him about a year ago, at the first and only AA meeting I'd ever attended. That's when Tara and my now ex-girlfriend, Janie, got together and "intervened," as they called it. For Tara the few joints a week I smoked, the six pack or so that helped quench my dry mouth and round off my buzz, made me a doubtful risk around her son. "You've got to be a better role model for him," she said, knowing how much I depended on his company.

Janie's reason for wanting me sober was more complicated; it was another aspect of the situation that forced me to move out of the rented bungalow we shared, the one on the river bank where their used to be an amusement park almost a hundred years ago. I've seen old photographs of a midway and a carrousel, and a ferris wheel at night all lit up and reflected in the black river. I can match up the shoreline to my fishing spots. I liked to tell Janie when we were in bed that that the wind rustling the leaves outside our window was the ghosts of happy people laughing. I moved out because Janie was pregnant—not by me, though I wish that would have been possible. Janie had the best one-time job I'd ever heard of—she was a surrogate. The fertilized egg of a rich woman had been implanted in her womb; she didn't know who she was bearing the baby for, only that she was to be paid a small fortune when the kid was born—exactly how much it wasn't my business to know yet, she said. She also received a monthly sum to eat properly, and a nurse visited once a week to check on the progress of her pregnancy.

Janie is beautiful and ambitious—she has a college degree, and when she was picked to be a surrogate, you'd have thought she won the lottery and bags of gold would soon be dropped off at our door. "You can't stay here," she told me. "They think I'm single. I signed something. You'll have to get an apartment, and I'll visit you there. And if I am going to visit, you'll have to change your habits. There'll be no smoking or drinking around this baby. He's going to be my down-payment on life."

I should have noticed that she said "*my* down-payment" and not "*our* down-payment." But I promised both Janie and Tara I'd go to an AA meeting, and I quit smoking and drinking. When Janie started swelling, I talked to the baby in her belly, which she let slip was a boy. Janie would sneak over to my tidy little apartment every weekend, at first, but she visited less and less frequently the more and more pregnant she got. She stopped letting me touch her. It wasn't that she wasn't horny anymore—she said she was "superstitious" about my fingers and tongue so close to "the portal," which would be the rich child she was carrying's access to the world. Sometimes I thought Janie was afraid I would contaminate the unborn kid with my ignorance—as if she had just enough class for him, but I'd never be in the same league.

When her nine months were nearly up—it was just after the night of that one and only AA meeting where I saw Mr. White Eagle— I suggested that we could deliver the kid ourselves, then take off with him and start our own family somewhere far away—a tropical island or a village in the Brazilian rain forest. I thought it was a funny idea to have to kidnap something inside of you. I never saw her again after that night. I don't know where or on which day she had the baby, and when I returned to the bungalow on the site of the old amusement park, there wasn't a scrap to indicate she'd ever lived there, let alone a note.

But while I waited in the dim fluorescence of the Methodist church's meeting room for that AA meeting to begin, I'd thought I was opening a new chapter on Janie's and my life, not closing the final one. About two dozen folks, mostly men, sat in three rows of folding chairs. Despite the ban on tobacco, the room reeked from clothing steeped in smoke. The people in charge were welcoming, but there wasn't much chit-chat. Everyone was too intent on publicly nursing a private woe. I thought I'd be required to share my story, and I decided I'd tell the assembly about the testicular cancer that left me single-balled and sterile. I'd reveal that I'd never be able to father a child of my own, and that the heart-wrenching disappointment had driven me to anesthetize my sorrows in drugs and drink. The truth is, I'd never had cancer, just a sperm count approaching zero—I'd been tested periodically because I'd grown up in a tract house my folks bought that was built on a nuclear waste dumping ground. That situation involved some mismanaged lawsuits, and if anyone in my family reaped a penny from it, I never knew. But a cancer story would draw more sympathy than a lawsuit story, I concluded. I imagined the eyes of these hardened substance abusers filling with tears at my tale of woe.

Tara and I don't talk about it, but she grew up over the same nuclear waste I did, and maybe her irradiated eggs caused Danny's problems. Her husband left after the weight of Danny's turning out to be the kind of kid he is cracked marital ice that was already thin. Tara and Tim didn't have it in themselves to deal with the situation as a team, which is why I'm scooched up next to my nephew at this scout meeting while Mr. White Eagle has resumed sounding melancholy notes on his flute. When I look at him, I can't believe I didn't recognize him immediately from the Methodist church basement.

There, he sat in the first row, and when he popped up to tell about his tribulations, he made no effort to dim the effect of his frightful eyes: they were like dimes floating in black ink.

"I have been a conman and a terrible human being," he began. His tale was set "in another city" where he had custody of a little girl, a toddler "not really my daughter." To make his very long story short, somehow he'd managed to scam the congregation of a church into believing that this child entrusted to his care was dying of "something like leukemia." He'd thrown himself on the mercy of the big-hearted congregants. "The good people organized a fundraiser," he told us, and netted a "blessed" profit in the thousands from the gullible church folk before skipping town.

"I have paid my debt for that and other offences," he said, by which he meant he'd done prison time, "and as a confirmation of that payment I inked my eyes." I shivered. I hadn't known it was possible to tattoo your eyeballs. "These eyes are my public admission of the midnight thoughts that always lurk inside. They warn everyone I meet, 'Trust me if you dare.' Being seen as I am is part of my daily battle."

Anonymous no longer, here he is, "George White Eagle," toodling his flute and yammering about *Blah-dee-blah* to a pack of Cub Scouts for the sake, I assume, of fifty dollars. How, I wonder, had the scout leaders found him? How had Mr. White Eagle advertised himself?

I'm fidgety, and at a loss as to what to do with my knowledge. Is there a statute of limitations on anonymity? What if Mr. White Eagle's got a bigger scam in mind than just that fifty? "You okay?" I ask Danny, mostly to calm myself down, and my nephew doesn't respond, but the father next to me shushes me and gives me a look like I've just violated *Blah-dee-blah*. I raise an eyebrow at the shusher and cock my head toward Mr. White Eagle, but the dad misses the signal. His plump son's mouth hangs open as if the nonsense Mr. White Eagle is feeding him is better than a cream-filled donut.

What I should do is get up and take my information about Mr. White Eagle to the Cubmaster. He stands at the back of the room, smiling at the stage; but if I leave Danny, I'm afraid he'll start howling, like he did when I left him on a movie line with a nice old lady so I could get the wallet I'd left in our car.

Mr. White Eagle has stopped playing and addresses us again. His silver and black eyes gleam. There's a beat in the pit of my stomach like a tom-tom.

"*Blah-dee-blah*," Mr. White Eagle intones.

"*Blah-dee-blah*," almost everyone replies. Danny makes his own sound.

"Boys," our guest says, "you make my heart glow. Your ways, the ways of scouting, are the ways of my people. And there are two things we must value as much as *Blah-dee-blah*: Truth and Vigilance."

Heads nod, though I'm sure few of the boys know what "vigilance" means. This is the real deal, dads are telling themselves, this is why we signed our boys up for scouting. Not to tie knots. Not to carve race cars out of blocks of pine. Not to earn badges for taking out the trash. But to grab hold of those old virtues, Truth and Vigilance. *Virtue*, I think, and that's when I decide that it's up to me to unmask Mr. White Eagle. I'm panting, and the hand I rest on Danny's knee is damp.

"And so," our guest continues, "I offer you myself as a lesson in Truth and Vigilance." He bows deeply. I brace myself—there's the kind of hush that Danny often fills with a wail. But his breathing is regular, and for a moment I understand the relief of fitting in. Who would it hurt to let the whole thing slide? But then Mr. White Eagle smiles—for the first time this evening—and the way his face twists beneath those eyes hits me like a blow to my manhood. I'm being disrespected—no *Blah-dee-blah*.

I remember the first father-son Cub Scout project Danny and I undertook. Tara had dropped Danny off on a Saturday morning at the bungalow I'd re-occupied after Janie's desertion. He sat at my kitchen table with a milk mustache while I whittled away at a Pinewood Derby car with a steak knife, the closest thing I owned to a tool. The magic marker for Danny to color the raw wood had dried up, so I gave him a Bic pen, and he slashed stripes along one side of the car, again and again and again, hundreds of them, then said, "TV," and I said, "Okay." We brought the car to Derby night, where other scouts displayed glossy, aerodynamic racers they seemed to be handling for the first time. Their dads swapped details about weight distribution and wheelbases, decals and metallic paint. Compared to the others, our car looked like it had been gnawed into shape by squirrels. I caught one father looking at it and muttering to another with a shake of his head, "You'd have thought..." The other dad shook his head too, staring at our scarred chunk of wood. The first dad repeated, knowing I was in earshot, "You'd have just thought." I turned to my nephew, who clutched our car to his chest like it was a gold ingot. "Who the heck is Akela, Danny?" I demanded. "Why can't anybody tell me that?"

So I have no choice. Mr. White Eagle must be exposed. But I'm still waiting for a sign that the moment is right when he beats me to his own unmasking.

"Truth," he says. "The truth is, I am not who you think. There is more to George White Eagle than meets the eye. I was baptized George DiBello, but I have gone by many other names. I have been William Smith. In prison they called me Willie Freeze." His words seem to echo from a pit that's opened beneath us. The blood has drained from the Cubmaster's face. "Truth: I was not born a Creek Indian. I am of Italian and Greek descent." He grins, and his eyes flash. "And now you think I have deceived you. That's good—you're being vigilant. There are those who will tell you lies, boys—you will meet such people as you journey through life."

Confusion reigns—dads look to the Cubmaster and to each other for some kind of reassurance, but there's none to be had, and as the boys feel their fathers' grips loosen, their eyes round with fear. It's frightening and exhilarating at the same time. It's a feeling I wish I could get credit for creating.

"But even now I have fooled you," Mr. Whoever says. He waggles a finger. "Truth and Vigilance— I became a Creek in prison. My cellmate was Creek, and after an intimate ceremony, we became blood brothers. He assured me I have full tribal rights. Then I had my eyes inked—I gave up their whites. And now, the blackness is a symbol. As I look out at you, my darkness is behind me. So, learn this lesson, just as I learned the lessons of my adopted people, the Creek—don't trust what you see. Don't cast judgments until you know the whole Truth. That trooper who pulled me over? He was wrong about who he thought I was—but he was also right, do you see? But in the biggest way of all, *Blah-dee-blah*, he was wrong."

Silence. There's too much to digest to understand it all. But the Cubscout oath prevails: "*The cub scout shows good will.*" A unified opinion settles like a golden cloud on Mr. Dibello-Smith-White Eagle's audience: *The subject was Truth. No one has been deceived. Good people chose this speaker. We will all sleep well tonight.*

"Thank you, boys, fathers, Cubmaster." Our guest is reluctant to leave the stage. I'm waiting for one more "*Blah-dee-blah*" when I feel Danny seething next to me. He's rocking on his haunches, forward and back. His lips part.

"Boo," Danny says, the sound a burst bubble that only I hear, because everyone else, all the dads and their kids, have begun to clap—louder and louder, applause that grows bolder as it justifies itself. Danny tilts his head back, and his jaws seem to unhinge. "Boo!" he bleats. "Boo, Boo, Boo!"

"Shh, quiet!" the dad behind me growls, and "Hey" and "Quiet" and "Shh" erupt around us. "Get him out!" another dad nearby hisses, because Danny won't shut up —"Boo-boo-boo-boo-boo—" he rattles like a machine gun. Outrage swells, and in a second I'm on my feet, and I pull Danny up, too. He's looking at the floor, and he stumbles stiffly after me as I lead him out the emergency exit that takes us into the parking lot and the night. "Boo-boo-boo-boo-boo," he's muttering. I haven't once told him to knock it off. Behind us I hear the Cubmaster's enthusiastic voice, muffled, then more applause. Did he just thank the speaker—had he apologized for my nephew and me? I take Danny into the darkness, onto the playing field stretching beyond the parking lot, walking him almost all the way to the trees at the far end. It's a cool evening, and it feels good to move. After a while Danny stops booing.

"Look at the stars," I say, catching my breath. I drape my arm over his slight shoulders. He doesn't say a word, but he lifts his eyes. "There's the Big Dipper," I say, "and the Milky Way." I haven't really found them, but I know they're up there somewhere. Danny's staring up— at the stars or the spaces between them. I plan to stay out on the field until the parking lot empties. Then I feel Danny freeze—he senses before I do that we've been followed across the field.

"The Seven Sisters," a voice whispers. It belongs to the man I first saw at AA. He points at the heavens as he circles around us until he blocks our way. "The Creek tell a story about them." His back is to the trees. There's an odor from him like incense. He lowers his gaze and I can feel its blackness spreading over us, thicker than the night. "You booed me," he says, addressing me, not Danny. "Do I know you?"

The truth is, maybe I did boo him. Maybe Danny got

the idea from me. I don't say anything for a few seconds. Up close he's not very tall, almost a head shorter than I am. His grin is tight, hiding his teeth. "We're just tired," I say. "It was a long night."

"There's something wrong with your boy," he says matter-of-factly. *There's something wrong with your eyes*, I want to say, but hold my tongue.

"He's my sister's kid." The moment I say it, I feel bad. "I can't have my own," I add, but it's too late. I have never before in my life hit another human being, but I'm feeling the instinct for it. My arm tingles and my hand closes into a fist. The man holds his flute like a club, as if it's heavier than anyone would think, and I assess how much it might hurt to block a swing with my forearm. Then I ask him, "Who's Akela? You should be able to tell me that."

"Akela? It's another name for the Great Spirit. Shawnee, I think."

"Wrong," I say. "It's Hindi. It's *Indian*-Indian, not Native American. From Kipling's *Jungle Book*. Akela is the lone wolf—the lone wolf who leads the pack." A lot of truths can be found on the Internet.

"I'm a hypnotherapist. And a homeopathic doctor," he says. "Maybe there's something I can do for the boy. For you, too." I twitch as he reaches into his jeans pocket, but he pulls out a card. I relax my hand to accept it. "Give me a call. We can work something out. No charge for session one." He looks at Danny, whose gaze has fallen from the starry sky to the turf. "*Blah-dee-Blah*," the Creek adoptee says. He salutes us with his instrument and turns toward the trees. I see now that there's a path through them to a lit street not more than fifty yards beyond, and he's striding toward it. "Boo," he throws back over his shoulder, followed by a laugh that turns into a smoker's wheeze.

By now my sister will be wondering where we are. I

might have to tell her we're done with scouting, and I'm trying to think of how to break the news. Maybe I don't have to say anything; maybe on Tuesday nights Danny and I could just do something else, like bowling or a movie. What we won't do yet is visit Dr. DiBello—that's the name on his card. The parking lot looks empty now, but I no longer care. The school's big classroom windows are bright yellow, and we can see the late-shift custodians moving around. I palm Danny's back and guide him forward.

"Akela" I say.

"Boo," my nephew says, his eyes on the night-blue turf he kicks at with each step.

Gregory Wolos

Having raised two children and spent more than three decades as an educator in upstate New York, he currently resides with his wife of forty-four years in a small town not far from Boston. He holds a doctorate from the University at Albany.

Gregory's has published over 100 stories in journals and anthologies that include *Glimmer Train*, *Georgia Review*, *Michigan Quarterly Review*, *descant*, *Florida Review*, *The Pinch*, *Post Road*, *Baltimore Review*, *Los Angeles Review*, *Tahoma Literary Review*, *Southern Humanities Review*.

He has four story collections: **Women of Consequence** (Regal House Publishing, 2019), **Dear Everyone** (Duck Lake Books, 2020), **The Green Ray and Other Stories** (Scantic Books, 2022), and **The Thing About Men** (Cervena Barva Press, 2023), and a novel, **T'ings**, by Silver Bow Publishing (2024).

Also by Gregory Wolos

FICTION

T'ings (A NOVEL)
Silver Bow Publishing, 2024

The Thing About Men
Cervena Barva Press, 2023

The Green Ray and Other Stories
Scantic Books, 2022

Dear Everyone
Duck Lake Books, 2020

Women of Consequence
Regal House Publishing, 2019

 Acknowledgments 

"Svengali," *Down the Rabbit Hole IV*

"Knothole," *Solstice*, reprinted in *Versal*: Finalist, *Glimmer Train* Very Short Fiction Award

"Marigolds," *Coachella Review*; winner, White Eagle Coffee Store Press Award for the Long Story

"Leaving Loathsome Cave," *Orca*

"Old Yeller," *Underground Voices*; Finalist, *Glimmer Train* Very Short Fiction Award

"Claustrophilia, Outer Banks," *Pinball*

"Nuzzi Great Grandpa," *Emrys Review*; winner, Sue Lile Fiction Award

"Iota," *Qwerty*, reprinted in *Stone Crop Review* as "The Green Ray"

"Balance," *descant*; winner, Frank O'Connor Fiction Award

"Glorious Vessel," *Shooter Literary Review*

"Blue Madeline's Version," *A cappella Zoo*

"Pinocchio— New Hampshire—1993," *Lit 'n Image*

"Amabelle's Children," *Altered States*; Finalist, Rick Demarinis Fiction Award (*Cutthroat*); Finalist, *Glimmer Train* Family Matters Award

"The Dry Boys, Paris—1995," *MadHat Lit*

"An Evening with Willie Freeze," *Baltimore Review*, winner (as "Who's Akela?"), *New South* Fiction Award